KILLING ME SOFTLY

Also by Christie Watson

FICTION

Moral Injuries
Where Women are Kings
Tiny Sunbirds Far Away

NON-FICTION

No Filters: A Mother and Teenage Daughter Love Story
Quilt on Fire: The Messy Magic of Friends, Sex and Love
The Courage to Care: Nurses, Families and Hope
The Language of Kindness: A Nurse's Story

KILLING ME SOFTLY

Christie Watson

PHOENIX

First published in Great Britain in 2026 by Phoenix Books,
an imprint of The Orion Publishing Group Ltd
Carmelite House, 50 Victoria Embankment
London EC4Y 0DZ

An Hachette UK Company

The authorised representative in the EEA is Hachette Ireland,
8 Castlecourt Centre, Dublin 15, D15 XTP3, Ireland
(email: info@hbgi.ie)

1 3 5 7 9 10 8 6 4 2

Copyright © Christie Watson 2026

The moral right of Christie Watson to be identified as
the author of this work has been asserted in accordance
with the Copyright, Designs and Patents Act of 1988.

All rights reserved. No part of this publication may be
reproduced, stored in a retrieval system, or transmitted
in any form or by any means, electronic, mechanical,
photocopying, recording, or otherwise, without the
prior permission of both the copyright owner and the
above publisher of this book.

All the organisations and characters in this book are fictitious, and any resemblance
to actual organisations or persons, living or dead, is purely coincidental. Where a real
organisation or person is mentioned, this is based on the author's imagination and does
not reflect who they are in reality.

Professional Standards of Practice and Behaviour for Nurses, Midwives
and Nursing Associates © Nursing and Midwifery Council;
https://www.nmc.org.uk/standards/code/

A CIP catalogue record for this book is
available from the British Library.

ISBN (Hardback) 978 1 3996 1312 5
ISBN (Export Trade Paperback) 978 1 3996 1313 2
ISBN (Ebook) 978 1 3996 1315 6
ISBN (Audio) 978 1 3996 1316 3

Typeset by Born Group
Printed and bound in Great Britain by Clays Ltd, Elcograf S.p.A.

www.orionbooks.co.uk
www.phoenix-books.co.uk

For Jess – the best of nurses, and best of friends

NURSES' CONDUCT

3.2 recognise and respond compassionately to the needs of those who are in the last few days and hours of life

8.5 work with colleagues to preserve the safety of those receiving care

8.7 be supportive of colleagues who are encountering health or performance problems. However, this support must never compromise or be at the expense of patient or public safety

9.1 provide honest, accurate and constructive feedback to colleagues

9.3 deal with differences of professional opinion with colleagues by discussion and informed debate, respecting their views and opinions and behaving in a professional way at all times

11.2 make sure that everyone you delegate tasks to is adequately supervised and supported so they can provide safe and compassionate care

13.3 ask for help from a suitably qualified and experienced professional to carry out any action or procedure that is beyond the limits of your competence

14.1 act immediately to put right the situation if someone has suffered actual harm for any reason or an incident has happened which had the potential for harm

16.5 not obstruct, intimidate, victimise or in any way hinder a colleague, member of staff, person you care for or member of the public who wants to raise a concern

20.3 be aware at all times of how your behaviour can affect and influence the behaviour of other people

20.6 stay objective and have clear professional boundaries at all times with people in your care

Professional Standards of Practice and Behaviour for Nurses, Midwives and Nursing Associates (Nursing and Midwifery Council), 2024

Ways to Kill a Patient

Drug error: NB nanograms/micrograms look similar
Omit basic patient observations
Do not escalate deterioration
Administer known allergen
Dislodge endotracheal tube
Paralysis before/in absence of sedation
Potassium in infusion
Unplug haemofiltration/ventilator
Air/blood/fluid in arterial line
Lack of oxygen – empty cylinder
Insulin/morphine overdose
Turn off/speed up infusion pump
Give intramuscular drug intravenously
Contaminated blood/drugs
Non-sterile/bad aseptic technique
Equipment failure
Misreported scans
Badly managed resuscitation

Allocate the patient the worst nurse on the unit

PROLOGUE
Sophie

Sophie liked to eat alone. She tried a new restaurant every month, always sitting at a window table. Instead of watching the world go by, she would listen to a true-crime podcast or read a second-hand novel that smelt even more delicious than the food. This food was mouth-watering, though. Japanese, a new place, buzzy, and Sophie had ordered sashimi, which was silky and beautifully presented on top of ribbons of tsuma that reminded her of Purkinje fibres, the microscopic muscle threads inside the walls of a human heart – structures that made us all beat.

She lifted the daikon with her chopsticks and took a bite. It tasted of pure electricity. Would a human heart taste similar? After all, everything living in this world is simply matter; humans are atoms and fibres and electricity. That was the most disturbing, comforting fact of all. We are simply made from stardust. A nurse's job is to play in the sand.

The couple at the next table were onto their second bottle of red and talking loudly enough that even wearing earbuds, Sophie could hear every word. It was entertaining enough.

'Honestly, Aoife, if another one of the FY1s asks for a mental health day, I'll shoot myself in the face.'

Doctors. City Hospital was around the corner, so that made sense. Still, Sophie was impressed by the unprofessionalism so close to work, the fuck-it attitude, the loud drunkenness. The man was smartly dressed, slightly red-faced, a few tiny capillaries patterning his nose and cheeks; a drinker. Probably nearing fifty, he looked like the kind of man who'd been extremely good-looking a decade ago, and had muscle memory, but was also crumpled by life, cynical, possibly angry. The kind of man Sophie liked to fuck. Nostalgic. Grateful.

The woman next to him, Aoife, was also in her late forties. She wore a floaty dress and trainers, and was soft in every sense: body, face, eyes. There were silver bangles on her right arm that jangled every now and again. She looked like a woman who picked wildflowers and wore them in her hair. 'Bless them, they're an anxious lot. But I mean, if you're a very anxious person, don't get yourself a job in ED.'

Surely the Emergency Department at City was the only A&E around here? After all, they were moments away. These two might well be her new colleagues. Sophie slipped an earbud out and pretended to read her battered copy of *Kindred*.

The restaurant was a mixture of minimalist and not. Heavy velvet curtains and chandeliers alongside sleek surfaces: marble and glass. There were ghost chairs and elaborate candlesticks on the tables, and every single member of staff she'd seen had a buzz cut *and* a septum piercing. The whole place was loud and heaving, but the fuckable man on the table next to her was the loudest. He laughed and coughed in equal measure. He had exactly the right amount of stubble. A silver fox. 'They're so entitled. Out of medical school for five minutes, then expecting to be consultants. I had Ben requesting another weekend off and telling me that working over forty hours in any given week was in breach of the legal maximum working-hours limit. Forty hours in a week. Ha! I worked forty hours in forty-eight at that age.'

Aoife poured more wine into his glass. A siren wailed outside. 'You still do, Michael.' Her voice was softer, harder to hear. 'But those were the days of a child with a saucepan stuck on their head. It's now a war zone. My nurses are struggling too.'

Sophie turned her head further towards them. *Nurses. My nurses.*

They spoke like this and gulped their wine until Aoife had dark red edges to her lips and was staring at Michael as he slurred. Sophie took another bite of sashimi, letting it melt on her tongue as she watched them. When the bill arrived, Aoife got her purse out, but Michael wafted her away and paid. They left together, leant close. Were they lovers? It was hard to tell. Familiar, certainly, and more than friends, but colleagues in the NHS were closer than lovers. Despite being only eighteen months qualified, Sophie knew that much already.

This was only her second real job. At twenty-four, her schoolmates were already having babies and marrying men named Dave who worked as scaffolders or Sky engineers, or dealt cocaine to support a habit. Sophie craved a different life. Childhood leukaemia and hundreds of hospital appointments and painful procedures had given her a respect for blood and death. She could have become a serial killer, but she wanted to get paid. So, instead, she became a nurse. She'd spent years around nurses and understood that nursing was a language with many different accents. It wasn't the compassionate, kind nurses she emulated. It was the hard-edged nurses, the ones who were in charge of their own universe and knew *everything*. Women with endless grit.

Sophie saw the commotion before she heard the screaming. There was a crowd gathered at the centre of the restaurant, anxious faces, waiting staff running, a few people clustered on the peripheries.

'Can we have some help here? Someone call an ambulance.'

She picked up her book and turned the page. Boring. It would be a panic attack or, at best, a choking. During her hospital induction, the resuscitation team had told all the new recruits that the place where the most choking deaths happened in the UK were restaurant toilets, because the British would rather die than feel embarrassed in public. She had switched off at that point. Everyone knew that the British got off on public humiliation. I mean, everyone knew that. Still, the atmosphere intensified. She lowered her book and took the other earbud out.

'We need a doctor. Any doctors? Is there anyone medical here?'

Sophie looked at the empty table next to her and glanced at the restaurant door, but Aoife and her companion were long gone. They were drunk anyway.

'Help. We need some help!' A waiter was shouting, yet still carrying a full tray of drinks, which Sophie thought impressive. She carefully folded the page she had been reading, closed her book and took a last bite of sashimi. Then she walked towards the drama.

People had stood up at their tables, and others crowded together around the scene. A few were filming on their mobile phones rather than actually helping. Sophie was short and skinny and could easily get lost in crowds, but the group parted for her as though they understood her authority.

'I've called an ambulance.' The waiter balancing the tray gestured to the woman on the floor, who was almost purple, the colour of an aubergine on the turn. The woman wore jeans and a sequined top, and cowboy boots. Her hair had half fallen out of a ponytail. Nobody seemed to be with her. Maybe she was waiting for a friend, or perhaps, like Sophie, she dined alone.

Sophie knelt on the floor as time slowed down. She felt for a medical alert bracelet on the woman's wrists, then took her pulse, which was strong and regular, around 90 BPM. Her own heart beat in her ears, steady and strong. She tuned out all the noise and focused on what was right in front of her. The woman flapped around, a fish yanked from water, flailing and gasping. Sophie ran through the ABC list of priorities. Airway was first above everything else; without an airway there was no oxygen, and with no oxygen the brain and the rest of the organs would soon be dying. Sophie put her ear close to the woman's lips and looked and listened carefully. A high-pitched squeak. A tiny amount of air was getting in and out, but not for long. Her face was blotched, and there was a rash rising up her neck. Her throat and tongue were swelling up.

'Does anyone have an EpiPen?' Sophie glanced at the waiter. 'Check in her bag. Where's the ambulance?'

The waiter nodded. 'There's someone waiting outside for them now.' He put the tray down on a table, then turned and waved his hands over the diners crowded around. 'Please. Go back to your seats. Please. Give her some room. Anyone?'

'She needs adrenaline. Who has an EpiPen?'

Sophie looked around. Some people were crying, holding their hands over their mouths in shock. The fear was palpable, but nobody had what she needed. Sophie forced her face to look sad, with a touch of anxiety, but her heart remained steady as ever. It felt like a film she was watching, a scene she was outside of. It always felt like that. She never panicked. Instead, her skin goose-bumped.

'Nothing in her bag.' The waiter held up a rucksack in front of him. 'We have her name, though. Sylvia, can you hear me?'

Sylvia had stopped moving and squirming around and her eyes were now rolling back in her head. Sophie could hear death whispering in her ear. 'Get me a sharp knife,' Sophie said. 'And a chopstick.'

'Are you joking me?' The waiter had sweat moons underneath his armpits. 'A chopstick?'

'I'm serious.' Sophie glanced at him as he ran towards the kitchen, then back down at Sylvia. The hissing noise she made was barely detectable. 'Are you sure nobody has an EpiPen? Come on now, we're in London.'

Blue lights, slamming doors, shouting.

'What's the story?' A paramedic wearing a parakeet-green shirt and carrying a large red backpack and portable defibrillator rushed towards them and knelt down opposite Sophie. 'I'm Claire,' she said, looking up and smiling. Like so many paramedics, she was young, attractive and had thick forearms covered in tattoos.

'Anaphylaxis,' Sophie said. But Claire had already set down the kit and was giving Sylvia an injection of intramuscular adrenaline in her thigh, through her jeans. She ripped open the defib pads and pulled Sylvia's T-shirt up, her torso by now covered in angry welts. As she attached the defib pads, another paramedic arrived, pushing a trolley with a stretcher balanced on top.

Sophie stepped back so they could take over. Sylvia was breathing more easily almost immediately, and soon regained consciousness. She reached out a hand towards Sophie, but Sophie wasn't the hand-holding sort.

The waiter finally ran back from the kitchen carrying a smaller tray, upon which were three different-sized knives, and a single chopstick. 'Is this what you need? Sorry I took so long.' He stopped, and looked at the paramedics lifting Sylvia onto the trolley and strapping her in. The other diners began returning to their seats.

Claire looked at the tray, and then at Sophie. 'What's that for?' She laughed nervously. 'Wait, I didn't catch your name. Tell me you're a medic?'

Sophie didn't answer but waved the waiter holding the knives and the chopstick away. 'Not needed now,' she said. 'The cavalry arrived.'

The other paramedic shared a look with Claire, who raised an eyebrow. 'What exactly were you planning to do with those?'

'She was moribund,' Sophie said, nodding at Sylvia, who by then had both eyes open, the redness already lessening. 'I suppose I thought it might act as a bougie.'

'So, you're a doctor. You look twelve years old. Where do you work?'

Sophie shook her head. 'Nurse. I start at City ED tomorrow, so I'll probably see you around.'

Claire's smile dropped slightly, and she nodded for her colleague to push Sylvia out to the ambulance. 'Show's over,' she said, and the waiter disappeared. The diners had begun chatting animatedly. Claire stood close to Sophie and leant in next to her ear, whispering. 'I mean, Christ alive, what were you thinking? A chopstick and a kitchen knife? Fuck me, have you been watching *Grey's Anatomy* or something? You could have killed her!'

Sophie stared, unblinking. 'She was dead anyway.'

ONE

Eden

'I will be an excellent nurse.' Eden whispered the words. It was her first day at City ED. She'd imagined it to be high tech and cutting edge, but the hospital was shockingly run-down. The mirror in front of her was cracked and there was a scruffy noticeboard up next to it, with a staff wellness sign-up sheet: 'Lunchtime Yoga Sessions – All Welcome'. Underneath someone had scrawled in biro, *I didn't get to piss for twelve hours yesterday. Namaste.* The changing room smelt of pickled onion Monster Munch. There were pairs of black clogs balanced on top of the metal lockers, scrubs strewn everywhere, and there were two cans of cheap lemon air freshener underneath the sink, next to an overflowing bin. Eden closed her eyes for a brief moment and visualised a thick pine forest, breathing deeply. Then she opened them and smiled at herself in the mirror, before reciting out loud: 'I am doing the work that works for me. I am worthy of love and respect. I breathe in love and breathe out negativity. I am wise and kind and I control how I respond to others. I am deserving.'

Moments like this throughout the day felt a bit silly but were important. Every evening, no matter how late Eden got home, she wrote in her journal. Every morning, before any shift, she stole a few moments for positivity. Gratitude was underrated. Her mentor at university had reminded her that personal protective equipment wasn't simply about preventing infection. Putting on psychological PPE, with essential self-care strategies, was just as vital as gloves and aprons in order to protect nurses' mental health. *One nurse a week tried to take their own life last year,* the mentor had told them all.

'I will make a good impression,' Eden chanted. 'My first day will be a success.'

She stopped, noticing smoke curling up behind her head, above the toilet cubicles. Then, the smell of cherries.

A young woman came out of the toilet, the vape still in her mouth. 'Hey. Nice affirmations.'

Eden's jaw fell open. 'Oh no. How embarrassing. I didn't know anyone was in here.' She turned around. 'Wait. Are you *vaping*?' For a moment she was speechless, but then she shook her head. 'You can't do that in here. You can't smoke or vape in hospital grounds.'

The woman shrugged, then put it in her pocket. She walked over and looked in the mirror. 'Do you have any eyeliner?'

Eden blinked and looked at her chest for signs of an ID card. Was she a relative? 'I have no idea what you're talking about. These are the staff changing rooms,' she said. 'You need to use the toilets in the relatives' room.'

The woman leant towards the mirror and pulled her eyelid down. 'God, I look anaemic.' She turned and faced Eden. 'I *am* staff.' Then she winked and walked out, leaving behind the smell of cherries, and a dumbfounded Eden.

Eden swiped her ID and pushed open the heavy doors to the main reception area. She had read up as much as she could about City Emergency Department, poring over the guidelines; the 'Advice for New Starters' pack that HR had sent to her. She knew that it would be overwhelming; it was one of the busiest departments in the country. The staff turnover here was eye-watering. One hundred and forty nurses on roll.

'Beep-beep.' A porter rushed past her, pushing a bed.

Eden stood to the side next to the queue of patients. A woman in front of her scratched away at large blisters all over her face, which were already open and weeping, the man with her shouting, 'Fuck's sake!' Another patient at the back of the queue had a cardboard sign that had 'JESUS SAVES' painted on it. He was the skinniest man Eden had ever seen – even from 20 feet away she could see every one of his ribs through his T-shirt.

She carried on, following the direction of the porter, swerving a man in an electric wheelchair, oxygen cylinder balanced on the front, and then a family, a mum and dad holding the hands of a young, bald child.

Eden's eyes watered. She forced her feet to keep walking. She pressed the automatic door sign, and when nothing happened, she leant on the heavy doors marked 'MAJORS/RESUS'.

There were two signs on the wall in the next corridor, one that said 'Aged 12–50? Please let the nurse know if you may be pregnant'. *Twelve?* Eden thought. The next was a warning about Mpox, advising patients to tell the staff if they had recently been to various central African countries, including the DRC and Burundi. A nurse in scrubs shouted a name out from a doorway, and a morbidly obese man wearing pyjamas stood up, moaning in agony, and limped over. When Eden swiped and walked into the clinical area, at least three people tried to follow, and she had to close the door firmly behind her.

She walked past a line of four tall, bulky security guards in black wearing yellow high-vis vests with 'SECURITY' written on their backs. One of them nodded at Eden, and crossed his eyes by looking at his nose. Eden didn't smile. She turned to another man who was sitting in a doorway on a plastic chair. Inside the room a small person shouted, screamed and banged their head against the wall. The man in the doorway ignored them and began chatting to the cross-eyed security guard, all of them relaxed and laughing as if they were oblivious.

Eden continued, breathing deeply, but still, she felt dizzy. Her hands were tingly, and she had pins and needles in her feet. Patients were everywhere, sitting on plastic chairs, or standing next to the walls or doors, pain etched on their faces. They looked half dead, leaning their heads against the wall behind them. A woman in a hospital gown was shaking and trying to get a paper cup out of the holder by a water machine. Eden's heart twisted. She placed her hand on the woman's back. 'Let me help you.'

After she had given the shaking woman a cup, other people asked for water, clearly too unwell to stand unaided and too weak to pull one from the holder. The strip lights above were flickering brightly and the alarms and the screaming were overwhelming. How was this a place of healing? Eden glanced down the corridor. It was clogged up with trolleys, upon which even sicker people were lying comatose, unattended, soiled. One elderly man had half fallen out; there were no sides on his trolley. Beyond that was another nurses' station, and Eden could see the ambulances lined up outside, the paramedics all running between them. All the staff were rushing, doctors in dark-green scrubs, nurses in navy blue, volunteers in bright-orange T-shirts with terrified expressions walking around with packets of sandwiches or incontinence pads or cardboard urine bottles. A nurse rushed past her, pushing a bed upon which a young boy was strapped, head down, neck braced, a look of utter desperation in his eyes. She walked past a man sitting on the floor next to the side of the cubicles, who was vomiting into a Tesco bag for life.

Eden took a deep breath and strode, almost marching, forcing her legs to be confident, though her hands were shaking, but crashed into an equipment trolley, sending a kidney dish full of blood bottles and needles onto the floor. She knelt and picked everything up quickly, knowing that she should be wearing gloves to handle bodily fluids and needles, glancing around to see if anyone had noticed, but everyone was too busy.

She found the nurses' station on the right side of the department. A few staff were there on computers or telephones. A woman sat at the desk, a receiver balanced against her ear. She was wearing civvies, and while her name badge clearly said 'Here to Help', her expression said otherwise.

'Hi, good morning, Pam? I'm Eden, one of the new nurses.' Eden smiled widely, despite the knot of fear in her stomach.

The woman tapped on the computer with aggressively long acrylic nails, then gestured to the other end of the ward. 'Handover's in the coffee room down the end. And it's Pamela.'

Eden smiled even more widely. 'Oh, sorry. Pamela. I know about handover, that was in the information pack. I just wanted to let you know that somebody was vaping in the changing room.'

Pamela let the phone drop from her ear. 'Vaping?'

'She said she was a member of staff, but obviously not. Shall I mention it to security? It's my first day, so I'm not really sure . . .'

Pamela snorted. 'Are you for real?'

Eden stopped talking.

'Well, my girl, you're in for a baptism of fire here, if you're wanting to report someone puffing on a vape.'

'I thought – I don't know. I mean, I didn't know who to report to.'

The security guards ran past them towards the blare of a siren, one of them speaking into a radio. 'Entrance to Resus.'

'Handover's in the coffee room,' Pamela repeated, as if nothing had happened. She pointed with a long nail, jabbing the air.

As Eden walked away, she heard Pamela talking to a nurse who had been on a telephone behind her: 'We've got a live one here.'

Eden had been on ED for about ten minutes, and she felt like crying already.

She went into the large room packed full of nurses sitting on threadbare sofas and plastic chairs, feeling small and unimportant. It was like starting secondary school. 'Hi. I'm here for the handover but then doing the orientation day. I'm Eden.'

'Welcome, welcome, Eden. Come on in. I'm Aoife. You'll already know Obi, and Rhian – that's right, isn't it? I understand you all moved into Rose Cottage at the weekend? There's another new starter today, so you won't be alone.'

Eden sat next to Aoife, who had such comforting energy: a green aura. She gently squeezed Eden's arm.

'Hey.' Her new flatmate Obi grinned. Eden smiled back. It was reassuring to recognise someone. Eden had moved in at the weekend and was still in the process of unpacking boxes and organising her room, but whenever she heard anyone in the communal kitchen area she made an excuse to say hello. Obi and Rhian were both nurses on ED with her. Ben was a junior doctor, also working on ED, and had been working there for two months already. He was less likeable, a bit full of himself, a know-it-all.

Eden scoured the other nurses' name badges. Mary, the one in charge of the night shift that had just finished, was older, red-eyed and grey-skinned. The staff room smelt like the changing room: feet. 'Grand,' Mary said. 'Welcome, Eden. Right, let's get going. We've three sickies already and Rosy hasn't turned up yet.'

A whip-thin nurse with psoriasis patterning her arms sat opposite. 'Busy night?'

'Hell.' Mary sucked her teeth and stretched her legs out in front of her. 'Rhian, you'll need to cover breaks, we're thin on the ground.'

Groans from around the room. Eden counted twelve nurses. Was that enough for Majors, Minors and Resus?

Mary yawned, then picked up a piece of paper. 'We've six on the way in and two chest pains in ambulances outside, so brace yourselves. Cubicle one is a sixty-two-year-old man post-aneurism. He's having decerebrate posturing, and the neurosurgical team want to do a CT this morning before making a plan. Two is a forty-one-year-old, Isabella – history of drug use and depression, drank a bottle of bleach and her trachea is now annihilated. Cubicle three: psychosis and waiting for a mental health bed, specialed but the mental health nurse, Priscilla, is vomiting and had to go home. This one's been screaming all day and currently been waiting eighty hours in cubicles. Believes he's the Archangel Gabriel. Apparently, he told Priscilla she was carrying the son of God, right before she started vomiting, so that's exciting.'

There was a smattering of laughter, then Mary carried on talking. Eden didn't find it funny. She jotted down the basic details of each patient but every now and then had to stop writing and take a deep breath. Eighty hours? Had she heard that correctly?

'In Resus,' Mary continued, 'Craig, had a sudden cardiac arrest while running, which is a good advert for not running in my book. HEMS were on the scene, and he had ROSC within five minutes but he's not fully regained consciousness, and GCS is nine. He's sitting on BiPAP awaiting an HDU bed.'

Eden wrote down *HEMS? ROSC? BIPAP? GCS 9?*

She glanced at the nurses on duty, who all seemed nonplussed by these tragedies. Of course, she expected sadness – after all, this was emergency medicine. But as Mary spoke, Eden felt tears pricking her eyeballs, and her abdomen felt heavy, leaden. These poor people. Poor families.

'Also in Resus, DV. Thrown down a flight of concrete stairs apparently,' Mary said. 'She's likely straight to theatre this morning for halo traction; they're setting up. She's immobilised but her spine is unstable, so please, please, decent log rolls. Perfect, and I mean perfect. Looks likely she's fractured at T2.'

The coffee-room door was flung open.

'Hello, hello, sorry I'm late. I'm Sophie. Starting today.'

Eden's eyes widened. It was the woman she'd caught vaping. She was now wearing dark-blue scrubs and clogs like the rest of them, except Aoife who had on a nurse's dress. She'd pulled her hair into a ponytail on top of her head, stuck a biro into it and put an ID badge on: *Sophie Ibrahim. Senior Staff Nurse.*

Senior staff nurse? That must be a mistake. What kind of nurse, senior or otherwise, vapes at work? Sophie plonked herself down next to Eden, still smelling of cherries. She was chewing gum. Aoife watched her, Eden noticed, with a slight frown. Sophie frowned back. Did they know each other?

'Hello,' said Aoife. 'Sophie, is it?'

Mary coughed. 'You'll need to get the handover from someone else,' she said. 'You've missed most of it. We start at eight on the dot.'

Sophie nodded.

'Well, we've all had a first day. Just to reiterate,' she said, looking around the room, 'especially for new starters.' Mary glared at Sophie. 'Log rolls on an unstable spine can make or break an entire life. Right. Hope you girls have a good one. And gent,' she added, turning to Obi, who grinned. 'And that's me over and out.' Mary slid on her shoes, yawned again and stretched. 'I'm offsky.'

Eden looked around the room. Mary's words echoed off the wall somehow, full of lightness tinged with threat. It occurred to Eden that the vast majority of nurses in the room, aside from Mary and Aoife, were young, maybe early twenties, like her. She'd imagined a much more balanced mix. Where were all the older, experienced nurses? She leant slightly closer to Aoife.

'Sleep well, Mary,' Aoife said. 'You back tonight?' She glanced up from her large black diary. Eden tried to see what she was writing, so she could emulate it. Her own scrappy paper looked like a child's doodle, and everything she'd written down had a question mark next to it. But Aoife snapped the diary closed.

Mary shook her head and performed a little jig on the way to the door, then left.

'Right, you motley crew.' Aoife's eyes shone as she spoke, and the entire team hung on to every word. 'Eden, you can shadow me today. Sasha, you can take Obi with you. Roberta, cubicles and lovely Rhian. Rhian, love, watch she takes her breaks, OK? She's a terror for forgetting. Sasha, can you be corridor nurse? Breaks by four, latest. Let's ship out the walking wounded and make space for the chest pains.'

Aoife kept talking as Eden wrote on the piece of paper in front of her and handed it to Sophie. *You were VAPING?*

Sophie didn't look up. Instead, she wrote something down and folded the piece of paper, holding it in her hand. As people left the coffee room one by one to attend to their patients, Aoife sat down opposite them. 'Right. So. I want to hear all about where you've come from and your experience and everything, but let's get the boring stuff out of the way first, OK? Fire doors and alarms and I'll show you round the unit, give you the secret access codes and all that. I'm sure you'll settle in in no time, but always ask any questions. We are a great team here, and you'll find everyone very helpful and friendly. OK, lovelies?' She held out her hand, squeezed Eden's. 'Ah, you'll be grand. Some days are a bit scary for us, let alone when you're new.'

Sophie nodded and stood up, following Aoife to the door. 'Thank you,' said Eden. As they filed out of the coffee room, Sophie handed Eden the slip of paper that she'd folded. They fell back a few steps behind Aoife, and Eden opened it. Sophie had drawn a smiley face and next to it written the words: 'SNITCHES GET STICHES.'

The streets surrounding City Hospital were lined with crumbly buildings and skinny pavements with alleyways shooting off them where people had dumped used nappies, old clothes and empty bottles. There was a small café with outside metal tables, where people all hours of the day or night smoked while they waited for a bacon sandwich. Next to that a launderette, the smell stopping Eden in her tracks. She stood outside for a moment and took a breath. She felt like a different person already, a before and after, as if one day working in the ED could alter a person's DNA forever.

She walked on. A few other small shops on the main road sold everything from Tupperware to rat traps, and giant colourful feather dusters burst from the crates outside, peacocking out like tropical birds. The pavements were uneven, and potholes pock-marked the road, causing cars to swerve dangerously close to the pedestrians. Ambulances and buses, police cars,

Ubers, even an old-fashioned rag-and-bone man on a horse and cart. Random people crossing the road in front of traffic: often disabled, mentally ill or drunk; sometimes all three. Eden had lived her entire life in leafy Keston, just south of London, a place her parents described as a chocolate-box village, but which was increasingly, in her opinion, like something from *The Only Way Is Essex*. The women had fake tans and eyelashes, and the men worked in finance. Everyone had a hot tub.

South London suited Eden far better. Her parents kept asking if she'd live at home to save money, and cut out articles from the *Daily Mail* about stabbings and schizophrenia and gang violence on the streets of Peckham, but Eden was ready to leave Kent. She'd moved to Edinburgh for nursing school to get as far away as possible, and not, as her parents had teased, due to her obsession with *Harry Potter*.

The only way to actually afford living independently anywhere near the hospital in London was to live in nurses' accommodation. Aoife told her she was lucky. Nurses travelled for two hours each way on top of their twelve-and-a-half-hour day to get to work and home, at odd hours of the day or night and with dodgy trains. 'It's great, and it's rare, that you've got subsidised accommodation for the first year,' Aoife had said. 'Though Rose Cottage has a bit of a reputation as a frat house!' She'd laughed but didn't elaborate.

Rose Cottage did not seem too crazy. If anything, it felt homely. Eden got to choose her own bedroom – the bigger of the doubles with a bay window looking out onto a block of flats, but it was warm, and the bed was comfortable with a new mattress. Moving-in day wasn't particularly stressful, not like the first day at work. Eden had a large suitcase, and a few boxes of books and sentimental items, including her brightly coloured bedspread and a few cheerful pillows, dreamcatchers, tarot cards and her teddy bears from when she was little. She had yet to properly spend time with her flatmates but had at least said hello. Rhian had moved from a paediatric oncology ward, had a thick Welsh accent and had hugged her warmly. Ben had told her the first night that he went to Eton but got thrown out for taking cocaine in the school toilets, a fact that Eden would have assumed precluded him from medicine. 'It was a long time ago,' he said, despite being only twenty-five. Obi had already been working in the Emergency Department as a staff nurse for a while. He was ridiculously good-looking and spent most of his time in his pants. Eden found herself gazing at his physique and had to make a conscious effort to appear less impressed. The last flatmate was yet to appear. The accommodation office told them it was a last-minute swap as the clinical fellow from Spain who was about to move in had suffered a breakdown.

Eden unlocked the heavy front door and stood in the hallway. There was a sideboard piled with dozens of unopened letters – bills most likely. Who didn't open their letters? People confused Eden. The hallway carpet was muddy and damp and smelt of old people. Rose Cottage was the largest flat, above a few smaller, self-contained family apartments, mostly inhabited, Ben had told her, by overseas doctors that the NHS had poached from Kuwait, Syria and Afghanistan. 'Even Ukraine,' he said. 'Like those places don't need doctors.' Eden hadn't met the residents yet, but she had heard the constant screaming, shouting and playing of young children, the thud of angry footsteps and the slamming of bedroom doors.

'Hello, hello.' She stepped in and walked past the bedrooms to the open-plan kitchen and living area, where there was a functional work surface, double oven, large fridge with a shelf each for them, a sofa with stains on it and a small square coffee table.

Obi was drinking a protein shake and smiled. 'Settling in? It's a bit extreme, isn't it?' He had the most incredible dimples Eden had ever seen.

She nodded. 'Kinda. It was pretty hectic.'

Obi swigged his drink. 'I know what you mean. There was this guy in Resus today who had a glass shoved up his arse, suction end first.'

Eden blinked. She felt her neck get hot.

'His boyfriend smashed it with a small hammer, apparently, to get it out. Ruptured his spleen.' Obi laughed awkwardly and clapped his hands together.

'Oh my goodness,' Eden started, her voice a bit strange, but then there was thumping at the door.

They both walked over but by then it was being unlocked and opened, and a woman was standing outside with a suitcase. She was carrying a taxidermy owl.

'Sophie.' Of course it was. She might have known. Still, Eden had to fight her own face to stop her frowning.

'Hey.' Obi reached out a hand to help. 'The final one to move in. Sophie! Claire and Tanya were the paramedics at that restaurant and said to look out for you. I thought I'd recognised you in handover from Claire's description. What the hell happened there? She said it was a near-miss prison sentence.' Obi laughed. 'Chopsticks.'

Eden stared at Obi – she had no idea what he was talking about – but they were ignoring her in any case.

'How did she describe me?' Sophie grinned at him.

'Small, beautiful, dangerous.'

Sophie shrugged. She turned away from Obi and stared straight at Eden. 'Oh, goody,' she said.

TWO

Aoife

Aoife *always* wore a dress. No matter how much starch she used, and how well ironed, scrubs never looked as smart as a dress. She arrived at work long before the shift started and stayed late and never complained, no matter how tired she felt. Instead, she'd wake before the birds, sneaking around so as not to disturb Sam. He was not a morning person. She'd quietly pack her work bag with the freshly washed dress, and the belt, with its large silver buckle – a gift from her mum, also a nurse, before she had died – and then write a Post-it note, sticking it on the fridge:

> Sam and James, my two favourite men. Be good and, James, if you can't be good, be careful. Love you.

James, who was eighteen and still awkward, would no doubt roll his eyes at what he called her 'dad jokes', but they both liked her silly Post-its, especially when she had a string of long days and would be working non-stop. Family was everything, but nursing was the blood in her veins. Of course, the job had changed beyond belief since she'd started her training in the early 1990s, but its core remained the same. It had always been about kindness, compassion and dignity. Aoife had risen through the ranks to become the senior sister on ED, the most capable captain at the helm. Her colleagues loved her, and junior nurses looked up to her. Most importantly, patients felt safe with her in charge.

Michael also got to work early. 'Bunch of new nurses started this week,' she said, as they stood outside the mortuary while he smoked a cigarette and gulped a coffee. 'Sophie, Eden, Rhian.' She sipped her green tea and waved the smoke away.

'At least they aren't new doctors. I'm dreading when they arrive in August already.'

'You say that, but I've already got Datix incidents coming at me, and the new director of quality and governance told me earlier this week that she'd attend all our morbidity and mortality meetings, because there needs to be, and I quote, *a new sheriff in town*.' Aoife flapped the smoky air between them. 'That'll kill you, you know?'

'Please, God,' he said. 'Who wants to be old?'

'We are old.' She laughed. It was true she and Michael had known each other a million years already. Neither of them had ever left City ED, their second home. Sam sometimes got jealous of Michael, who he called her work husband, pointing out that they spent more time together than she did with her family. 'It's the job,' Aoife told him. But really, it was more than that.

'Sophie, my new senior staff nurse, was vaping in the changing room apparently.'

Michael laughed. He'd always liked the leftfielders. 'Kindness has its place,' he'd once told Aoife, 'but that place is not ED. We need *badasses*.'

Aoife disagreed.

'Let's get back to it,' he said. 'We've a whopping brain tumour in status arriving any minute and my FY2 today is Ben.' He sighed exaggeratedly. 'Ben. There's a rumour afoot that he starred in an am-dram performance of *Puppetry of the Penis* during med school, which just about sums him up, really.'

Aoife giggled. 'Ah, he's not that bad. We were young once. Green around the gills.'

'Never,' said Michael, and gently squeezed her arm as they walked. The main ED entrance loomed before them in the largest of the hospital buildings, a helipad on the roof housing the helicopter emergency service, for those trauma patients sick to the extent that even a blue-light ambulance would be too late.

It was true they'd been naive and idealistic, like everyone young. Aoife remembered Michael's first day at City, as a house officer back then. He looked like he'd never been near an iron in his life and cut his own hair. He was sent for 'a heavy, long weight' on this first day, and spent two hours diligently standing in the anaesthetic room of the cardiac theatres, after his boss, an old-school consultant, insisted medicine required such initiations. Those were the days when tricks were ten a penny. Even she had once been Plaster of Paris-ed from the waist down and, when completely immobile, pushed in a wheelchair into a lift and sent to the management floor. HR was more of a silent partner in the old days.

Aoife had been a staff nurse for a few years by the time Michael arrived, and was already married to Sam, but she remembered the first time Michael had touched her, shaking her hand, and the slight static electric shock they had both felt, which made them laugh. 'That's a sign,' he'd said. How many times had he touched her now?

Eden's long mullet was clipped into a neat ponytail. She wore a rainbow lanyard and yellow name badge: 'My name is Eden Walsh. Staff Nurse'. A small brooch from Edinburgh University was pinned to her scrub top, and she had an overstuffed bumbag around her waist, and some alcohol hand gel attached to it with a large silver clasp. She looked shiny and professional. Even her regulation black shoes were brand new.

'You'll be shadowing me again today, Eden, you poor thing.' Aoife smiled.

Eden looked relieved. 'Thank you,' she said.

They began a more in-depth tour of the Emergency Department, Aoife scanning each area to avoid taking Eden anywhere that a patient was kicking off; she wanted her eased in as much as possible. Plenty of time for Eden to get used to dealing with violence. Her nurses had been spat on, strangled, punched and kicked. Only last month a nurse had had her jaw broken by a relative of a patient in cardiac arrest and they were about to start trialling body-worn cameras for all staff. For now, orientating Eden to the environment was the priority; that, and trying not to frighten her. They couldn't afford to be any more short-staffed.

'ED is all ground floor, and shaped in a long rectangle, with different areas off each side, and it's divided into level of need. You can't get through any door without your swipe card – make sure you always have that on you, or you'll be waiting an age. It's a bit of a maze, but think of it as the entire ground floor, virtually, of this hospital building and on the one side is the ambulances, then Resuscitation, then Majors, then Minors, the Acute Medical Unit, then the reception area. If you walk in, you're likely to need the less extreme care; if blue-lit in, then you start off at the opposite end, in Resus.'

Eden smiled at the angry-looking reception staff in their booths. 'Is that bullet-proof glass?' She laughed faintly.

'It is. Safety's the priority here, for patients and staff. We record all the ED wait times, document outcomes and performance against monthly targets. All of the governance is about patient safety.'

'Gosh.' The colour drained from Eden's face. 'It's a lot to take in. I'll need a map to find my way around. So much to learn, too.'

'There is. But it's your first week, so give yourself a break. You'll get tons of support, and if you're unsure about anything, always ask.'

As they walked around the ED, Aoife pointed out the large equipment room, the quirky way the drug fridges opened, the alarms underneath the desks, the trolleys that had assessment equipment on them. Eden interrupted every moment: *How long is the average wait for people? Are there specific mental health cubicles? What kind of patients do you see in Minors? Are there a lot of deaths?*

'Right, let's save the questions for now. I want to show you the arterial blood gas machine.' Aoife patted the top of the metal box as if it were a small child. 'Eight thousand pounds if it goes wrong, so this is important. Never put bone marrow samples in here, and don't attempt to use it if it's calibrating, just wait for it to do its thing. We can run through blood gas interpretation later. It's complicated, but you'll get the hang of it.'

They were standing in the dirty utility room, which was lined with cardboard bed pans and bottles, and had a large tank where bodily fluids were deposited. The whole room smelt of urine, but Aoife was immune to reacting.

Eden coughed and covered her nose. 'Sorry, something's making my eyes water. What's that smell?'

Aoife smiled. She nearly said, *Foetid humanity*, but stopped herself. 'It doesn't seem possible, I'm sure, but you'll get used to anything. OK, let's go set up and test the portable oxygen cylinders. You'll be using those a lot now we're treating so many people in corridors.'

Aoife opened the sluice door and Eden bolted out, gasping dramatically. If she thought that smell was bad, she was in for a shock. Depending on the day and the patients, ED smelt of faeces, burnt skin, chemicals, urine, ketotic coffee breath, perpetual body odour, feet, gases, blood. There were specific smells that Aoife could recognise, and even diagnose from, predicting exactly what infection a person had, and what antibiotics they needed: a pseudomonas bacterial infection was present when there was a particularly putrid smell of a patient's sputum; melena, the black, tar-like stool that suggested a gastrointestinal bleed, smelt of gone-off food mixed with stagnant water; the foul, sweet, almost fishy smell of bacterial vaginosis occasionally wafted from the crotches of patients – and sometimes staff. Aoife could smell necrosis, the dying of tissue and flesh, before a person's skin changed colour. She could smell cancer.

Like all experienced nurses, Aoife could walk onto the department and gravitate towards the sickest patient, or the patient who was about to 'go off', without any kind of information other than gut instinct. Nursing was taste, smell, sound and touch. It was *feeling*.

Eden continued breathing deeply and coughing a bit as she followed Aoife closely back to the patient area and into the cubicles.

'Toni here had a seizure at home, brought in via ambulance, and has a deteriorating GCS. Today seems to be a day of coma. It goes like that. ED is weirdly thematic. We'll get a rush of strokes, then stabbings, then head injuries. Makes scans tricky as the department gets backed up, but Toni had a CT scan already – it showed swelling and we're not sure the cause of that. He needs an MRI, then a High Dependency Unit bed, and they're full. To make things worse for the poor chap, his wife went into labour at twenty-four weeks. Stress, most likely. She's with the baby in the Neonatal Unit now. What a situation.'

Aoife whispered despite Toni's comatose conscious level. Toni may have been showing a Glasgow Coma Scale of eight, and not really responding to anything except pain, but who's to say if he could hear them or not? One of many research studies being conducted on ED and ICU was about hearing and death. The patients during cardiac arrest were told a specific word during the time they had no output, so were technically not even alive. It astonished Aoife how many patients post-arrest could recall the word they'd been told: 'oranges'. One even swore he could taste them.

'Let's do another GCS, then have coffee?'

Eden nodded. 'Absolutely.' She washed her hands, put on an apron over her scrubs, and took a small pen torch out of her bumbag. 'Toni, my name's Eden. I'll take good care of you. You're completely safe with me.'

'Oh, great, Sophie, I was hoping to catch you today. How's it going?'

Sophie didn't look up from her book. She wore white, scuffed trainers, what looked like yesterday's make-up smeared around her eyes, a pen in her hair. She shuffled up slightly so Eden could sit down next to her, and Aoife sat opposite them. The coffee room was large and had at least a dozen chairs dotted around the place. There was an industrial fridge, sink, draining area and long table in the corner, which housed the coffee granules they all relied on, as well as a loaf or two of white bread. Someone had left an article on the smaller coffee table between them about the gut microbiome and next to it was a basket of leftover Quality Street, only the strawberry creams remaining.

'What are you reading?' Aoife put a plate of anaemic toast on the table between them all. 'The fire brigade was constantly called out for burning toast, so we now have the toaster on some special setting,' she said. 'It's more like warm bread, I'm afraid.'

Sophie shrugged and closed her book.

'Tell me about you both, then.'

Eden grinned and reached for some toast. 'I'm newly qualified, so not much to tell yet.'

Sophie ignored her. 'What do you want to know?'

'Well, where you're from, your experience so far, that kind of thing. It's not an interview, don't worry.' Aoife laughed. 'I really need to stop scrolling and get back into reading. Any good?'

Sophie took a piece of toast and flashed the cover at Aoife. 'Cormac McCarthy. It's pretty dark.' She nibbled the edge of the toast. 'Is that Stork margarine?'

'It's hardly the Ritz. There's a staff fridge there.' Aoife nodded at the small fridge in the corner, which always had out-of-date food in it and Tupperware with Post-it notes stuck to the top: *FOOD THIEF: BACK OFF. DO NOT EAT.* They all knew that the food thief was any and all doctors. Thanks to the FY2s, the Lucozade that used to be present on the crash trolley to treat hypoglycaemia was now in a locked drawer.

'No wonder you're avoiding the toast,' said Sophie.

Aoife smiled. 'Ah, I'd love some. But perimenopause has me eating nothing but seeds and low-fat cottage cheese.'

Sophie frowned. 'Sounds brutal. You should probably read some Mary Oliver.'

'Love Mary Oliver,' said Eden, looking between them. 'I trained at Edinburgh Infirmary, where I did placements and my elective on ED, so hopefully it won't be too terrifying!

I always wanted to be a nurse, as long as I can remember – cringey but true. What else? Oh, I'm living at Rose Cottage.' She paused. 'With Sophie and a few others, most likely for six months anyway. I want to be near the hospital and do as many extra shifts as I can.'

Aoife smiled. Eden was very warm, if a little saccharine. She reminded Aoife of herself in her early twenties. Keen, thoughtful, people-pleasing. She was naive and overly optimistic, but this place would cure that in no time.

'Have you worked here for long?' Eden asked.

'Ah, you don't want to know. Put it this way, I'm part of the furniture.'

Sophie rolled her eyes. A tiny bit, but enough for Aoife to feel her skin bristle. Sophie was *not* a people-pleaser. 'What about you?' Aoife asked her.

Sophie put her bitten toast back down on the plate. 'Nothing much. I worked eighteen months at Blackpool Royal – ED, but not as you know it. Level two mostly. It was a good unit, but obviously it was Blackpool. So here I am.'

'I went to Blackpool a million years ago with Sam, my husband. I seem to remember us arguing on the Big Wheel. I'm sure it's changed a lot.'

'It's less like a holiday destination now, very deprived. Crack central.'

'What was ED like there?'

'Like a scene from *Pirates of the Caribbean: Dead Man's Chest*.'

Aoife raised an eyebrow.

Sophie took her phone out of her scrub pocket again. 'I've got to make a call, sorry.' She smiled and stood up, dumping her toast in the bin on the way out.

After she'd closed the door behind her, Eden waited a few moments and leant towards Aoife. 'She's very hard to get to know.'

*

The afternoon passed in a blur. Aoife was called away three times, leaving an anxious Eden flying solo. She had an M&M meeting, the weekly catch-up in-house to discuss the morbidity and mortality of all the patients on the unit, to highlight red flags and identify any unusual areas of concern. She had to prepare an expert witness statement for a case that had ended up in the Royal Courts of Justice. The off-duty rota didn't even get a look-in, and four nurses called in sick for the night shift, which they'd need to find cover for. 'I'm so sorry, Eden. The last thing I wanted to do was leave you alone on your second day.'

Eden was doing another set of obs on Toni. She looked up and smiled. 'It's OK. Honestly. I've been fine.'

Aoife looked at Toni. His posture had changed, stiffened. She could see his jugular pulse. 'What's his blood pressure?'

Eden clicked on the computer where she'd recorded it. 'His blood pressure is 220/130. Oh. That seems very high. Shall I let the docs know?'

Aoife shouted, 'Help here, please!' and Kemi, one of the anaesthetists, rushed in alongside a healthcare assistant. They busied themselves drawing up drugs, and Aoife pulled Eden to the side. 'If there's any observation outside the norm, get help immediately,' she said. 'You can see the NEWS scale? That BP put him in the red.'

Eden's shoulders shuddered. She looked like she was holding in tears. 'I'm so sorry. I'll do an incident form. I'm so sorry, Aoife.'

Aoife took a breath. She held the outsides of Eden's arms. 'Don't worry about that. If we wrote down every near miss, we'd be here until midnight.' She nodded at Kemi. 'Under control?'

Kemi smiled. Like all anaesthetists, she was unflappable.

'Right. I've asked a porter to pop up to NICU to bring his wife down here to visit. I called up – she's been waiting an age, apparently; they're super-busy and short today too. I'll do the antibiotics and drugs; sure we're a bit late with that.'

Eden looked up, less anxious now. 'Of course. I could also get Toni's wife. I mean, if it's quicker. I can easily go. She'll probably be going out of her mind.'

'That would be helpful. You can bring her down from NICU and then get the porters to take her back up. She's on a chair, not a trolley, so only needs one person. I'm sure she's desperate to come visit. His wife is Nicola. Do you know where to find the Neonatal Unit? Seventh floor.'

Eden nodded enthusiastically. 'Yes, I know where NICU is. I popped up there last week to see if they had any extra shifts going, but they want six months' experience, minimum. Those tiny babies! They're so teeny I can't even . . . I'll be super-quick.' She skipped out.

Aoife watched her for a few seconds. It wasn't Eden's job to collect a relative and bring them to ED, but nurses, good ones at least, did all sorts of jobs outside their official role. Eden would no doubt be a decent nurse once she calmed down a bit.

'The guy waiting in area four has no sats; his oxygen levels are not recording at all.' Sophie appeared, and sounded almost bored.

Aoife glanced past her at the corridor where dozens of people were sitting on plastic chairs, leaning their heads against the wall. One man had slumped over and folded in half. 'Sorry, what?'

Sophie shrugged. 'I've whacked a bit of oxygen on him, but he really needs seeing.'

Aoife stared at Sophie. Then she pushed her aside and rushed towards the waiting area.

*

The rest of the day sped past, and before she knew it Aoife had handed over to night staff and was heading for the exit. A good day, overall. She had somehow managed to keep people alive, despite the odds. The patient in Resus who'd been thrown down the stairs was safely in theatres. Aoife had made sure they'd log-rolled her when the new starters were on a break, rather than risk them anywhere near a fractured spine, and they'd managed to arrest her husband. It was hard to imagine, being married to gentle Sam, what it must feel like to live with a monster, but violent men were ten a penny in ED.

Toni was safely transferred to ICU before he had a stroke due to the dangerously high blood pressure that Eden had somehow missed reporting. He was hovering between life and death, but thanks to quick work during the golden hour – the time immediately after a traumatic injury or, in his case, severe medical emergency, when proper treatment may prevent death – he made it. She'd managed to get Sophie's patient with very low oxygen levels into Resus, where the team had assessed and reviewed him before finding him a bed on the respiratory ward. Another five minutes of Sophie's seeming lack of both competence and empathy and it might have been a different story. Still, all's well that ends well, as Aoife often mumbled at the end of such days, especially with new starters.

'City ED is a place of miracles as well as sadness,' she told Michael as they stood in the ninth-floor corridor looking out over the London skyline. This was the spot they caught the best sunsets, and sunrises, when they could snatch the time. 'Golden hour in more ways than one. Look.' She gestured to the rich-orange glow streaming in through the grotty NHS windows. The smog outside gave the sky fire and blood. 'I'm going to get changed, don't wait for me.'

Michael looked at her. 'Your lilac eyes in this light,' he said, 'kill me.' He had his coat on and walked with her to the heavy doors out onto the atrium where they usually waited for the lift with other tired staff all going home after a long day too. But this time he didn't open the exit door. He looked left to right, then pulled Aoife into the equipment cupboard.

They stood opposite each other in the darkness for a few moments. 'We'll be caught sneaking around.'

'Shh,' he said. 'Nobody saw us come in.'

'I'm a married woman!'

'You're a married ED nurse; different rules apply. In any case, it's never stopped you before, and this place hides all secrets . . .'

Aoife knew he was right. The hospital was rife with unseen affairs. It was a perfect environment for infidelity, with wildly unpredictable working patterns and a heightened respect for living in the moment.

She leant against the door, expecting him to move closer. Instead, he pulled open a drawer on one of the trolleys and rummaged through needles, catheters, endotracheal tubes, spare gauze squares, pericardiocentesis kits, chest drains, arterial blood syringes, until he finally found what he was looking for. Aoife's eyes had adjusted to the near darkness now. He turned around holding a tube of KY Jelly. 'Bingo.'

'Michael,' she whispered. 'You're not serious.'

'Deadly.' He squirted some onto his fingers, put the tube back and moved towards Aoife, kissing her gently, before dropping to his knees in front of her. He lifted her dress, and slid his hand into her knickers, then pushed his fingers inside her so hard and fast she had to move away from the door in case it rattled.

Neither of them noticed Eden watch them go in. By the time they came out, the corridor was dark and empty; golden hour was over.

THREE

Sophie

All hospital staff in the UK understood what the term 'Rose Cottage' really meant. It was used every day, all over the NHS, as secret code for the mortuary: 'We've got a patient in bed five ready to go to Rose Cottage,' or 'Pick up and transfer to Rose Cottage,' or 'Mrs Bradley in ten looks like she'll be off to Rose Cottage by the end of the day.'

Sophie loved the idea that somebody had named their functional yet ugly hospital accommodation flat after the mortuary. She had always admired the macabre.

There were five of them sharing, four nurses, and Ben. It was fairly social, though their shift patterns prevented it from being the frat house Aoife had warned her and Eden about. In any case, Sophie preferred to be in her room, listening to music, reading novels, daydreaming. Her room was decorated with taxidermy she'd collected from boot fairs and antique shops and markets over the years. Ben nicknamed her Dahmer, but what could any of them say? Rhian spent half her time in the historical re-enactment society dressing as a knight and jousting with fake weapons, and the other half on OnlyFans to supplement her Band 5 salary. Obi had applied to *Love Island* and regularly blocked the toilet due to the amount of protein he was consuming, and Ben was Ben. They were misfits, but they were all OK. Each to their own.

Sophie did find Eden a bit annoying, though. After the first time they all hung out together and it turned into a late-night confessional chat, she told them that she was sapiosexual and the only two people in the world she'd have a threesome with were Jeremy Corbyn and Taylor Swift. She asked Sophie if she wanted to hang out at Ruskin Park on their day off, to join a local protest group activity and 'fly kites for Gaza', to which Sophie scoffed, 'Sure, that's going to make all the difference in the world.'

They cooked for themselves – noodles, packet stir-fries, pasta – but sometimes hung out together after an impossibly long or stressful day, smoking weed until late in the night. Ben took every drug known to man and spent his evenings scrolling Grindr. Once, he'd left his computer open, and Sophie had checked his search history to find an array of pornographic horrors, but the biggest, most tragic repeated searches were for porcelain veneers, hair plugs and abdominal liposuction. He'd googled Ozempic and Mounjaro, despite being a doctor, and his latest search was 'Sharon Osbourne Rapid Weight Loss'.

'It's the trenches,' said Rhian. 'London, I mean. Tall, bearded, hippy types who live in East London, still smoke actual fags and never call you back. I've basically stopped dating anyone.'

'You could date me!' Obi clapped his hands together. 'Gorgeous Rhian. We could be the Rose Cottage power couple.'

Sophie sucked on her vape and watched her flatmates interact with interest. They were in the sizing-up phase, only a month in, working out if they might become actual friends.

'You need to avoid fuckboys.' Ben was making dinner for them all. Once a week, they would chip in a tenner each and take turns cooking.

'I do, actually. Hence you' – Rhian kissed Obi on the cheek – 'are out of the question.'

Obi wiped an imaginary tear with his finger. 'You're not exactly my type.' He chuckled. 'But, oh God, that would make my dad happy.'

Obi must be the last gay man in London who had not come out. Sophie didn't get it. Surely his parents already knew. Still, what could she say about communicating with parents? Sophie hadn't spoken to hers since around the age of eleven, when her grandma had come to the house to collect her and taken her back to the Isle of Man to live with her in Onchan. Gee's cottage smelt of Bovril and lard, and was full of love and treasured taxidermy mice playing tiny instruments, which her late grandad had spent his life making.

Ben shouted with his head in the oven. 'Fuck.' He stood up, red-faced and sweaty. 'Fish is off, I'm afraid.' He pulled the tray out.

'That's decimated,' said Obi. 'Reminds me. We had this burns patient yesterday, kept saying he couldn't feel any pain, which is obvs because the burns were so bad they'd gone through the nerves. He was literally charred. Jumped in a firepit at a BBQ after taking magic mushrooms, apparently, then set fire to a nearby house. Smelt like pork.'

Already, ED nursing in London was making them a bit numb. They were matter-of-fact about things no person should ever be matter-of-fact about.

'Ooooh,' said Ben. 'I have mushroom tincture. Who's in?'

They must have got to bed at 4 a.m. and Sophie was working at eight. She couldn't afford to be late again. Aoife had already given her a ticking-off about yet another patient in the corridors who was about to arrest due to low oxygen levels. If it hadn't been for Sophie checking his SaO2, he *would* have arrested, but she didn't mention that. She'd already noticed how powerful Aoife was in ED. It was her kingdom.

Sophie had also noticed how Aoife did not fill in a Near Miss form, despite saying to Sophie that the most important priority for all nurses was patient safety. No senior nurse wanted the adverse incident rates on their ward going up. It reflected badly on them, after all.

The alarm beeped again. Sophie forced her legs out of bed, then stood up and stretched. Her room was tidy and organised as ever, the piled papers on the desk next to the window, the table against the bookshelves, which were full of books, trinkets and small curiosities. A fox with one eye was in a glass box on the table, feral, vicious-looking. She'd never stuffed anything herself, even after years spent watching Gramps in his workshop, taking animals apart and turning death into something lifelike. But her first part-time job aged fifteen had been in a butcher's, where she learnt about sinew and tissue and bones, how to carve flesh and slice organs open. By the time Sophie was a nursing student, she was an expert with a knife.

She slid her feet into flip-flops, her head throbbing. It was still dark, and Ben was asleep on the sofa, lying next to a pizza box. She liked Ben, damaged as he clearly was. He was exactly as he seemed, no hidden agenda or fake niceness. Eden was harder to get to know. She wore a badge on her rucksack that said 'Everyone Deserves Kindness'. Eden had scowled when Sophie had asked about it: 'What about Jimmy Savile? Fred West? Surely that message doesn't apply to child killers, rapists, paedos?'

'Actually,' Eden had said, smiling, 'I think it does. The NMC code of conduct is basically that. Nurses should be non-judgemental. Completely objective.'

'There's no objectivity in nursing,' Sophie had said. 'You and I both know that some people are more deserving than others. I guess we'll have to agree to disagree.'

'Morning.' Ben groaned and opened one eye. He was perfectly crumpled.

'Hola. Want a smoothie?' Sophie began to tip frozen berries into the blender.

'Mate, I'll puke. What time is it?'

'Around six-forty-ish.'

'Fuck, fuck, fuck.' He jumped up and started waving his arms around, grabbed a slice of cold pizza and ran towards his bedroom.

Sophie stood for a few moments in the near darkness of the stale-smelling room, downed her smoothie, then went to shower and dress, before leaving the flat wearing huge sunglasses.

Aoife had her head in her hands and was sitting in darkness in the staff room. Sophie heard Gee's voice inside her: *All that glitters is not gold.*

She switched on the strip lights. 'You look how I feel. Rough night?'

Aoife looked up. 'Ah, I'm bracing myself for today. We've no room at the inn already, and half the day staff are off with the new wave of Covid. We've had to poach ward nurses. Ben's having to be a nurse today, and at this rate, so will Michael.' Aoife gulped.

Her face was wet, Sophie noticed. The day a senior sister as experienced as Aoife cried at work was surely the End Times. 'Are you OK?'

Aoife wiped her wet cheeks with the palms of her hands. 'Not really. We're in total breach of the four-hour target, and the death rate this week is off the scale. It's shot up in the last few weeks, to the extent that the powers that be are conducting an internal review.'

'That all sounds pretty heavy,' Sophie said, closing her eyes. A death rate going up rapidly would shake even the most experienced of nurses, but it wasn't uncommon these days. The NHS was fucked. Humanity was fucked. Those two facts colliding became perfectly dark bedfellows.

Aoife sighed, 'Ah, I'm sorry. I was meant to be taking my son, James, to a uni open day and I've had to let him down so I'm feeling a bit sorry for myself today. I shouldn't be offloading to you. You've only been here five minutes.'

'A month, actually.' Sophie grimaced. 'I'll be needing the drug-cupboard keys, please. I won't be able to function until I've had a root around for Tramadol.'

'Sometimes I don't know if you're joking or not,' Aoife said, laughing.

There was an awkward pause. Sophie hovered in front of Aoife, then held out her hand.

'You can't be serious. You know that's an opiate, right?'

'I had a touch of cancer as a kid,' said Sophie. 'And the only good thing about it was Tramadol . . .'

'Oh, Sophie, that's awful!'

Sophie shrugged. 'Long time ago. Still, this hangover is giving me flashbacks.'

Aoife was silent a moment, staring at her. 'God, I'm sorry, Sophie. Perhaps that's what led you to nursing. I can give you some paracetamol from my own supply, but you can't take anything from the drug cupboard, I'm afraid.'

Sophie shrugged then watched Aoife reach for her handbag, pull out some Nurofen and paracetamol, and hand her two of each. She dry-swallowed them in one go.

The morning was a struggle, and her brain felt increasingly foggy. There were so many patients at death's door it was hard to know who to prioritise – yet another day of firefighting. Still, the staff seemed to thrive in extremis. Sophie knew that ED was a place for adrenaline junkies. At Blackpool she'd worked with a nurse who hovered by the red emergency phone and had actually punched the air when a call came in about a bus full of people that had fallen off a bridge. She'd lowered her hand when she saw her colleagues staring at her, and said, 'How terrible.' Nobody berated her. It gave you a warped relationship with danger and excitement, this job. But she'd yet to meet a single nurse who didn't love emergency medicine. On days like this, with so many sick people pouring into ED, Sophie focused on the patients quietly suffering. Those easily missed. The Emergency Department was no place to be dying from cancer, but it happened all the time.

Sophie put on two aprons and two pairs of gloves and closed the curtain. Dealing with shit and piss and blood and vomit usually had no effect on her, but nausea had not left her all morning, and the stench was putrid. She could almost taste it. Mr Francis was a big man, and there was nobody to help move him, so she did the best she could: a packet of wipes, three new incontinence pads, a yellow clinical waste bag opened and ready at the foot of the bed. She wiped him clean as much as possible but gagged when scooping out the faeces that had crusted up in his skin folds. Luckily his skin hadn't broken down, but it was red and angry when she dried it. This man needed things that the NHS didn't provide. Talc. Nutritious food. Family.

'Mr Francis, I'm going to put a bit of barrier cream on your thighs as it's all a bit sore down there, OK? We'll get you comfy on the ward as soon as we can.'

He was out of it but lifted his hand a fraction. Sophie picked it up for a moment. His fingernails also needed cutting; they were thick and gnarly. She rolled him slightly off his left leg and onto his right, her back twingeing a bit, a hazard of the job.

He coughed, a sort of rattlesnake death cough, fluid bubbling in his chest. He was on high-flow oxygen delivered by a non rebreathe oxygen mask that was inflated like a small balloon. 'Mr Francis, I'm going to wipe your mouth.'

Sophie shouted into his ear, but he didn't respond. She glanced at the closed curtains around them and looked closely at Mr Francis's face. The smell of shit hung over them in a cloud. His skin and cheeks were puffy, his eyes bulbous and shadowy. She looked for clues – people's bodies could tell you anything – and glanced over the medical information, but that didn't say much about this man's life. Sophie liked to know what kind of person she was really looking after. Whose arse she was wiping, whose heart she was keeping alive. Whether they were deserving or not.

The man's bag was on the foot end of the trolley, with his wallet inside it. Wayne Francis. He had a Nectar card, a membership for Sidcup Library, a packet of stamps that were no longer in use and a black-and-white photo of a woman about Sophie's age with thick dark eyebrows. She'd found all sorts of things in patients' possessions. A small bag of cocaine (Ben verified that); a war medal; a zombie machete; a photo album entirely made up of pictures of vulvas; once, a ferret, which a woman had put into her handbag the moment she had chest pain, and was subsequently rushed to the ED. Sophie had heard a squeaking and wondered if it was a mouse or rat, which were rife all over the hospital. But then she'd found the ferret and phoned the patient's next of kin. 'I'll take it to the RSPCA,' she'd said, 'if nobody is able to come get it.' She had no intention of taking that animal to the RSPCA after staring at its black marble eyes, and feeling the texture of its fur, which reminded her of Gee's winter coat.

Wayne Francis had no animals in his bag, and nothing of note. She put everything carefully back, leant towards his face and hesitated, thinking about Aoife's words.

The death rate on ED is off the scale.

'We'll get you to the ward soon, Mr Francis.' She leant closer still. He had that smell of chemotherapy, the metal poison of it unmistakable. 'You're dying,' she whispered. 'It's your time. But there's nothing to be frightened of.'

Then she pulled the oxygen mask from Mr Francis's face and put it over her own nose and mouth, breathing in as deeply as she could.

FOUR
Eden

Eden liked to masturbate while she was reading, one hand holding a book, the other touching herself. Multitasking. Sometimes she would orgasm and drop the book, but not always. She held it high in front of her face, which was getting hotter and sweatier, her other hand moving faster underneath her pyjama bottoms. She must have momentarily closed her eyes and was pressing her mouth closed tightly to stop any noise coming out.

'Holy fuck.'

Eden shot upright, whipping her hand out of her pyjamas, dropping the book onto her quilt.

Sophie stood in front of her, wide-eyed.

How did she get in without Eden hearing her bedroom door open? How long had she been standing there? Eden forced her breathing to slow down and fake-stretched. 'Oh, hey.' But her voice sounded shaky.

'Holy fuck,' Sophie repeated.

Eden sat up further still and extended her head from side to side.

Sophie was standing in front of her desk and leant back onto it. 'You're sick in the head, Edes.' Her eyes were sparkling. 'A sick puppy.'

'What do you mean?' Eden looked down at the book, a depiction of Florence Nightingale holding a lamp on the cover. 'Oh, this. I was reading it last night, must have fallen asleep—'

Sophie shook her head. 'Liar, liar, pants on fire.'

Eden stared at her. Sophie would tell everyone about this, and she'd be laughed at forever. 'I don't know what you think you saw,' she began. Her stomach spasmed.

Sophie held a hand out. 'Let's not do this,' she said. 'I mean, you're really fucking weird, Eden Walsh.'

'Why are you in my room?' Eden pulled the quilt over her chest, which she could feel burning underneath her pyjama top. 'Didn't you knock? Where are your manners?'

Sophie lowered her hand and smiled. 'Eden, you were wanking to Florence Nightingale.' She paused. 'I mean, if *Notes on Nursing: What It Is, and What It Is Not* by Florence fucking Nightingale makes you thirsty, you might need to get out more for a hook-up, or to see a therapist.'

Eden's tone hardened. 'I was reading, that's all.'

Sophie shrugged. 'I came in to borrow your deodorant, but I can see you're busy, so I'll come back later.' She stood up straight, laughing. 'Just so you know, Rhian has a First World War vintage nurse's uniform in her wardrobe if you want to borrow it.'

'You burst into my room without knocking and now you want to shame me? This is my bedroom. My safe space. Get out, Sophie.'

Sophie threw both her hands in the air. 'You're right, you're right, and I'm sorry for teasing. No judgement, let's never speak of this again. I'll leave you and Florence to it, and next time I'll knock. Loudly.' She glanced at the book, then winked and left the room, closing the door behind her.

Eden spent the next ten minutes lying in bed, staring at the ceiling. Masturbating was the most natural thing in the world and, if anything, it was Sophie who should feel embarrassed. Having flatmates was not at all what she'd imagined. She'd pictured group meals, movie nights with popcorn and late-night chats, sharing their experiences on the unit. She had not expected to feel this lonely.

Nursing wasn't what she'd imagined either. Despite excellent handwashing, Eden had already contracted nits, scabies and impetigo in her first month, as well as two bouts of diarrhoea and vomiting and a constant productive cough. The patients were not grateful and sweet, but rude, smelly, drunk, aggressive and sometimes – often – violent. They blamed the nurses rather than the government for the ridiculous wait times; they swore, shouted and sobbed.

'Watch it.' A nurse carrying a giant cup jumped out of the way, spilling coffee onto her scrub top.

'Ah, sorry. I was miles away.'

The nurse smiled, but as she walked off Eden heard her muttering, 'Idiot.'

She ignored her and pushed on. A group of teenage boys clustered together outside the Breast Clinic were playing EDM from a small speaker, and Eden noticed a line of women, all shapes and sizes and ages, all anxious, waiting for the clinic door to open, the line already snaking around the corner. One woman at the front was leaning against the wall and had her hands pressed over her ears. She wore a scarf over her head.

'Can you turn that music off or move somewhere else?' Eden pointed to the exit.

'You move, man.' The boy holding the speaker lifted it high in the air, making the beat sound even louder.

Eden put her hands on her hips, shouted, 'There are sick people here, and there's plenty of space outside to listen to music.'

The tallest boy made a gun sign at Eden with his hand and the others laughed. The woman wearing a scarf pressed the Breast Clinic door buzzer repeatedly.

Eden walked around the corner to Radiology and leant across the desk, picking up a phone: *2222 Need Security, outside Breast Clinic, Ground Floor, River Wing.*

Security arrived in seconds, the fastest response team at City. Eden watched the teens slink away on sight of the security guards twice their size. The women waiting in line clapped noiselessly. Eden felt her jaw unclench.

She was surely late now, though. A shortcut took her outside opposite the mortuary building, and the viewing room next to it, where the casket was lined with maroon silk, the tissues the expensive balsam kind, and the air smelt of copper. Eden paused a brief moment, breathing deeply, then walked quickly, almost running, ignoring the man shouting to the air, and the teenagers from earlier, now arguing by the bike rack. Then she stopped. A man with one leg was balancing on a crutch and smoking a cigarette through his tracheostomy hole in his neck. Eden stopped in front of him and blinked. He stared back at her and continued, sucking in the cigarette smoke until the tip turned orange, then blowing it out of his neck hole.

'I don't think that's a good idea,' she said, in a crisp and accusatory voice, before noticing he was tearful. She softened her words, her face. 'Do you have someone with you? Can I help? I mean, that's not going to do you any good, is it, smoking like that?'

The man looked at her and shot back in a voice like a robot. 'Bless you, nurse, but no point giving up now.' Then he started coughing and a large green chunk of phlegm flew out of his neck hole and landed on Eden's cheek. 'Oh God, I'm sorry, nurse.'

By the time Eden had washed and then wiped her cheek repeatedly with alcohol gel, there was a flurry of activity at the entrance of the Acute Medical Unit. The staff, mostly nurses but a few doctors, were congregated around a couple.

'Morning, Eden. You remember Toni and Nicola?' Aoife's eyes were sparkling, her smile wide. 'This is the best part of our job.' It was difficult to understand Aoife, and why she'd disappeared into the dark equipment room with Michael, as Eden waited outside the door, holding an ECG, listening to the sounds coming from the other side. But whatever the state of her marriage, Aoife was an excellent nurse and mentor, there was no denying that.

Eden smiled back and whispered, 'Sorry I'm late.'

Eden recognised the couple next to Aoife immediately, the man using a wheelchair, and the woman she'd met in NICU. She'd loved watching those impossibly small babies, bubble-wrapped, a few even in miniature sandwich bags to preserve their heat, with their alien heads and all-knowing eyes, not quite alive yet; not quite human; fragile, delicate ghosts.

Toni was almost unrecognisable. His skin shone bright, his eyes were clear and he was clean shaven and dressed in smart clothes, sitting upright. 'Eden?' He held out a hand for her to shake. 'Aoife told me you looked after me too. I can't remember much, to be honest, even in ICU. A&E is a complete blur.'

Eden leant down and hugged him. 'Oh, my goodness,' she said, standing upright to hug Nicola too. 'You look amazing.'

'Thanks to the expertise of the nurses and doctors here. Thanks to you.'

Aoife clearly hadn't told him about her misdemeanour, that Eden had not reported his dangerously high blood pressure. He might have had a stroke because of her. She kept running it over in her mind, all the what-ifs, and even chatted with Rhian, who listed all the mistakes she'd made when she was newly qualified. 'It's a wonder any of my patients survived,' she said.

Eden stood next to Aoife as the other nurses drifted back to their patients. An alarm sounded from across the ward. 'How are you? How's the little one?'

'She's good. Growing. They're talking about moving her to Special Care in a few weeks if she carries on doing so well – if they can get staff, that is. They're so short of nurses!' Toni looked down into the AMU and the other side where he was being nursed in Majors. 'It's so weird, I can hardly remember anything.'

'Well, you were as sick as they come,' said Aoife. 'But sometimes, occasionally, we get a miracle here. That's the glue that holds us nurses together.' Aoife was beaming. She looked as if she'd won the lottery, or it had been her who'd recovered from a serious illness.

Eden looked at Toni's face, astonished at how well he looked, how quickly he'd recovered. He had been written off by the doctors – Michael had looked at his scan and commented that his brain matter resembled shepherd's pie – but Aoife had kept up hope.

Toni took a photograph from his pocket and handed it to Aoife. 'For your board.'

'Oh, wonderful. I'll pin it up on the wall of fame.'

Eden loved the giant pinboard in the corridor outside ED, covered in photographs of people who had survived serious accidents or illnesses, and hundreds of thank-you cards. For every card or thank-you note there were a dozen complaints, Aoife had told her, but still, it was important to hold on to the good. 'What's her name?'

'Jocelyn. Small but mighty.' Toni grinned.

'And how's the recovery going? You've defied the odds, but I'm guessing it's not linear . . .' As Aoife kept talking, Eden felt the sound of her voice become distant. She thought about tiny baby Jocelyn. She'd have a dad, partly because of Eden, definitely because of Aoife. What a feeling.

Eden looked at Aoife and let her body fill up with something close to awe.

Aoife handed the photograph to Eden. 'You can pin it up – you've earnt that honour.' She moved back towards Toni and Nicola. 'This one's newly qualified and gives me hope for the NHS.'

Eden swelled with pride as she looked at the photograph. Jocelyn in the NICU, hooked up to all manner of machines, but with wide, open eyes. She touched Nicola's arm and smiled at Toni, before walking towards the corridor, leaving them talking and laughing.

As she approached the pinboard, Eden looked at the photograph again. Jocelyn was small enough to fit in the palm of her hand. She looked at the pinboard in front of her and the many hundreds of messages, cards and photographs, then looked again at Jocelyn's face and slipped the photograph into her scrub pocket. There wasn't much room on the board in any case.

'It's Dickensian,' she said out loud, as she rubbed moisturiser onto her stinging skin. This time, a patient had ripped out a line and she'd had to clean herself again with Hibiwash because she was covered in droplets of blood. It had been a week, and Eden had been monitoring Sophie closely. She'd studied her body language, tone of voice, actions, all for any small changes, but Sophie was Sophie, same as usual. She had not mentioned the bedroom incident, or *Notes on Nursing*. The best thing Eden could do was pretend nothing had happened and put it out of her mind.

She'd been planning an evening by herself, but after another unbelievable day, she needed company. 'I look like Stephen King's Carrie half the time.' She walked into the living area where her flatmates were all gathered, wearing a dressing gown her mum had bought her, thick and cosy and covered in love hearts. 'What even is this job?'

'There was a woman outside Resus today,' said Sophie, 'eating a live guinea pig.'

The room was silent a moment, then the others erupted into nervous laughter. The barometer of normal, of humour, of political correctness, was off. She couldn't believe some of the things they found funny. Being a newly qualified nurse was like living in a fever dream.

'I don't understand how it's so brutal. I never experienced this in Edinburgh. It was busy, sure, and we had our fair share of social deprivation, but this feels like the End Times.'

'Nobody ate guinea pigs in Blackpool,' Sophie said. 'But they did eat a lot of ketamine, sniffed glue, old-school aerosols and all that. People are people.' She puffed on her vape and made a large smoke ring.

'South Wales was a vibe,' said Rhian. 'Even in paediatric oncology; full of fights on the ward, and overdoses in the toilets. We had one family drinking all the alcohol hand gel on the unit, like a warped version of *The Tiger Who Came to Tea*, and another broke into the controlled drugs cupboard.'

Eden sat down on the sofa and let her head flop back. 'I don't know if I'm cut out for this. I should have studied anthropology after all.'

'Course you are,' said Rhian. 'You need to let off a bit of steam, that's all. Work hard, play hard. Come out with us tonight.' Rhian jigged around excitedly; she could never sit still – even when they watched TV she was constantly moving her legs and feet. She said it was ADHD that had led her to the ED, as paediatric oncology was slow, and the children were often too sick to be children.

Eden did not feel like leaving the flat. She wanted to lie in her cosy dressing gown, in the sanctuary of her bedroom, and do a bit of journalling and a lot of Netflix bingeing. But maybe Rhian had a point.

She dressed in jeans, hoodie and Converse, put on the seven silver rings she wore on days off and left the flat with Obi and Rhian – the others had gone ahead – and the three of them walked slowly in the late-evening sunshine back towards the hospital. 'I won't stay late.'

'Nor me. I'm off the booze because of the *Love Island* application,' Obi crossed his fingers as they walked, 'so I need to shred; there's a group audition coming up next month.'

He'd grown a moustache and reminded Eden of a classic film star.

'Gay *Love Island*,' said Rhian. 'About time.'

'Nah, it's straight, but I've identified as bi. So if I get in there will be peak family drama – as a minimum, an all-night deliverance vigil at Christ Paradise Assembly of God Church. My dad may never speak to me again, but I'll risk it for the brand partnerships.'

Rhian laughed. 'You can buy your dad a new church building with a Boohoo deal. Win him over.'

They walked down the cobbled, uneven streets towards the pub. The pavement was too narrow for them to walk side by side, so Eden kept dropping back and missing snatches of the conversation. She sped up behind them. 'Wait, *Love Island*? I genuinely thought you were joking about that. What about ED? Aoife is no way going to give you months off work, not even unpaid.' They all revered Aoife. Eden had toyed with telling them that she'd watched Aoife and Michael disappearing into the cupboard together, but it felt important and loyal to keep what she'd witnessed secret. First, do no harm.

Obi laughed. 'If I get on *Love Island*, there's no chance I'm going back to nursing. I'll be free of ED and loaded.'

Eden smiled. 'I know it's intense, but doesn't it make you feel alive? ED, I mean.'

Nobody answered, but Rhian nodded. They turned the corner to the already busy bar, seeing colleagues who had spilt out into the street and the last of the sunshine. It was the same crowd, always socialising. Even on Monday mornings ED staff would go out after a string of nights and drink pints of beer at 9 a.m. with the market porters and local police force, also finishing their night shifts. Eden heard stories about the Messy Mondays, after drinking all day and with broken circadian rhythms, which involved extremes of behaviour that shocked and scared her. An orgy at the police station. A nurse being admitted to ED herself, unable to maintain her own airway she was so drunk. Another who defecated in the street one Monday lunchtime and was arrested for indecent exposure.

Monday evenings were quieter. The nurses ordered bottles of white wine, and when asked how many glasses, somebody would inevitably say, 'Just a straw,' but nobody drank to obliteration. Instead, everyone smoked and chatted outside, even the non-smokers. They talked shop, but in code. *Did you hear about the adenosine person? The RTA was an FLK. Frequent flyer was back again in Minors.*

The bar was heaving. ED staff sat or stood around a large wooden table, all deep in conversation, laughter and familiarity. Over by the exit, Sophie and Michael were particularly friendly; almost uncomfortably so, Eden noticed. Michael was clearly a massive flirt. Sophie was staring up at his face and Michael kept looking away, discombobulated no doubt. Sophie had this way of making you feel awkward, a strange power.

Eden bought a beer. She never knew where to stand. Her arms felt too long, swinging by her sides. Pamela, Fran and Aoife were sitting on bar stools at the table, a bag of crisps torn open between them. She hovered near them for a moment.

Aoife smiled and pushed the crisps towards Eden. 'Sustenance,' she said.

Eden sat and chatted with them a while. Pamela had been nicer to her since that first day but was still a bit patronising. Fran was the oldest nurse on the unit, still doing night shifts, somehow. Aoife was lovely as ever, which made the Michael thing all the more shocking. Eden looked back to where Sophie and Michael had been standing, but they had disappeared from view.

Fran started telling a story about an elderly patient who had testicles so swollen he had to push them on a trolley in front of him, so Eden excused herself and went to look for Sophie. She hated the idea of patients' lives being gossiped about; confidentiality breached. The Code of Professional Conduct was explicit about confidentiality – *5.1 Respect a person's right to privacy in all aspects of their care* – and with good reason. That poor man was somebody's grandad. All bodies failed eventually.

It was getting dark, the moon covered by clouds, and her colleagues' cigarette ends lit up like fireflies. She couldn't see Sophie so walked on across the courtyard and around the corner. Michael was leaning – or being pushed – against the wall, Sophie's arms raised around his neck. Eden tried to look away, but she couldn't take her eyes off them. Her stomach contracted. Michael's hands circled Sophie's waist, then moved down towards her bum. They hover-stared for a few seconds. Eden felt the hairs on the back of her neck stand up and her skin prickle. She watched, biting her lip, as Sophie and Michael kissed.

FIVE
Aoife

'Full again today and outliers in AMU, and we've no less than fourteen ambulances backed up outside with patients being treated by paramedics. Who'd be a paramedic these days?' Michael was drinking the largest cup of Starbucks Aoife had ever seen. She sat opposite him in the doctors' office, which was stuffy and windowless, the desk cluttered with coffee mugs and books, research articles and, for some reason, an old copy of *Vogue*. The wall was pock-marked blue where notices had gone up and down over the years, and there was a constant humming sound, the source of which nobody had ever discovered.

'Fun times,' said Aoife. She looked across at Michael and noticed his eyes were hooded and tired. No surprise. Every week they had this, the morbidity and mortality meeting, to discuss the things that had gone wrong and any learnings they could take. The data was grim.

'We've had to open the sink space again. That poor patient gets splashed with water every time anyone washes their hands.'

'Better or worse than the corridor?' Michael slurped his coffee.

'It's bad or worse, never better or worse. I've had enough. Thinking of running away if you want to come?' Aoife smiled but then yawned almost immediately. She was exhausted, but although the nursing buck stopped with her, Michael's level of responsibility was even greater, and his hours even longer. August was fast approaching, along with a bunch of new doctors who, as he always commented, didn't know their arse from their armpit. Whilst it was always a dangerous time, the summer lull that usually happened in ED, when respiratory infections and winter viruses were reduced, hadn't materialised, and the workload was steadily impossible.

'It'll be a long meeting today, sadly – there's been lot of deaths. Too many.' Aoife sighed. 'Apparently, all our cardiac arrests and medical emergencies are now being audited by the Resus department. I mean, can they not see the ambulances backed up around the block? The nursing numbers are shocking.'

It was Michael's turn to yawn, then he grinned. 'Not our first rodeo. How long have you been a nurse now? Surely you deserve a medal.' He was not his usual grumpy morning self, despite the dire straits of ED and his apparent exhaustion.

It was hard to believe that it had been thirty years since she'd started at City, almost twenty since she and Michael had first met. 'Too long. But Fran's at forty-two years and going strong, so she wins. Nearly half a century, and that deserves an award for sure. I'm a wee baby at thirty years, but still, I imagine we've lost a chunk of life expectancy due to this job. The nights alone knock a decade off.'

'Ah, you love it. And I can't imagine Fran retiring, can you? She's climbing Ben Nevis to raise money for the sensory room this year.'

Aoife smiled. 'They don't make 'em like that anymore. Between us, it's not been easy orientating the new nurses. There was a complaint from a relative – remember Mr Francis, metastatic cancer? Apparently one of the junior nurses whispered, "You're going to die," to him. They're all denying it, and frankly it could be any of them, but my money's on Sophie.'

He frowned. 'Sounds a lot more like delirium than anything so sinister, surely?'

'Maybe, but she doesn't play by the rules. Sophie, Eden and the others have been here six weeks, and they're still taking up most of my time. Obi asked for annual leave yesterday to go to a TV audition, and at this rate Sophie's going to have to do some in-charges.'

Michael glazed over a bit. 'I think you're wrong about her. She's got the makings of brilliance, I think.'

Aoife pretended to stab herself in the heart. 'Sophie's half your age,' she reminded him. 'In case you're developing a slight crush.'

Michael put his coffee down and reached across the desk, grabbing Aoife's hand momentarily and squeezing it gently.

The door swung open, and Michael snatched his hand back. A piece of A4 paper marked 'Confidential Meeting' fell off as Rohan came in. Aoife retrieved it, sticking it back on the door, lest they get constantly interrupted.

Rohan was a quiet and thoughtful man who always brought in cakes that his wife had baked for them all. He was followed in by a few of the other junior doctors, including Ben, and a medical student, who had terrible acne.

'Welcome, everyone, let's go around and if you can sign in that would be helpful,' Rohan began. 'Shall we look at the numbers? We have had seven morbidities and/or mortalities since the last meeting, so a lot to discuss. Let's start the first case so we can get out of here before midnight.'

The medical student with terrible acne took a gulp of Diet Coke, then burped. 'Gosh, I'm terribly sorry.'

They all ignored him and looked at Rohan. 'Tuesday, we had a patient, Gordon Seales, twenty-four, motorbike accident, clean snap at C6. He's currently in ICU, maxed out on Norad and dopamine. Basically, we spent the day trying to stabilise him before transfer to the Spinal Unit, and he spent a good ten hours on a spinal board, immobile. A few days in and he now has a grade-four pressure sore that is positive to group A strep and he's developed nec.'

Aoife's head pounded. Pressure sores were preventable and entirely down to nursing care, and necrotising fasciitis was life-threatening within hours if not surgically removed. No person should be left for hours on end on a spinal board, least of all a disabled or immobile person. 'That poor guy. Oof.'

'Doesn't look great,' Rohan continued. 'He was whisked to theatres straight away but now he's having further debridement on Intensive Care, and they will take out a bit of bone no doubt too. We've recorded a serious harm and National Patient Safety are reviewing. It's all pretty serious.'

'Jesus,' said Michael. 'Who was looking after him? How long was he waiting on a trolley for?'

'Eden Walsh.' Aoife sighed and raised her eyebrows at Michael. He shrugged.

'More bad news, I'm afraid. We had an unexpected death Wednesday night, a John Bedwell, referred to the coroner, so we'll likely be dragged to the coroner's court again. This patient walked in with mild symptoms,' Rohan paused, 'and never walked out. The family is threatening to go to the media and have been posting on TikTok. They've shared a video of John looking pretty well aside from a hand injury, drinking a cup of tea, with a voiceover basically saying this was my dad minutes before City ED killed him.'

The medical student belched again, louder this time. 'I need to stop drinking fizzy drinks,' he said.

Michael put his coffee down on the desk, stood up and stomped out, slamming the door on the way.

The meeting lasted a while, and there was plenty more bad news before Rohan wrapped up and they all dispersed. Aoife found Michael queuing for a sandwich in the hospital café and put her hand on the small of his back. 'That was brutal, but you know it goes like this sometimes.'

'Ah, I'll be OK. Hot-headed as ever. That dick of a student was really pissing me off, though.' He groaned. 'And we're going to fuck the mortality ratio with this death rate. The hospital insurance rating is already on a knife edge, and I don't want to be the one sending City into special measures. What the hell is going on this month?'

The café was staffed by angry-looking young people. A few of them raised their eyebrows as Michael spoke, so Aoife quietly shushed him.

The air smelt of tuna. 'I'll have a large latte with an extra shot – actually, make that two extra shots – and a ham-and-cheese croissant.' Michael turned to Aoife. 'What do you want?'

She squeezed his arm. 'Ah, just a fruit salad and yoghurt for me. I'm trying to maintain my six-pack.'

He laughed. She loved making him laugh. He often told her she could 'make every bad day at the office so much better'.

'Are we having dinner Tuesday? Shall we go to Queens?' It was a tradition they'd continued for at least the last decade, at least once a month, usually the first Tuesday. They'd share a meal, a vat of wine, a lot of laughter. This was their medicine, even more than the illicit sex. Whatever the job threw at them, however bad the day looked – and the worst days seemed to be getting increasingly frequent – she and Michael prioritised this time together to put the world to rights.

'*Absolument.*' Michael grinned.

Sometimes they stayed in a hotel, other times they went back to his. Once, he'd been to her house, just once. Sam had taken James on a weekend away to camp out in the wild and *get back to nature*; he'd been watching a lot of *SAS: Who Dares Wins*. Michael had walked through the house and looked at the photographs of Aoife's family dotted around the living room and then couldn't get an erection.

Since then, they'd snatched moments at work, on unused wards that had been designated for bird flu or SARS or the next pandemic. They presented at any medical conference they could, sneaking in and out of each other's rooms. It never felt less than magical, even in a Premier Inn. Theirs was an intense relationship – sometimes it felt like they were the only two people on the planet who really understood each other.

Aoife watched Michael in the sandwich queue, biting his nail as he waited, hopping slightly from leg to leg, never good at standing still. He noticed her gazing at him, and took his hand away from his mouth, then winked at her. 'You're impatient,' she said.

'I'm starving. I'll be hangry unless this food arrives soon.'

She smiled and stood close enough to him to smell Polo mints and the lemon shower gel he liked that was a bit overpowering. It felt so natural to be close to him. Aoife had wondered if they would end up together properly – after all, they'd always been so close – but after Layla left him, Michael hadn't suggested that she leave Sam and they start afresh, as she had thought he might. He seemed content loving her and having her love him. 'Let's not spoil it with labels,' he said. 'We don't need to break hearts. We can be French about this.' It was best, they both agreed, for Aoife to keep her worlds separate. Two lives. Work and home.

This was enough, Aoife always agreed. It turned out to be entirely possible, perhaps even healthy, to love two people at once. In any case, she had James to consider. He was off to university soon, but he was a fragile soul; causing him pain would be unforgivable. And besides, she didn't want to leave Sam. She'd loved Sam immediately.

'He's tall, dark and handsome,' she'd told her nurse friends after they met. 'Drives, has his own flat, a real job, something business-ish, and he's so different – I don't know, so steady.'

By then Aoife was already sick of hook-ups, the random students she met during nights out with her peers, who soon tired of a nurse girlfriend's schedule, working so many nights and weekends. She'd gone along with a blind date and Sam had arrived at the restaurant with a bunch of yellow roses. They'd eaten three courses and then he'd ordered a cheese plate. When Aoife asked how he stayed so slim, he laughed, and said he'd do anything to extend their first date. She took him home, and that was that. He never really left.

She hadn't been planning on Michael. But life without Michael was unimaginable.

They moved along the queue and stood by the collection area, the smell of tuna intensifying. 'Tuesday. Any chance you can sneak out a bit early? If so, I'll make sure I'm not in charge.' Aoife could rarely leave early, but Mary was on duty Tuesday and so it was possible that she'd at least get out on time.

'Yes! My favourite night of the month, our clandestine date night.' He looked up at the ceiling, then back at Aoife. 'I don't know what I'd do without you, Aoife. This fucking job is killing me . . .'

Aoife smiled and moved even closer to him, her arm touching his. His skin felt hot, and impossibly soft, and, she noticed, a bit shaky too. 'You need to stop drinking so much coffee,' she said. 'I quite like having you around.'

He looked at his smartwatch, and around the sandwich crowd. 'Quick fag?'

'How you run for miles and continue to smoke is beyond me.'

They grabbed their food and coffee and exited out of the revolving doors. These were heavy enough that at least one elderly person a day got stuck inside, banging on the door, like an insect in a glass. Aoife and Michael stood to the side of a giant industrial bin, and she picked at her fruit salad while he smoked.

He put his cigarette out, then reached across and stroked her back. The action was hidden from passers-by but felt dangerous enough. Loving, too.

Aoife stepped forward slightly. 'Not here, not now,' she whispered.

Michael put his hands in his scrub pockets. 'Safest way.'

She smiled and leant towards him, glancing around to check nobody was in earshot. 'By the way, I came the other day in a shop changing room. I couldn't stop thinking about fucking you, and before I knew it I was touching myself, thinking about you. About us . . .'

Michael's eyes shone. 'Tell me more . . .'

Aoife hid her face with her hands. 'Michael, it's so shameful.'

'I need details. What shop? And is that actually true? God, that's fucking hot.'

She never behaved like this with Sam. But there was something about Michael that made her impulsive. 'Massimo Dutti.'

They stopped whispering a moment as a senior midwife they both knew walked past and smiled. Then Michael turned to Aoife, and they stared at each other before starting to laugh. Michael laughed so hard tears appeared at the corners of his eyes. 'Oh, Aoife. You banged one out in Massimo Dutti?'

She was laughing too. 'God, it sounds so weird now. All of it. In the cold light of day. A bit seedy.'

But he linked arms with her as they walked into the entrance. 'Sexy, not seedy. And by the way, I couldn't love you more,' he whispered.

*

Aoife was frazzled by 8 p.m., and more than glad to hand over to the night shift. One of her nurses had a heavy period and had bled all over her scrubs with no opportunity to change. She'd carried on dealing with the emergencies at hand, her navy-blue trousers turning darker. Aoife could smell blood in the coffee room.

'Aoife, Mary said you're looking for me urgently?' Eden walked into the staff room as the night staff filed out. Aoife was rubbing the sides of her head. The throbbing was getting worse, despite paracetamol.

Aoife stared at Eden, who appeared animated, excited even. 'I need to talk to you.' She patted the chair next to her. 'Come. Sit. I hope you're OK. What a day.'

Eden sat next to Aoife. She had the straightest back of anyone Aoife had ever seen; she must have studied ballet as a child.

'I need to talk to you about the patient who you cared for in Majors. The man who developed a serious pressure sore. We had an M&M meeting and there is going to be an investigation. It could be quite serious, Eden, for the patient; and for you and the team too.'

Eden's eyes opened wide. Her hands were shaking. Aoife reached out to take them. It was hard not to feel empathy for her. She was young, bright and compassionate. Of course, like all newly qualified nurses she had a lot to learn, but still, she was kind, and that mattered a lot in this game. It wasn't the only thing, but in Aoife's book, it was by far the most important.

'That sounds serious,' Eden said. 'Where is the patient? What will happen? God, I feel like I'm going to be sick. That poor man.'

Aoife softened her voice. 'I'm afraid he now has nec – necrotising fasciitis – so it will have to be investigated, but look, don't beat yourself up, OK? We learn from mistakes and that is why investigations are important.'

Eden nodded. 'Thank you,' she said, but then she slumped forward and groaned. 'I feel so bad for him.' She sat back up and stared, wet-eyed, at Aoife with a strange expression on her face.

'Is there anything else wrong, Eden?'

Eden hesitated and went to speak but then closed her mouth.

Aoife instinctively pulled her close, and Eden rested her head on her shoulder, crying a little. 'Hey now, come on, we all make mistakes. Let me get you some tissues and we can talk about next steps and the systems we have for clinical errors.'

But Eden put her arms around Aoife and squeezed her so she couldn't move. Aoife knew what to do in every situation, but for a moment it felt so awkward being bear-hugged by a junior colleague that her mind went blank. Eventually she managed to extricate herself, stood up and brushed herself down, laughing, catching her breath. 'You nearly squeezed the life from me. Perhaps it's best we avoid hugging colleagues,' she said.

Eden shook her head and stood up. 'Nothing else is wrong,' she said, almost smugly. 'And nurses are more than colleagues.' She stared at Aoife. 'We're *family*.'

SIX

Sophie

'Another day, another dollar.' Michael walked beside Sophie, having almost run to catch up with her on the way into work. 'How are you getting on? It's been a stressful time on ED.'

'All good.' She studied him. He was tall, with a broad swimmer's back and a neck a few inches too thick; a snorer, no doubt. Most of what he said was cringey: he spoke in clichés, old-fashioned ones at that, but there was something about him that intrigued her. He walked like a man who owned the room, marching almost, with no regard for anyone in his way. It made people step aside as he approached. He wasn't the kind of man who would sit with his legs so wide on the Underground that he took up two seats, more that people instinctively gave him space. She liked his smell, too: a mixture of Polo mints, lemon and chlorhexidine. 'It's going OK. Busy, but good busy,' she said, and smiled in such a way that he looked away. 'I like how you walk.'

He half laughed. 'I like how you disarm me.'

They had been heavy flirting for a few weeks. He'd kept on suggesting dinner while they were on a unit night out, but she'd looked him dead in the eyes and said, 'Let's not confuse this with a date,' and watched his face redden with excitement. She'd reached out then, to prove her point, and, surrounded by co-workers who were all chatting and drinking, had pressed her body against him until she felt his dick get hard.

Now, Sophie ran her fingertips over her collarbone. 'Do you want to hook up this week? I'm off Tuesday.'

He glanced around, suddenly a bit flustered. 'I can't do Tuesday, I'm afraid.'

'No biggie. And just to reiterate, I wasn't suggesting a date. As in, I don't want to go out anywhere and I'm not looking for a relationship.'

He stopped walking, then started again but slowed as they approached the hospital entrance. 'Tonight? How's tonight after work?'

She laughed, stared at him, unblinking. 'Sure. I'm triaging, though, so who knows when I'll finish.' Sophie turned and nodded towards the changing room.

'Ah, triage, the domain of the great unwashed. Stinks in that room.'

'True. But there's an NHS air freshener ready to go.'

Michael was breathing heavy and fast, Sophie realised. His respiratory rate was twenty-two. She watched him stride away through the double doors.

The small triage room was at the back of the reception area. Patients arriving in ED queued up for Reception One and gave their details: name, GP, date of birth, and the presenting problem (chest pain; back pain; head pain; leg pain; always pain). Then Sophie popped out and shouted the patient's name and they'd shuffle in, sometimes alone, sometimes accompanied by a family member looking more worried than they did. Sophie would run through the questions that were designed to catch any major red flags and bump them up the system. The computer did most of the work, prompting her to ask standard questions: chest pain? Allergies? Diarrhoea and/or vomiting?

Recent travel abroad? The answers led her down the appropriate rabbit hole of further questions, before deciding whether a person should be directed to Minors (twenty-five-hour wait), Majors (twelve-hour wait), Resus (varied) – or might be better off going home.

Mabel was not better off going home. Sophie could see it immediately. Obi walked into triage holding her up, almost carrying her. 'Hey, Sophie, I've queue-jumped with Mabel here. I know we're not supposed to have favourites, but, well . . .'

Mabel smiled and looked up at him. She was half his height. 'Thank you, doctor.'

'Nurse,' he said. He gave Sophie a flash grimace over Mabel's head.

Sophie helped Mabel sit down onto the chair as Obi left. 'He's a charmer, isn't he?'

'Lovely lad.' Mabel winced. She was the colour of a pigeon's back.

Sophie could already see that Mabel was having a heart attack. There was a particular grey sweat that slid down her face. She smelt like an oily puddle, and yoghurt – the smell of dead people.

Mabel was curled over. 'I'm sure it's nothing, love.' She touched her chest with her fingertips. 'I'm so embarrassed to take up your precious time. I probably should have stayed at home.'

Older women died quietly. But not on Sophie's watch.

'Mabel, I think we'll get you straight over to Resus. My guess is you're having a problem with your heart, but it's your lucky day because the team here are experts and they're all as good-looking as Obi.'

Sophie called for back-up, and spoke in nurse code: 'Can I have a hand in triage, please? Got a patient here – Mabel – who will need a review in Resus, or a transfer to Rose Cottage seems likely.'

Mabel was whisked away within moments, and thanked Sophie profusely on the way out.

Young women were a very different entity. They arrived in droves and caused a lot of waiting-room issues. They regularly started fist fights and had to be banished – after all, if they were well enough to fight, their airways were sufficiently protected and they'd be unlikely to go into respiratory arrest. They swore and screamed like pirates. Rage wasn't listed as a presenting problem, but it often was one. Sophie had been called all manner of names in ED, but most anger came from young, drunk women. It was nothing she couldn't handle. Blackpool had been a training ground for deflecting physical abuse and ignoring verbal; the nurses had been offered self-defence lessons. Sophie understood the rage of women, albeit misdirected.

Hurt people hurt people. Frightened people frighten people.

'Jasmine Bell?' Sophie scoured the reception area, the queue of people waiting already stretching out of the door and around the block. Everyone looked either extremely sick or extremely pissed off, which said everything about who did and didn't need to be here.

There were only five metal chairs in the reception area, spaced 10 feet apart and chained to the floor. People nicked anything from hospitals: chairs, clocks, staff handbags; someone had even dug up and stolen all the plants from the volunteer-run 'Zen garden'.

A pale and terrified-looking woman was sitting on one and glanced up. At first, Sophie assumed she was Jasmine, but then she noticed the shadowy figure behind her, leaning against the wall: a young teen, dead-eyed and heroin-thin, deep scars laddering her arms. She moved slowly away from the wall and followed Sophie into the triage room.

Jasmine sat down, her mum next to her, though they might have been a million miles apart. The air between them looked darker, somehow. Sophie often heard death: the sound of a whisper, bubbles deep in her stomach, a low humming. The sound filled the room with Mabel. But although Sophie listened hard to her body and looked at Jasmine's far-away face, she now heard nothing. Then Jasmine's mum sniffed.

It was the mothers that Sophie found hard to assess, beyond her understanding. She'd never learnt about what it means to be a daughter, or what it means to have a mother. Her own mother had disappeared after Sophie was diagnosed as a child with leukaemia, a cruelty that she'd never be able to understand – or forgive.

Sophie put on her glasses and logged on to the computer, tapping in the information as she received it. She turned to Jasmine. 'Can I check your name and date of birth?'

Jasmine talked slowly, with an entirely flat tone and expression. She was severely depressed. Regardless of the words she used, Sophie could tell from her eyes that she didn't want to be here on earth.

'I'm going to run through all the boring questions, then do a few observations, OK?' She put the clip onto Jasmine's finger to record her oxygen saturation levels, and noticed her fingernails, bitten down past the white, the gnawed edges. She wrapped the blood-pressure cuff around Jasmine's arm and could tell immediately by the looseness of her skin that she'd stopped eating suddenly and recently. She put the digital thermometer into her ear and noticed the old ligature mark, a thin pale silver-pinkish line across her neck, shiny like the trail of a slug after rain.

'She's suicidal. She doesn't sleep. Doesn't eat. Doesn't leave her bed.' Jasmine's mum began to cry. Sophie continued tapping information into the computer, directing questions at Jasmine as she did so:

Have you made actual plans to kill yourself?
How long have you been feeling like this?
Have you taken any tablets or harmed yourself in any way?

It sounded so perfunctory to speak about suicide in this way, but it was important. All day long Sophie triaged teenage girls – sometimes boys, but mostly girls – who were sad and desperately unwell, seemingly from nowhere. It was an epidemic that was largely silent outside hospitals, aside from the odd news story. And the Emergency Department was no place to manage it. You could kill yourself here and nobody would even notice.

Jasmine pulled up her T-shirt. 'It won't stop bleeding,' she said.

Her mum stopped talking, and Sophie stopped typing. Both of them stared at Jasmine. Sophie felt winded, unable to catch her breath.

In the centre of Jasmine's chest, she had carved a word deep into her skin.

HELP.

Sophie followed all process to the letter. She made good time, triaging all patients appropriately, and cleared out much of the waiting area, but still, the unit outside was utter carnage when she walked past Resus.

'We need rapid sequence intubation drugs, bay four.' Michael was at the head end of a patient who was thrashing around violently. 'Now.'

'Coming up.' Sophie walked quickly to the large fridge and took out a small cardboard tray labelled RSI. There were three syringes inside: a small saline flush, one large syringe labelled in yellow 'SEDATION', and another large syringe in red, 'PARALYSIS'. She marched back to the Resus bay.

Eden was hovering at the foot end of the patient. 'Can I help?'

Sophie handed her the cardboard tray. 'Give the drugs, then a flush? Sedation first, obvs.'

'Yes,' Eden said, wide-eyed. 'Of course.'

Michael was trying to hold the breathing mask in place. 'Fuck it,' he said. The patient was turning blue; his oxygen levels were dangerously low on the monitor. Sophie stood near him, trying to hold the patient still so that Michael could deliver breaths and oxygen, but it was near impossible with him punching and twisting around, trying to get up.

'He's like the Incredible Hulk,' Sophie said, already sweating as she tried to stop him from hurting Michael. 'What's the story?'

Michael pressed the mask over the patient's nose and mouth with one hand, the other gently squeezing in oxygen. He had a stethoscope in his ears, but the monitor was screech-alarming by then. 'Eden, get the RSI in now!'

Eden knelt at the side of them, pushing a syringe of medication into his vein.

Suddenly, the patient stopped moving.

Sophie let go of his arms, which dropped like dead weights, and Michael delivered a breath, watching his chest rise with ease. She glanced at the monitor. 'His oxygen levels are coming up, but his BP is through the roof. Jesus, his systolic is over 200, and heart rate 140 and climbing.'

Michael looked up, frowned. Then he looked at the patient. 'Fuck.'

Sophie followed Michael's eyes to the patient's. They were bulging, open wide, in absolute terror. 'He's awake!'

The patient's eyes looked as if they would burst out of his skull, but it was the fear in them that was most shocking.

'Was that sedation? Tell me you didn't give the paralysis

medication without sedation first?' Michael stared over to Eden, who was flapping now, picking up the remaining syringe and holding it up: yellow, *SEDATION*.

'Should I give the sedation? This one?'

Sophie ran around the trolley, and shoved Eden out the way.

'Take a breath!' Sophie reached out for Eden's arm and pulled her to the side, next to the pile of used oxygen cylinders and large yellow sharps bin waiting to be collected by the porters.

'How would I know you're meant to give sedation before paralysis. How?' Her voice was squeaky.

'Because I told you to,' Sophie hissed. 'If he'd died, you'd be in a world of shit. His BP was off the charts.'

'I haven't had my RSI competencies signed off yet,' she said, shaking her head. 'I should have said something. I'm sorry, I guess I didn't think.'

'Are you having a laugh? This is ED, not the Duke of Edinburgh Award.'

Eden looked over to the now-empty space where the porters had pushed the trolley towards theatres, the patient having stabilised with the proper treatment. 'Are you going to tell Aoife?' She looked afraid, and much younger then. 'It's all I've ever wanted, to be a nurse.'

'You still don't get it, do you?' Sophie glared at her.

Eden looked confused as Michael appeared, holding the tray of empty RSI drug syringes. He held up the empty, red-labelled PARALYSIS syringe. 'Lesson one: never, ever give a patient paralysis before sedation,' he said, 'and try not to accidentally kill anyone else today.'

Michael was angry enough that his face had reddened, and as he spoke Sophie noticed a tiny burst blood vessel in the white of his eye.

'I'm really sorry,' said Eden, her face softening, her own eyes blinking back tears. 'I'll do a Datix form, and I promise it will never happen again.'

A man walked past wearing a hospital gown that was undone at the back, his saggy bottom in full view. None of them commented or paid any attention.

'Look, let's say lesson learnt, I hope, and not get into red tape,' said Michael, dropping the used syringes into the large neon-yellow sharps bin. 'It's probably best to delete this incident from our memories.' He shook his head, then walked off towards Majors, leaving Eden looking a fraction relieved.

Sophie nodded at Eden. 'Let's hope the patient can forget it too. Have you ever had a nightmare where you can't move a muscle, and you're literally paralysed with terror? Times that by a million.'

Michael met her outside after work, loitering near the side entrance. 'What's the plan, Stan?'

'Let's go to your place.' She liked to get a sense of people from their things, the books on their shelves, the clothes in their wardrobe.

He looked surprised but smiled. 'I figured you'd insist on a drink in a hotel bar or something, as anonymous as you seem to like to keep things. OK, great, I have the car here. Though you'll need to excuse the mess.'

Sophie briefly considered her hairy legs, vulva, armpits. She thought of the smells she'd picked up at work after twelve and a half hours in triage. The man who came in vomiting faeces, due to a bowel blockage, the rancid smell of it lingering on her own skin. But Michael was surely used to the reality of human bodies. That's what she liked about him; he was as raw as she was. Neither of them gave a fuck about mess.

He drove a Volvo that smelt of mildew and was full of crap. The backseat held piles of papers, journals and, Sophie noticed, some medical notes that had 'DECEASED' printed on the front. 'That's probably illegal,' she said. 'Carrying patients' notes around in your car. Surely, they're all electronic now anyway? What decade are these from?'

'Safest place for them,' Michael said. He was driving but kept looking at Sophie rather than at the road, like a dog with a steak. 'It was only last year that one of the respiratory professors stopped collecting bits of lung in jars, and I know an ophthalmic surgeon who has a drawer full of eyes. Few old notes here and there is nothing.'

Sophie stared out of the window.

'Penny for them?' He indicated left and followed the road towards Greenwich.

'You can't have my thoughts. They're all mine.'

'Bit of a shit day, wasn't it? Eden is a sandwich short of a picnic, if you ask me.'

'Ah, she's all right really. It's not easy being newly qualified and dropped into this.'

'You're right. It's bad enough when you're a dinosaur like me, and it's getting worse. One more investigation and we're fucked, frankly.'

Michael lived in a new build that had underground parking and primarily housed escorts, newly divorced men in a high-income bracket and Chinese university students.

The car park smelt of chlorine. Sophie assumed the building would have one of those fancy gym and pool areas that never really got used. They went up to the eighth floor, and he tapped his keycard on the door. 'God, I miss keys,' he said.

His flat was tiny. Almost a studio apartment, but for a

miniature living area populated with a two-seater sofa opposite a giant TV. There were no books, bar medical textbooks – huge, old and no doubt out of date. *Dermatological Disorders* was acting as a doorstop. He noticed her looking at it. 'Not bedtime reading. Might turn your stomach, and from what I've seen at work, you're made of tough stuff.'

She walked through the hallway, the small kitchen to the left with a bag of bagels on the counter, at least a dozen empty wine bottles, a sink full of coffee cups and cereal bowls. The bathroom was next door: no hand towel, unwashed bathmat, spots of black mould at the back of the shower, Head & Shoulders, a tube of athlete's foot cream, a few different aftershaves, a lemon shower gel and a cracked mirror. Michael had one of those shower curtains that stuck to your skin, rather than a screen. He was clearly single.

The bedroom was neater. A large bed, made, and two side tables with framed photographs and lamps. Sophie lifted a few of the photos. Children. Michael with children – his, she assumed – of varying ages and stages. A black-and-white wartime-looking photograph of a young woman, clearly his mum, and a photo of a very young-looking Michael and Aoife wearing matching pink T-shirts that said 'Beat Ovarian Cancer Fun Run 2015'.

She turned that photo away, towards the wall. 'Feels like God is watching.'

Michael looked shifty all of a sudden, scrunched his face up. 'Shall we have a drink? I've a good whisky. Some decent red wine?'

Sophie shook her head. 'Take your clothes off,' she said.

Michael's eyes widened in shock. Then he pulled his T-shirt over his head in one movement and swung it around above him, throwing it across the room. 'My kinda girl.'

Sophie stepped forwards and held his arms, then ran her

hand over his chest, which was toned, almost skinny. He had one of those divorced, Lycra-clad cyclist bodies, like so many male ED consultants. He probably spent his days off cycling from London to Brighton to ward off the combination of loneliness and PTSD, an ultramarathon sort. The gentle exercise the doctors recommended to their patients did not apply to them, being, in their own minds, superhuman. Immortal. She touched his warm chest, his arms, his soft skin, before undoing his belt and pulling his jeans down. 'I like your body,' she said, and put her finger to her lips. 'Let's not talk.'

SEVEN
Eden

It was the first weekend in May. They had been at City two months before having a full day off together, except for Ben who was working through the bank holiday. Obi insisted they try a new bakery in Camberwell that had gone viral on Instagram. The queue was an hour long already, even at 11 a.m., and Sophie groaned. 'It's worse than ED. Are we really doing this?'

Rhian nodded. 'Be worth it, I think, or there wouldn't be a queue.'

Eden looked at her phone. 'Shall we do shifts?'

'Honestly, is this a joke? We're seriously waiting in line all morning on our one day off for a croissant?' Sophie flicked her head up and down the line. 'This is tragic. I'm calling it.'

'Just wait until you try the baked goods, Soph.' Obi took out his phone and started taking selfies.

'Let it be known that I object to this and am only standing here due to peer pressure.' Sophie crossed her arms but didn't leave.

They waited forty minutes, during which time Eden popped to the newsagent to buy them bottles of water, and Rhian smoked three roll-up cigarettes. After buying overpriced pastries, they walked over to Camberwell Green and sat on the grass, chatting and eating. Nobody talked about ED. Instead, they discussed music, films and Obi's future career as a TikTok sensation.

'Mental health,' said Rhian. 'Position yourself as a mental health guru, send out some motivational words and be performative about your expertise. That's how stardom is reached on socials now.'

'Ha, you're so right,' Sophie said. 'Everyone's a fucking expert. So why not you, Obi?'

Eden leant back onto her elbows, watching Sophie. Maybe she had her all wrong? She was different to anyone Eden knew, but she was acting friendly enough towards her at last. She enjoyed listening to them all chatting around her, the banter and joking, and the increasing sense of familiarity. It had been such a wobbly start at Rose Cottage that she'd been homesick like never before. But this felt good. 'You need to have a brand,' Eden said. 'A trademark name or message.'

Obi nodded, clearly enjoying the attention. 'Let's have a brainstorming session.'

'Obi-wan Kenobi,' said Rhian, immediately. 'You're my only hope.'

Sophie rolled her eyes, but Obi took his phone out to write it down.

Ivy was ninety-two and had arrived in ED with chest pain, which, in Eden's view, should put her at the top of the list to be treated. Instead, she was lying, frail and alone, on a trolley in a cubicle in Minors. 'I'm Eden and I'm going to be your nurse. Is it OK if I call you Ivy?'

She nodded, barely. Her eyes were sunken and her skin was extremely dry, Eden noticed.

'We're waiting for the doctors to review your ECG and blood results, then we'll try and get you a more comfortable bed as soon as we can.' Eden reached out and touched Ivy's hand. It was ice cold. 'I'll do a set of obs on you too. How's the pain?'

Ivy's rheumy eyes watered as she spoke. 'Not too bad, love.'

Eden flicked her head out onto Minors. She could hear the alarms, the calls for help. She was late checking a diabetic patient's repeat blood sugar, and she'd done no documentation at all; the observations and drugs were all late. There was so much to do, and she ought to be playing serious catch-up, but Ivy's face stopped her. She perched on the side of the trolley. Ivy was sparrow-slim, and her skin was covered in bruises of different colours where they'd repeatedly tried to take blood. 'Have you had heart problems before?'

She shook her head and shakily attempted to wipe her wet eyes with her forefinger. Eden reached out and held her hand. 'You've really been in the wars. If there's a problem with your heart, you're in the right place.'

Ivy sniffed and shook her head. 'Oh, you're kind, nurse. But this is where he died. Right here in this place. I told the ambulance people I didn't want to come but they brought me anyway.'

Eden gently stroked her hand and nodded. 'Best to get checked out,' she said softly. 'But I know it's not nice.'

'My husband died of a heart attack. We'd been married sixty-four years. I expect that's hard to imagine for someone as young as you.'

'Oh, I'm sorry. I'm so sorry. And to be back here must be horrid. Let me check on the doctors to see if I can hurry them along and check you over.'

Ivy smiled. 'You are kind.'

'I'll snaffle you some biscuits too, Ivy.'

'Thank you, nurse.'

Eden left the curtains open so Ivy could see and be seen, and walked quickly to the small kitchen area at the back of Majors. She could send a volunteer, but it would be quicker going herself, and she wanted Ivy to have some comfort, at least. She reminded Eden of why she'd wanted to be a nurse in the first place: to deliver kindness, compassion and caring.

There was a shriek of laughter from the doctor's office as she walked past, and Eden slowed down enough to hear voices: Michael and Sophie. She stopped, not meaning to eavesdrop, but the door was slightly ajar.

Michael groaned. 'Could she not work in Dermatology outpatients or something?'

'She's never going to set the nursing world on fire, but she's earnest,' Sophie said.

'Earnestly dangerous.'

Sophie laughed. 'I've stuck her in Minors today so she can't do much damage.'

'Excellent plan.'

Eden's head slumped towards her chest as she listened to them laughing. She'd really thought that they might be friends after all, but it was clear that Sophie was simply pretending to be nice. She took a breath in, tapped her forehead ten times and then stood up straight, striding away. Sophie was a snake. She didn't deserve her friendship – or any loyalty at all. But Aoife did.

The following day, Eden knocked on the office door thirty minutes before shift. Aoife was early, as expected, and despite it being just gone dawn, she looked immaculate, hair blow-dried, wearing her starched nurse's dress, and a pair of small diamond stud earrings. She had perfectly manicured short nails, Eden noticed, feeling a bit self-conscious about her own hands, dry and eczema-covered from constant washing and industrial-strength scabies treatment.

'Morning,' she said when Aoife called her in. 'Just a quick thing but I wanted to say thank you for being my mentor. It's been a bit overwhelming to be honest, but I feel I've learnt so much from you.'

'Eden. I'm up to my neck in it, but have a seat. That's nice to hear. Everything OK? I've been a bit worried about you.' Aoife pulled a chair out from the small round table in the corner and sat down, beckoning for Eden to sit next to her. She smelt of a perfume that Eden recognised, maybe her mum's.

She must have looked like she was about to cry, because Aoife reached over and lightly touched her elbow. 'There, oh dear! What's going on?'

Eden pulled herself upright and cleared her throat. Despite herself, it all came pouring out. 'I'm sorry, it's just I'm trying my best, and my anxiety is so bad at the moment. I need to tell you something, but I wasn't sure if I should, or how, and you've been so kind to me and . . .'

She watched Aoife's face. Her eyes had narrowed a fraction, her gaze lingered, and she'd opened her hands, palms up, on her lap.

Eden had Aoife's attention, which she so desperately wanted. Surely she'd want to know about any issues? The Code of Professional Conduct stated that *any and all concerns about colleagues needed raising appropriately and in a timely fashion.* Eden wanted to do all she could to be a good nurse, to follow that nurse's bible to the letter.

'OK. Take a breath. What's happened? You can tell me anything, no judgement.'

Eden sat opposite Aoife. On the desk was a photograph of a very tall and smiley man, and a tall teenager, much taller than Aoife, skinny and awkwardly handsome, a bit spotty and not quite symmetrical yet.

'That's Sam,' she said, 'my long-suffering husband. And James, my son. He's mid A levels and about to burst with stress, despite me trying to reassure him. So much exam pressure these days and in the grand scheme of life it doesn't really matter much, does it? It's kindness that counts, I'm always telling him.'

Eden cleared her throat and swallowed audibly. 'It's about Michael,' she said.

Aoife stopped talking and frowned. She'd clearly not been expecting that. 'Tell me more.'

Eden took a deep breath, glancing up at the wall above Aoife, and the giant yearly planner with 'OFF DUTY' written at the top, colour coded and complicated. Aoife would surely be a code-breaker in Bletchley Park in another life. Eden hesitated a second, glancing again at the photo. But then she heard their laughter in her head. 'I saw something and now I'm a bit concerned that Michael and Sophie might be forming a very close friendship – too close, I mean. I'm not sure they're breaking any rules, exactly, but it feels a bit inappropriate. She's an adult, of course, but the power dynamic makes it wrong in my book. I know he's your friend, and I didn't know what to do.'

Aoife's face shifted. Hardened. A flash of anger passed through her eyes, but it was gone just as quickly, and she resumed her composed expression. 'Have you spoken to Sophie? Asked them about it?'

Eden shook her head. 'I wasn't sure. I mean, it's fine if they were to have a relationship, to have an age gap, no judgement, but Sophie has been here a short time, and although he's a doctor, he's surely sort of our boss? It feels a bit, well, off on both sides. Unprofessional, perhaps. I'm asking for advice, really.' She took a pause and let the information land.

Aoife stared at Eden. 'What exactly did you see?'

Eden tilted her head to the side. 'I think they might have been kissing, and I thought you should know, as the nurse in charge, but also . . .'

Aoife dropped her pen. 'Also, what?' She frowned again, picked up the pen.

Eden felt the skin on her forearms turn cold, but she smiled. 'Well, I just wanted you to know that, about Sophie and Michael behaving inappropriately.'

Aoife began to doodle in the large black diary on her lap. 'Michael's a big flirt. He always has been, but he's harmless. I wouldn't worry about it.'

Eden rubbed her forearms and stood up. 'Got it,' she said and walked over to the door.

'Thanks, though,' said Aoife. 'I appreciate you telling me.'

Eden turned back and smiled, then softly closed the door behind her.

EIGHT

Sophie

'Quick five minutes before handover.' Aoife beckoned Sophie and Eden into the coffee room. Like all the gold standards promised in the NHS, their weekly mentor/mentee meetings had been sidelined, and despite Eden being newly qualified and Sophie being new to City, they'd been thrown into deep water since day one. Still, Aoife was trying, at least.

They sat opposite her on the clapped-out chairs. Eden pulled her workbook out of her rucksack. 'I've most of my six-month competencies ticked off,' she said. 'Most' – she side-eyed Sophie – 'except rapid sequence intubation.'

'That's brilliant work, given how busy we've been since you started in, what was it, March? We can get the remainder signed off this week or next, I'm sure.' Aoife turned to Sophie, her voice becoming slightly clipped. 'Do you perchance have your competency book?'

Sophie tutted. 'You know I'm a senior staff nurse, right? I haven't used it at all.' That wasn't entirely true. She'd ripped a page off the back and written Michael a note after visiting his flat again the night before, handing it to him as she walked past. *That was fun. Let's hook up again next week.*

'Hmm. Well, how are things? It's still quite different than a level-two ED.'

It was true, there was an avalanche of information to remember. Sophie had an almost photographic memory, but still, there had been more to learn than she'd anticipated. 'We had some similarities. Lots of respiratory infections and heart disease, the odd exciting case.'

'It's all exciting to me,' said Eden. 'But it's traumatic, for sure.'

Neither Sophie nor Aoife responded. Both of them, Sophie suspected, knew that anything they said would encourage her to start talking for ages. Eden loved deep and meaningful conversations. Sophie found them a waste of energy.

'Well, the workbook might be useful but it's up to you.' Aoife glanced at the clock. 'Just make sure you ask for support from those around you, and don't run before you can walk. There's an ongoing internal review into our mortality figures, which, as you know, have spiked, and the CQC arrive next month, so let's be extra-safe, and please make sure you document everything meticulously.'

Mary poked her head around the door. 'Can we pile in?'

Aoife beckoned her in, smiling. 'Come, come.'

A stream of day staff arrived holding coffees and Stanley cups full of water, striding in straight and tall. Theirs was the only job, Aoife had once said, that could have a person shrink by a few inches in one day. She looked around. 'Can you cover Paeds today, Sophie?'

Sophie hated working with children. Paediatric ED was full of screaming babies and extreme social problems. Adult nurses were meant to stay in adult ED, but of course every hospital now got nurses to sign contracts, the small print of which specified that they'd go anywhere they were needed, trained for it or not. She didn't like even touching babies, or generally being around them. She'd once worked a shift in Paeds ED where a baby had come in with burns so terrible the entire ward filled with the smell of smoke. Sophie could still smell that baby's skin and see the expression on his mum's face.

'Rather not,' she said. 'I'm allergic to children.'

Aoife rolled her eyes but then softened, and a look passed between them. All nurses were haunted by something. 'OK. Sophie, you take charge of Resus, please. We've only Phoebe, the new student, and a healthcare assistant in there with you, I'm afraid, but Obi can come help with obs.'

Asthma was a bummer. Everyone assumed it was a nothing illness, something the fat wheezer kids at school simply grew out of, but it could be a killer, especially when it led you to the Emergency Department. In Sophie's opinion, asthma was the most dangerous of all the diseases they treated – you could put air into a person, but you couldn't take it out.

Liam was unconscious and paper-white with blue edges, the colour of a computer screen through anti-glare glass. 'His blood gas is shocking.' Sophie waved the small printout in front of Michael to look at. 'He's super-acidotic.'

'Bollocks,' said Michael. He kept swallowing, his Adam's apple bobbing up and down. He exhaled slowly, as if willing Liam to follow suit, and looked at his face.

'Are you OK? You look a bit green around the gills.'

Michael took a breath, whispering. 'I felt fine first thing, but safe to say I was probably a bit pissed still. To say I'm regretting that nightcap is a total understatement right now.'

Sophie's mind flashed to the early hours, fucking Michael so hard that afterwards he'd chugged amaretto straight from the bottle, to *settle his nerves.*

He leant forwards, before heading to the sink and splashing water on his face. 'I'll be fine.' He stood up and returned to the foot of the bed, taking another deep breath. 'I think we need magnesium. Wait, no, let's try heliox. I think, I – erm, wait.' Michael waffled on while Sophie flushed Liam's IV line with saline and wracked her memory for magnesium doses. She scanned the Resus area for another consultant, but the only other doctor around was Ben. It required precision of thought and a clear head to lead a resuscitation. Michael was falling apart, clearly hungover to fuck. He looked as if he should be in a dark room watching Netflix and eating carbs, not leading a respiratory arrest.

Sophie's eyes slid over to Liam's monitors. His heart rate was peaking at 160, his blood pressure declining. She pulled the stethoscope from Michael's neck and walked over to Liam's barely moving chest. Without glancing up, she spoke in a loud, clear voice. 'Fast-bleep the anaesthetist. He needs intubating yesterday.' With one hand she whacked up the oxygen until Liam's face disappeared behind smoke, and gestured towards Rosy, who had arrived on the scene with the crash cart. 'Rosy, can you get salbutamol IV, magnesium, another neb – we'll do back to back; Mary, defib if he loses output.' She pressed the stethoscope onto Liam's chest on either side, listening hard above the sounds of alarms and the hum of ED. 'Silent chest,' she said out loud, and touched his throat, gently holding his trachea between her thumb and forefingers. 'Trachea is central.'

'Sophie, you can go and help Rosy.' Michael's voice did not sound as confident as his words, and it was clear he was swallowing bile.

Liam stopped breathing. The alarms sounded; wave patterns flatlined in a row. Sophie pulled his bed forwards and stood behind his head, tilted it back, looked down his chest and felt for a carotid pulse. 'He's arrested.' She climbed on top of him, straddling his abdomen.

Three more nurses arrived, and everyone got to work. Rosy stood behind Sophie. 'Three, two, one.' She took over from

Sophie as Kemi ran towards them, setting herself up at the head end. Phoebe hovered nearby, white as a sheet.

Michael should be taking charge – he was the most senior clinician with the most experience running cardiac arrests – but he was not in a fit state. Sophie stood next to him, touched his arm. 'Go get some water,' she said, and turned to Phoebe. 'If you're a fainter then stand right out of the way. If you do faint, we don't want to be stepping over you.'

Phoebe's mouth opened wide enough that Sophie could see her fillings.

Mary called out, 'Oxygen away. Everyone stand back, please.' She made sure everyone was safely away from his bed, then glanced at the defibrillator monitor. 'There's a sinus-looking rhythm – does he have a pulse? Three-point pulse check, please.'

'PEA,' Kemi said. 'Back on the chest.'

Eden swooped in from nowhere and hopped from side to side as she realised what was happening. 'Shall I take over chest compressions?'

Eden looked directly at Michael, who was still standing motionless. He kept leaning forwards to clear his throat, and appeared as if he might puke or faint or both. 'Erm, yes, Eden, actually can you – I mean . . .' He stared at Sophie.

Sophie viewed the scene as if from outside it. The chest compressions were not effective: Rosy had been on the chest too long. Mary, on the defib, was flushed and flustered.

'Can you draw up adrenaline?' Michael looked at Sophie.

'He's in PEA,' she said. 'You need to run through reversible causes.' He blinked and she noticed the sweat on his forehead. Phoebe was wobbling, almost falling over. More people arrived, some of whom Sophie didn't even recognise – new doctors on the crash team. Ben appeared, holding a polystyrene box that he placed on the trolley at the end of Liam's bed. The box popped open and the smell of its fried contents filled Resus. Ben started trying to get peripheral access in Liam's foot, a pointless endeavour, but Sophie took the moment to grab his breakfast and drop it into a clinical waste bin before the smell had Michael throwing up all over a patient in cardiac arrest. Ben was wise enough not to say anything.

It was chaos. Carnage. There was no chance in hell Liam would survive if this carried on.

Moments later, at the next round of pulse checks, Kemi shouted out, 'He's now hyper-resonant on percussion and left side of chest not moving. Deviated trachea, I think.'

'Go get a big cannula, three-way tap, and syringe. And a chest drain,' Sophie said to Eden, who ran off to the equipment cupboard. 'Right, I'm taking charge.' She stood in front of Michael and glanced over her shoulder at him.

Michael coughed and stepped forward. 'I really don't think—'

She ignored him. 'Right, folks. Ben, stop dicking around with peripheral access, you won't get it. Get the EZ-IO drill and let me know when you're in. If there's a bit of bone marrow aspirate, test it for glucose. Obi' – she looked over at Obi, who was in the next bedspace taking the temperature of a woman who was unconscious – 'get over here and take over chest compressions. Let's put those biceps to good use. Kemi, how are things your end?'

'Three way-tap, cannula, syringe and chest drain here.' Eden was breathless and held out the equipment tray as if it were an offering; she stood in a half-curtsey.

'Ben, can you do a needle decompression after you get access, and let me know when it's done. Eden' – she looked at Eden's expectant face, almost puffy with excitement. 'Scribe,' said Sophie. It was the least dangerous job. 'Can you scribe, Eden? Everyone else, do one. Too many cooks and all that. If you don't have a job, go and tend to the sick and dying. ED goes on.'

'I'm in charge here!' Michael was shouting, red-faced now. 'Everyone, I'm in charge here!' Some of the team slunk away, and the remaining members looked from Sophie to Michael. Then they carried on doing what Sophie had asked them to do.

Sophie ignored him too. 'Three-point pulse check,' she said. 'Off the chest. Rosy, what say you?' And so it went, round after round, as Sophie went through the possible causes. 'Toxins. Any history?'

Rosy shook her head. 'Nothing. But let's get the medical notes up.'

Sophie zoomed in on the scene. She ran through the theoretical knowledge she'd retained and the practical wisdom she'd earnt, giving orders to each team member as if she'd been doing it for years. 'Hypokalaemia – what's the potassium on the arterial blood gas? Hypoxia we know about; hypovolaemia – can we push in a bag of saline, please? Do we have enough access?'

Michael finally relented. She didn't care either way. It felt natural to her, to take charge.

At the next two-minute point Kemi felt a pulse, and within moments Liam was waving his arms slightly, agitated.

'We have return of spontaneous circulation,' said Sophie. 'Well done, team. Right, keep bagging gently, Kemi, and let's get a chest X-ray, full bloods, arterial gas and proper assessment. Let's get him to ICU, pronto.'

She glanced at the doorway. Aoife was standing and watching. She flicked her eyes from Michael to Sophie and, instead of smiling, she looked disgusted.

Michael found Sophie after the ward round, no longer angry, but rather with a puppy-dog expression on his face.

'Hello, gorgeous one. I'm so sorry about earlier. I never get hangovers like that. I lost it and I'm sorry, but you were in-*cred*-ib-le! Made this old cynic feel alive just watching you manage that arrest. Pure poetry. A man lives today because of you, no doubt. How you pulled that out of the bag after getting home at, what, 2 a.m.? I'm impressed. And I apologise.'

'It's fine. We all have off days.'

'This place is sending me round the bend at the moment. In any case, you were amazing. I had no idea you were so clinically brilliant. All we hear about from high up are the number of near misses and the increasing death rate, and here are our nurses literally saving lives.' He looked at her with something between respect and awe. 'Badass.'

Phoebe walked in and hovered nearby. 'There's a sickle cell patient coming into Resus and the paramedic asked for morphine ready to go. I've checked this out with Fran, but I can't give it.' She held up a vial of IV morphine. Sophie checked the vial and double-checked the dose. Rhian had recently confused micrograms for nanograms and given the patient a thousand times the amount of medication he needed, though he'd somehow ended up walking out and going home, which baffled all of them. They kept that to themselves. The paperwork would have been eye-watering.

Sophie nodded and handed the drug to Phoebe. 'I'll be there in a moment to give it, then witness you dispose of the remains.'

'Witness?' Phoebe looked flushed.

'I'm the authorised witness for controlled drug disposal. Basically, making sure you don't pocket whatever's left and sell it to minors.'

Phoebe shook her head earnestly. 'Oh, I'd never do that.'

Sophie waited until she disappeared again before turning back to Michael. 'Is it me or are people a bit thick?'

'I think it's your deadpan sense of humour,' he said, pressing his lips together. 'She probably thought you were serious and was horrified.'

He was attractive. His eyes reminded her of a bird's egg she'd once found in a nest at Gee's house. She'd crushed the egg in her hand, crunching it to nothing but sharp pieces.

Michael's eyes were the same colour, a perfect green-blue. He had the right amount of chest hair visible at the deep V of his scrubs, and he'd folded the short sleeves, only once, as though they were cuffs on a pair of jeans.

It was nice feeling the adoration leaking off his skin, and Sophie was still buzzing. 'Ever been to a sex party?'

Before Michael had the chance to answer, or laugh, or even redden, multiple alarms sounded from the cubicles, and Eden was running past them both. 'Cardiac arrest, bay six. Another one.'

They were having a day of cardiac arrest dominoes. Sophie bleeped the site nurse practitioners to beg for some strategic patient-moving to free up Resus and Majors cubicles. Then she returned to the four-bedded Resus bay. At first, she didn't notice that the wall had been painted red. The patient – a twenty-four-year-old woman suffering with alcoholism – had come in screaming violently with abdominal pain, vomiting blood. Her skin was the colour of Dijon mustard, but clearly, Sophie could see as her eyes adjusted, she had developed oesophageal varices – thick, swollen veins in her throat, which had split open, like Ben's fry-up sausages. She ran over to the patient, who was spewing blood out of her nose and mouth onto the wall, showering Sophie.

Sophie pulled the red alarm and shouted for help. Phoebe ran in and clamped her hands over her mouth.

'Get help,' said Sophie. She flashed back to the other poor girl she'd cared for recently who had carved the word 'HELP' in to her own chest. Nursing did that, gave you firefly memories that then caused another to flash up. A terrifying dot-to-dot inside every nurse's brain. A constellation of fucked-up stars.

*

On their way home after shift, Eden walked quickly beside her, trying to keep up. 'You were amazing this morning, leading that asthma arrest. Honestly, I thought Michael was going to be sick. I had a terrible afternoon. I was looking after a girl with meningococcal disease. It was so sad. It looks like she'll lose her limbs.'

'Sounds grim.'

'Awful. They gave me prophylactic antibiotics. Rifampicin.' She was quiet a moment. 'I've got something else to tell you – I mean, I did something. I heard you and Michael talking and then . . . oh, I don't know. What do you think of him? Michael, I mean?'

Sophie slowed down. 'You're not making any sense.' They walked past the café, the smell of oven cleaner and grease wafting out, the same odour as a full-thickness burn or a loop diathermy. Nothing was separate from the job anymore, not even smells. She could no longer go into a butcher's shop. 'What are you getting at?'

Eden stopped walking and turned her body towards Sophie. She had such a lack of awareness about personal space. Sophie stepped backwards, almost tripping over a dog.

'Are you trying to hug me?' Sophie moved away. 'I'm not really a hugger, just so you know.'

Eden was silent for a few moments. They turned the street corner to Rose Cottage and Sophie fished her keys from her pocket. 'He seems to like you, that's all.' They entered the flat and dumped their bags. 'Did you go out late last night?'

Sophie ignored her and went into the living area.

The others were already there, sitting around in mufti, chatting and laughing. Sophie and Eden washed their hands at the kitchen sink and joined them.

'What's occurring?' Sophie walked over to the sofas. 'You been home long?'

'I'm here for a good time, not a long time.' Ben was rolling a joint on the living-room table. 'What a fucking day. You owe me a full English, babe.'

Eden, for once, didn't disappear into her room and open the window wide, or walk around the flat spritzing the White Company room spray her mum had sent her, which did nothing to mask the smell. She hovered around Sophie and moved slowly as if in pain, looking at her quizzically.

Obi laughed. 'Tobacco will kill you. You need to bong it.'

Ben rolled his eyes and snort-laughed. 'How council. What do you take me for?'

'You're so classist,' said Rhian. She was wearing some sort of medieval monk costume, something none of them commented on. 'Nothing wrong with being working class, and as it happens most working-class people aren't sitting around smoking bongs, they're *working*. Clue's in the title.'

'Ha! Have you been to a Wetherspoons midweek? Fucking packed out.'

Rhian kicked him, and Ben rubbed his leg, pretending it hurt.

'Speaking of working, how're all the perverts? Paying top dollar, I hope.'

'They're not perverts. Not all of them.'

Sophie enjoyed their chat. She took an apple from the bowl and began to cut it with a scalpel – much sharper than a paring knife. She liked the smell of Ben's weed. Earthy, green, new life; it was far from death and blood, and more wholesome than alcohol, that was for sure. As far as she could tell, they had no admissions at all to the Emergency Department for weed, except perhaps a few adolescent boys who did little else but smoke and came in with first-presentation psychosis.

'Are you joining us this evening?' Obi grinned at Sophie and then Eden. 'Understand it was a bit like *SAW III* in Resus today?'

'Well, it wasn't *Call the Midwife*, that's for sure. Where exactly are you going?' She ate a small piece of apple, the first thing she'd eaten all day; since arriving at City, her hip bones had started jutting out.

'Rose Cottage Carnage.' Ben had stupid names for everything, a hangover from private school. 'It's the first night in ages we've all been off at the same time.'

'Let's do something that doesn't involve drugs or alcohol for once,' said Eden. 'Cinema? They have late showings at the Ritzy on Fridays. Or a drink but with an activity? I heard about this night at the Pelican. It's a Sip and Stich cross-stich class where you get a free drink and all the equipment. It started at eight thirty but we might catch the last hour of it if we leave now? Might be fun.'

'Sounds insufferable,' said Sophie.

'Bowling or something?' Obi looped his arm through Eden's. A peacekeeper.

Ben roared. 'Fuck that. We're heading to Peckham for mayhem and overpriced cocktails. I have a mixologist friend who'll sort us for drinks.' He nodded at Eden. 'Even mocktails if that's your bag.' He passed the joint to Sophie and took a small bag of powder out of his jeans pocket, shaking it onto the glass coffee table.

Rhian made a victory sign. 'I'm in. Let's drown our sorrows.'

Ben grinned and took a twenty-pound note out of his wallet. He began rolling it, but Sophie stopped him.

'Hang on.' She walked to her room and opened her top drawer. It was full of equipment she'd magpied from the hospital. Bits of kit. She liked collecting artefacts, souvenirs, shiny things. It wasn't stealing, exactly – most of this stuff was out of date – but she liked equipment; she felt safe having lifesaving kit around. Now she wouldn't need to rely on a chopstick to open an airway. It was odd to Sophie that it was about four months already since she'd first arrived and eavesdropped on Aoife and Michael in the restaurant.

She pushed her hand into the drawer. Arterial forceps; a cardiocentesis kit; stitch cutters; various syringes of different sizes. She grabbed what she was looking for and opened the packet and returned to the living room, pulling off the plastic end piece. 'Endotracheal tube,' she said, handing it to Ben.

Ben shook his head but looked delighted. 'A breathing tube. You evil genius.' He stuck it firmly up his nose, leant down and inhaled.

It was then that Eden began to cry, loudly. Sophie glanced up and saw her face. 'Oh my God.'

'It was such a horrible day,' said Eden. 'Really shitty, and I wanted to talk to you all without you getting wasted. There were four deaths. Four! And one was a girl about our age.'

'Eden,' said Sophie, 'you're bleeding.' She walked over and gently stroked Eden's cheeks with the palms of her hands. 'You're crying red tears.'

Ben wiped his nostril on his forearm and looked up. Obi covered his mouth with his hand. Rhian rushed over and held Eden by the arm. 'Ede. It's true. You're crying blood.'

'That's pretty cool,' said Ben.

NINE

Eden

I will breathe negativity out. Eden sat cross-legged in her bedroom on a yoga mat. *I am kind. I am compassionate. I am deserving. I am trustworthy. I am a nurse.* She stopped whispering when she heard a knock on the door. She ignored it, closed her eyes and tried to visualise a green triangle. Someone had once told her about this, or perhaps she'd read it in a book about forest monks. Either way, it calmed her.

Another knock. Rhian's voice. 'Ede. It's me. Can I come in?'

Eden didn't answer but opened her eyes when Rhian came in anyway. She'd changed out of her monk's costume and into dungarees. She had a very short fringe, which made her eyes look disproportionally huge as she looked at Eden. 'I had no idea about rifampicin. Who knew a medication could make you cry red tears? When did you take it?'

'This afternoon. I was looking after this uni student who had meningococcal disease, and they said it would cover me for infection.' Eden snorted. 'The team knew. Aoife knew! Mary must have, and the pharmacists. Everyone knew, and not one person told me that could happen. Nobody. I am literally freaked out, and now my anxiety is off the scale.' She tapped her collarbone as she spoke.

'I'm not surprised. How scary to think it was blood. You OK now?' Rhian sat on the floor next to Eden. She smelt of grapefruit. 'We can still go to the cinema if you want – they have a late showing.'

'I'm not really up to anything now. And I don't know how I'll be able to work tomorrow. I've got four long days. I might have to call in sick.'

'Shall I text Aoife? She might be able to suggest a swap.'

Eden shook her head. She stopped tapping and pressed her hands into the floor. The last person she wanted to speak to was Aoife. She looked at Rhian. 'Have they all gone to Peckham now? Idiots. Honestly, can you imagine if the NMC found out they're doing coke, or the General Medical Council? All Ben does is take drugs.'

'Ah, I'm sure they're not the first healthcare professionals to take recreational drugs on a night out.' Rhian smiled. 'Shall we order a pizza? It's just you, me and Sophie.'

Eden found herself nodding, in a bit of shock that Sophie had stayed behind and wanted to hang out. 'Let's do it,' she said. 'Vegetarian chilli?'

The three of them squashed onto the sofa that had an unidentifiable stain on it. 'It's pretty incredible,' said Sophie. 'To think that a drug can make you cry red tears. I wonder how long it'll carry on. Do you think you'll piss red too?' She leant across Eden's legs and took a small slice of pizza.

Sophie hardly ate anything, Eden had noticed. She didn't drink much alcohol either, bar the odd beer, though Eden knew she had taken drugs with the others during nights out. She hadn't imagined nurses to be so wild. Many of the girls she went to school with posted their own university experiences on social media – that seemed to be mostly about studying and wellness routines. Meanwhile, Rose Cottage *was* like a frat house after all. Some nights, they didn't even go out until midnight.

'I just wish they'd told me,' Eden said. 'Surely that's negligent prescribing.'

'I'm sure the pharmacist has bigger things to worry about than one prophylactic tablet for a staff member. OK, that's me done. I'm showering, then out.' Sophie put the crust of her pizza slice down on the opened box on the table and stood up, stretching. 'Hope the reprobates don't keep you up all night. You're on days tomorrow? Been a shite few shifts. Can only look up, surely.'

Eden nodded. 'I'm feeling super-anxious, though, so that depends.'

Sophie laughed. 'Snowflake.'

Rhian rolled her large slice of pizza into a tube and pretended to smoke it. 'Hi, my name's Ben and I'm going to get fucked up, then lecture you all about socialism.'

Eden giggled. She was feeling slightly better, less lonely. Her flatmates were dysfunctional, but there were glimmers of closeness. She'd hated Sophie when she'd overheard her and Michael, but seeing her in charge of Resus, it was impossible not to be impressed by her. Could they be friends, after all?

'Where are you off to at this hour?' Rhian asked, a large piece of melted cheese hanging from her chin. Eden pointed to it.

'Just a hook-up. Nothing serious.'

'Will you be safe? It's really late already, and if you don't actually know this person in real life . . .'

Sophie laughed. 'I'll be fine. We're meeting at a craft brewery. Nobody ever gets murdered in a craft brewery.'

Eden watched as Rhian shrugged and Sophie left to shower. They both acted like it was nothing at all. 'Who's she hooking up with?'

'Some old dude, no doubt. Each to their own. Shall we watch a film?'

Eden leant back and sat cross-legged. 'I worry about her self-esteem.'

Rhian threw her head back and cackled. 'Sophie's self-esteem? I think she's good.'

They watched a Korean horror film. Rhian fell asleep halfway through, leaving Eden wishing she'd insisted on *Twilight*.

She wondered for a second or two if she should tell Rhian that Sophie was most likely going to meet Michael, and how ever since they'd arrived at City, he had been sneaking around with Aoife one minute, then kissing Sophie the next. But after Aoife's non-reaction a few months before, she thought it best to keep these secrets to herself.

Eden didn't mention the rifampicin tears, to ask why anyone hadn't warned her, but she must have been subdued at handover. Aoife allocated her the least sick person on the unit: a man named John who had muscular dystrophy and had arrived via ambulance with raging pneumonia. According to his carers, he was riddled with MRSA so was sent straight to the isolation room. 'Pitch perfect care today, team. I don't want any disasters.'

All the managers were twitchy about the increase in adverse events on ED in the last few months. But the governance of ED was a strange process. Unexpected deaths had to be reported to the coroner every time. Yet nobody reported the deaths of those who were *expected* to die, only those who died a little bit sooner than anticipated. Surely, Eden thought, by the time they ended up in ED many people were *expected* to die.

Still, at least today she'd be able to give the care she wanted to give. Eden liked the quiet hum of the isolation room. She closed the blinds and, aside from her semi-conscious patient, was completely unwatched, alone and in charge. Eden studied John's face: his perfectly long and curled eyelashes, wide-set eyes, thick curly hair. She stared at him sleeping a while, then checked everything and double-checked again. She shifted his position on the trolley every thirty minutes or so to prevent pressure sores, careful not to make the same mistake twice. John slept, mostly, while Eden nurse-buzzed around him. She checked the oxygen was working and the suction was set up appropriately. She made sure there was a bag valve mask in case of gas-supply failure for his breathing machine, and a spare, full oxygen cylinder at the end of the trolley. Everything was shipshape. Eden made her daily plan: she took note of what medications John needed and the timings, and checked the doses lest the doctors had made a medical error, which, to her surprise, was seemingly common. She recorded John's vital signs, his blood pressure, heart rate, oxygen levels and the numbers on his machines, then she performed a detailed assessment, listened to his lungs, heart and bowels with a stethoscope, and assessed his circulation, testing his capillary refill time by lifting his arm in the air, pinching his thumb for five seconds, then watching how long it took for the colour to come back. She checked his pupil reactivity with a small torch that she kept in her bumbag. She found herself humming, the stress of the day before lifting with each hour of doing exactly what she'd wanted to do all along: be a good nurse.

John was stable. All his bloods were back and in range, and he'd had a chest X-ray. There was nothing else needed; his paperwork was all up to date, his discharge planning filled in. The transfer to the High Dependency Unit was organised. Eden even had time to call his family and let them know he was still in ED but fine and going to HDU. The number of family members who burst in not knowing if their loved one would be there alive or not was astonishing, but the nurses didn't have time to call everyone.

Eden felt cocooned in the room with John. It was like a spaceship, a place of sanctuary. The quiet whoosh of his BiPAP machine, the trickling of the water from the humidifier and her own soft humming the only background noises.

'Hi, hi, go for a break.' Sophie came in, looking tired. Eden had listened out for the front door and hadn't heard her return from her so-called date until the early hours. Michael had turned up in ED that morning with a reddened face, stubbly, dishevelled and slightly animated. They had surely been together. Eden planned to watch them closely.

'He's off soon. I can wait. He needs transferring and there's no healthcare assistant to come sit with him. It's not safe to leave you alone, John.' ED was not ICU, and not the place for one-to-one nursing; it was way too busy and noisy. But many patients needed one-to-one nursing nonetheless.

'Aoife sent me and said you're to have your break now, come hell or high water.' Sophie laughed. She entered the cubicle pulling on a plastic apron. 'You'd not need to ask me twice. It's a fucking miracle when we get a break.'

John opened one eye and coughed.

'Hello, I'm Sophie. I'll be looking after you while Eden goes for a steak dinner. Small glass of wine. Nothing heavy.'

Eden ignored her. 'Right, John, I'll be gone thirty minutes tops.' She stroked his hair. He opened both eyes for Eden, which made her feel warm. He trusted her. 'I won't be long.' She nodded at the infusion of saline. 'His potassium was low so he's having a top-up. Keep an eye on the IV.'

'I know what to do,' Sophie said. 'I'll keep popping in, don't worry.'

Eden left the room, glancing behind her. John had already fallen back to sleep and Sophie was sitting at the end of the bed looking at the computer screen.

Eden took off her apron and gloves and scrubbed her hands. MRSA could spread like wildfire and put patients at risk. She walked quickly to the heavy exit doors and ran down the stairs, two at a time. There was a café at the bottom serving toasted sandwiches, which were ultra-processed but Eden had not made herself any lunch today, so one of those would have to do. It was rare to get a lunch break at all, Sophie was right, and she intended to get off the unit and enjoy it. A few moments of rest to recharge for the afternoon.

After twenty minutes, and having inhaled a veggie melt, Eden returned to ED. She stood outside the entrance for a moment, listening. Alarms sounded as ever but there was also the distinct sound of the crash bell, like the siren of a toy police car. She walked in, and could at once see the team clustered around the isolation room. John.

The floors were shiny and slippery, but Eden ran. She arrived breathless to see Sophie on John's chest, doing CPR, Aoife at the foot end of the bed in charge. Two junior doctors were dashing around.

'What happened?' Eden felt her heart speed up, her throat fill with acid.

'Stand clear,' said one of the doctors, in front of the defibrillator. She waited until everyone was well away from the bed, their hands in front of them to emphasise their safety, then continued: 'Off the chest. Shocking.'

John's body jolted awkwardly. Sophie went straight back to chest compressions.

'You're too fast,' said Aoife. 'Press harder and slower. You need to be about a third of the chest deep. Six centimetres.'

Aoife was tough on Sophie, Eden noticed.

Eden rushed to stand behind Sophie. 'I'll take over,' she said, and glanced at Aoife, who nodded.

Sophie counted, 'One, two, three,' and jumped out of the way, allowing Eden onto John's chest, pressing down with her elbows locked. His chest was skinny and his ribs prominent; she heard crunching noises as she pushed. But after only a few presses John moved his arm.

'Signs of life,' shouted Eden. She stopped chest compressions.

'Three-point pulse check, please,' said Aoife. 'Can you repeat his potassium?'

'He's breathing.' Eden looked down at his chest and relief flooded through her. A strange power, too. She had literally saved his life. She turned to Sophie. 'What happened? He was *fine*.'

That evening, they were so late home Eden went straight to her room and flopped into bed. She lay in the dark for a while, listening to the quiet. A strange sensation was making her skin feel tingly. Her body was tired but her mind was wide awake. Instead of trying to sleep, she opened her laptop and then Facebook and typed a name into the search bar. John Wheeler. She recognised the profile picture immediately, his long eyelashes, wide-set eyes, curly hair, and then she scrolled to photos of a family, friends, events he'd attended, holidays and weddings. It made her feel a bit sneaky somehow, accessing so much information about a stranger, but Eden found comfort and fascination at seeing his real life. His family. The people who would miss him if he was dead.

TEN

Aoife

Nobody did death better than Irish women. Aoife had grown up with it – exposure to the reality that everyone dies and it's normal and natural and, in many cases, a relief. She found it odd that Sam, who'd grown up in Reading, had never even seen a dead body. 'It's baffling to me,' she'd said once, after he asked if it was scary, being around dead people, 'that you never even saw your nanna when she passed. And, no, it's not at all scary. It's the living you want to watch out for, not the dead.'

She spent her childhood weaving in and out of front rooms, peering into coffins at the recently deceased, the dead person in a family living room and life simply playing out around them. Aoife talked to them as if they were still breathing, which was a comfort to her, and to the families. 'I'm going to give you a little wash,' she'd say. 'And open the window so your soul will be free.'

Aoife had seen it all. Patients long dead who exhaled loudly enough that it sounded like a sigh or a groan. Dead people occasionally twitched. They burped and farted. Sometimes they squeaked. People very rarely surprised her, living or dead, though once, a patient who was very much deceased had developed an enormous erection, which had baffled even Aoife.

'I'm going to pop a clean gown on you, after freshening you up.' The patient now, Alan, was eighty-four but looked a hundred. His face had caved in, and his limbs were twig-like and emaciated. He'd been transferred to ED after confusion and a fall at his nursing home, but he had a list of previous: cardiovascular disease, renal disease, diabetes, hypertension, dementia, peripheral neuropathy. He'd arrested en route and the team unanimously agreed futility, calling it on arrival. Some patients they only met in death.

Aoife couldn't do much to make this poor man's death dignified, but she could still make a difference. She took her time. A small silver tray on wheels contained a bowl of soapy water and a large mint-green sponge. She gently washed Alan's face, carefully and slowly, trying not to get soap in his eyes. 'There you go. We'll have you spruced up in no time,' she said. After his face, Aoife washed Alan's arms, legs and feet. She was careful, gentle and calm. She chatted constantly.

'Porters are here to take him to Rose Cottage.' Sophie came in and looked down at Alan's body. 'Shall I get a shroud?'

Aoife shook her head. 'It's fine, we can use a sheet. Could you refill that bowl with hot water and open up the window for him?'

Sophie didn't move, as though she hadn't heard Aoife, but then she nodded at Alan. 'You do know he's dead, right?'

Aoife looked up at her. Sophie was perplexed, a hand on her hip. 'We like to treat all people as if they are family here at City. As you know, good nursing care doesn't ever stop.'

'That's a patronising thing to say.'

Aoife shot her a look. 'Have some respect.'

Nothing had been quite right at City since these girls had arrived, and although the system was impossible, there also seemed to be something fundamentally lacking in their character, Sophie's in particular. Aoife had been floored by Eden's disclosure a few months before about Sophie flirting with, or even *maybe kissing* Michael. But she told herself it would have been innocent on his part; over the years she'd watched him flirt with patients, other nurses, doctors, men and women of all ages. He was charming, that was all, and he liked being adored. Still, even the *idea* that Michael might glance in Sophie's direction had Aoife feeling uneasy.

'Respect for you,' Sophie said, 'or for him?' She nodded at Alan's face. 'Because I can promise you, he doesn't give a shit what I say.'

Aoife took the sponge from the bowl and continued washing Alan. Her head flashed with heat. She ignored Sophie and focused on gently sponging the bottom of each of Alan's feet. They weren't dirty but this was the ritual.

Sophie reached up and opened the small window as far as it would go. 'You know, these windows only open an inch, to prevent people jumping out.'

'You should always open a window for the dead,' said Aoife, taking a comb out from the drawer and beginning to run it through Alan's wispy hair. 'That's how it's done. It's what nurses have been doing for centuries.'

'If you say so,' said Sophie. She had a wry smile as if she was about to laugh. 'I mean, there are hardly any windows in ED, and to be honest with you, I know plenty of nurses who wouldn't bother.'

'It's probably quite frightening, seeing this, but you get used to it.' Sophie was full of bravado, but she was still very young. James always acted like a brat whenever he was scared.

'Ah, I'm used to dead people,' said Sophie. 'The death rate at my last hospital was off the scale.' She looked at Alan, then at the window, and her eyes glazed over a fraction. 'I can always tell when death is coming, you know?'

Aoife opened her mouth to say something but then changed her mind. She didn't want to get into a discussion about her spiritual beliefs. Instead, she focused on very gently closing Alan's eyelids with her thumbs then attached an identification tag to his ankle.

Billy, one of the ED porters, came in pushing the adapted trolley, which was like a concealed coffin. 'Do we need a body bag? Any leakage?'

'No, we'll be OK.' Aoife ignored Sophie mock-retching, and pulled a sheet over Alan before standing up and lowering her head.

Billy positioned the trolley next to the bed so they could slide Alan onto it easily. Sophie left them to it.

After they had Alan's body safely strapped and secure on Billy's trolley, he nodded at Aoife. 'You OK, sister? You look a bit peaky.'

'These young nurses,' she said, 'are testing my mettle.'

'You should see the lads they're sending over to my porter's lodge. There's this one kid, straight out of college, said he can't work Tuesdays as he's got his talking therapy, and Occupational Health has said he can't collect any blood bottles or transfusions on account of his anxiety.' He made a whistling sound. 'Right then, fella,' Billy said, looking at the sheet covering Alan's face and body. 'Let's get you on your way.'

Michael grabbed Aoife's arm as she walked past him in the corridor. 'You still good for dinner tonight?'

'Absolutely. I've had a day and then some! Can you get away on time?'

'Sure. Let's be radical and go to Moon and Stars this evening? We've done Queens to death by now. I'll maybe even be a bit early, by some miracle. Lionel's covering the consultant rota again. He's working hundred-hour weeks to get away from Pippa, so I should get off a bit early.'

'Why doesn't he get divorced? He must be sixty already. Jeez, does any medical couple have a happy marriage?'

Michael half smiled, and paused a moment before clapping his hands together. 'Right then, I'll capitalise on Lionel's bad marriage and head to the pub as soon as I'm done. See you there when you can. I'll find a quiet corner, send you the menu.'

Aoife hadn't meant to mention marriage and certainly not to bring up happy marriages with Michael. The fact was, she *did* have a happy marriage; she was one of the lucky few medical people who managed it. If anything, she had two: Sam at home and Michael at the hospital. Entirely separate, but complementary.

She'd brought a decent outfit to work as usual on the first Tuesday of the month and kept a small washbag of make-up and shower gel in her locker. She changed after her shift, then texted Sam that she'd be late. She never said anything in advance – there was no need – things changed hour by hour, and a full day shift could easily become an overnight one.

She walked across to the Moon and Stars, a short walk further on than the All Bar One where their colleagues all went, and around the corner from Queens, their usual hangout, avoiding eye contact with anybody on the way. Michael was waiting outside the pub, texting on his phone. He smiled at Aoife and put his phone away, ushering her inside. They didn't touch in public, not visibly. 'Feels odd not going to Queens. Like we're cheating, somehow.'

'How's Sam?' Michael never asked about Sam. It was an unwritten rule. They talked about work, sometimes, and politics, often. They argued about books, what they'd read recently and why it was good or not. Michael read a lot of classics, and non-fiction, which Aoife considered dull. She would press contemporary fiction into his hands, and if he tried reading it at all, he'd scoff at everything but George Saunders. Sam didn't read. He hadn't read a single novel except *Cider with Rosie*, which he'd been forced to read at school. She and Michael once had a full-blown row about Sally Rooney. It was bliss.

'Sam's good,' she said. 'He's booked flying lessons at Biggin Hill Airport, but they're pricey, so only a few. He's trying to talk me into keeping chickens.'

'Blimey.' Michael smiled. 'He's a good guy.' They let that hang in the air between them.

He was right, of course. Sam was a good guy. He was thoughtful and genuinely cared about people. He was the only man she'd ever met who'd sent her a handmade thank-you card after she'd cooked for him. He'd done a tiny painting of forget-me-nots on the front, having remembered her mentioning that they were her favourite flowers. She'd kept looking at his beautiful handwriting.

Aoife and Michael shared a charcuterie board and a bottle of red, and made small talk, gossiping about colleagues and patients alike. 'Shall we get another?' Michael gestured to the empty bottle of Chianti on the table between them. It felt strange being in the near dark in July, drinking red wine in the shadows, a bit sexy.

'Let's do it,' she said. 'Though I'm in early tomorrow so I shouldn't go crazy. So let's keep it PG tonight.' She laughed, but really, she imagined they'd check in to the Travelodge, as they had last month, and there'd be nothing PG about it. She had lube in her handbag.

Michael grinned but didn't belly-laugh as she'd have expected. He was clearly tired. When he disappeared to the bar, she reapplied her lipstick, dabbing her lips on a serviette.

'We need to talk about Sophie,' Aoife said, when he got back carrying another bottle. 'I'm worried about her.'

She waited for Michael to forbid all work-related chat, but he put his hand to his forehead and whispered, 'So, you know, then.'

Aoife frowned. 'It's bad enough how rude she is, but she's unsafe, or perhaps even worse than that. She gave the wrong blood to a patient today waiting in an ambulance – wrong blood, wrong patient – and she's claiming it was about the lack of admission wristband, blaming the patient who could barely speak English, and the ED for not admitting before treating; anyone but her. Honestly, Michael, I think she might be intentionally . . .' Aoife stopped talking. She looked at Michael, who had his fingertips spread over his forehead, pressing hard enough for the skin to change colour. 'What? Wait, what do you mean, I know? Know what?'

Eden's words throbbed in her ears. *I think they were kissing.*

Michael put his hands on the table and looked at her. Then his eyes moved away.

Aoife felt the ground disappear beneath her. Eden hadn't been making things up or exaggerating. Her entire body grew hot. 'You and Sophie? Sophie Ibrahim? My junior nurse, Sophie?'

Michael poured two generous glasses of wine and lifted one to his lips.

Aoife took a big breath and tried to focus. 'We've been doing this for many years,' she whispered. 'And never, ever has there been a question of you seeing anyone else.'

Michael took another gulp of wine. He leant forwards and touched her elbow. For a second, she wondered if he'd kiss her, say she'd got it wrong and of course there was nothing going on with him and Sophie, or perhaps even that Eden had been right and Sophie had tried to kiss him and he'd pushed her away, silly thing, but he frowned. 'I didn't want you to find out from anyone else.'

'Find out about what exactly?' Aoife could hear her voice rising. 'A shag? A flirt? A fling? This is one of our junior colleagues we're talking about. It's totally inappropriate.' She stared at him.

The edges of her vision blurred. She could hear a whoosh of blood inside her head and she pressed her fingernails into the palms of her hands, hard. Michael didn't answer. 'I assume you've slept with her, then. You've slept with a much younger woman behind my back? No secrets between us. We always said that.'

Michael's pupils constricted. 'We did sleep together, yes. I'm telling you now. And of course it's not exclusive between us, you and me, in either direction.'

Aoife spoke slowly. 'What exactly are you saying?' Her voice was loud. She knew she had no right to anger, but Michael had always seemed happy with their arrangement. He'd forever assured her he didn't need or want anything more. 'Tell me you haven't said anything to Sophie about us. You surely wouldn't do that to me?'

Michael scratched his shoulder. 'I haven't, no. But I don't want ambiguity anymore. Or confusion.' He paused, reached out and held Aoife's hands in his. 'My feelings for you remain unchanged. You're my best friend and my most trusted person in the world, and I always want honesty with you. I love you, Aoife. Always will. You know that.'

Aoife's fingers softened in the warmth of his hands.

He paused again – a split second, but enough for his voice to lower. 'It wasn't a one-off, though. I've been seeing Sophie regularly. I delayed telling you, and I'm sorry for that. But I want transparency between us now.'

Aoife pressed her tongue against the roof of her mouth. She thought of Sophie's body, her perfect skin, her long neck. Then she began to laugh. 'Sophie is a psychopath! She's callous and dangerous and she's clearly using you. Why would a young woman like that be shagging a fifty-year-old? It's a power trip, Michael. You've lost your fucking mind.' As her words surged, tears began to fall.

He sat up straighter. 'Come on, Aoife, I know you're angry, but this isn't Sophie's fault. You'll never leave Sam, and I've always been fine with that, and you can't ask for monogamy from one party only. It doesn't work like that. I'm single as much as you're married.'

The room became darker still, and it felt like the whole world was exploding inside her chest. 'But we're together and have been since the beginning. We've been through so much, so many years, and it's always been us. Me and you. Why would you do this?'

'We never made each other any promises, Aoif. I mean, with you being so very married and all, how on earth could we?' Michael stared but his voice became softer. 'I get to be with who I want. Like you do.'

Aoife took a black cab home and cried all the way. She let herself into the quiet house and stood in the hallway for a few moments in darkness, before kicking off her shoes and putting down her bag. She checked the time on her phone: 11.45 p.m. Sam would be asleep, his work clothes laid out on the armchair next to his side of bed. She thought about sleeping on the sofa, so she could cry, but instead she padded upstairs and climbed into pyjamas, before lying next to Sam.

'You OK?' He was half asleep. 'Bad day at the office?'

'I'm fine. You know how it is.'

'I know, love.' He turned over and spooned her, his breath warm on the back of her neck. She could feel him getting an erection, which they both ignored. Sam stroked her arm a while, then reached around to her face and wiped her tears with his fingertips. 'Want to talk about it?'

She took his hand and held it against her heart. 'No need.'

ELEVEN

Aoife

'Denise, at last I've found you,' Aoife said, almost running down the corridor to catch up with her. 'You've vanished into management ether just like the rest of them – your PA said you've no space in the diary for the next three weeks! Busy playing golf, I expect?' This was the problem with nursing: anyone seriously good at it got promoted out of clinical care in the blink of an eye. Not Aoife, though. She had no intention of ever leaving her patients.

'Aoife! Lovely Aoife. What's your excuse, then? How's the coalface? We're long overdue a catch-up but it's been insanely busy.' She laughed. 'And you're right! It's all elaborate dinners and golf courses, first-class flights to the Seychelles, that type of thing.'

Denise was a bag of bones. Her eyes were sunken and her skin had a certain kind of pallor only found in the NHS management offices; Aoife had known Denise for decades before she'd become the director of nursing at City a few months earlier, and it was clear she'd lost her shine already. 'You look well,' Aoife said.

'That's a lie! I don't sleep anymore.' Denise leant towards Aoife's ear and whispered, 'One of the student nurses jumped in front of a train last night.'

'Jesus.' Aoife placed her hand over her heart, took a breath.

'Anyhoo,' said Denise, her voice brisk and louder, 'we should get a date in.'

'Actually, I need to speak with you now, Den. It's important.' Aoife put a hand on Denise's arm. A few people walked past wearing scrubs, and a kitchen porter pushing a large square trolley that smelt of chlorine and gravy.

Denise nodded, laser focused on Aoife's expression. 'Are you OK? Hey, you look worn out – all good at home? Sam OK? I can be a bit late for my next meeting. Let's head to the conference centre and find a quiet room.'

'Thank you. Promise I won't keep you for ages.' They walked along the corridor covered in posters and artwork. The walls were painted lime green, the paint peeling off at the edges. A few other doctors walked past them, and they side-stepped an industrial floor polisher and a healthcare assistant pushing another revolting-smelling meal trolley.

'Food smells as good as ever. Haute cuisine.'

'It's high on the agenda with the powers that be this year.' Denise waited until they were out of anyone else's earshot. 'Apparently the catering is no longer going to be outsourced, so I've got to organise annual in-house resus and fire training for a group of chefs, and they want to return to a weekly set menu for patients, with no extras. I'm bracing myself for complaints. Do you know, we get more complaints about the food than anything else? One of the relatives asked to speak to the chef after finding an actual mouse in her lasagne and his response was to tell her to fuck off, so that's fun.'

Aoife laughed. 'At least it was protein.'

'You on the crash team today? I heard ED is having to cover the crash bleep until we get the posts filled.'

'A few calls but nothing of note. There's a leak in the equipment room, though, so we're one portable defib down. Hopefully won't be too hectic a day.'

They made more small talk as they walked and eventually came to the atrium and an empty office. It had a few plastic chairs, an old ECG machine with a piece of paper sellotaped to it – 'BROKEN' – and a few out-of-date and dusty textbooks on the desk.

Denise closed the door behind them, and they sat down opposite each other. 'Right then, my old friend. What's going on? Everything OK with Sam?'

Aoife nodded. 'Sam's fine. It's a work issue, and, honestly, I don't really know what I'm saying exactly, other than sounding you out.'

'Go on. I'm listening.'

'OK, well, completely confidentially, of course' – Aoife looked at Denise, who nodded – 'I'm worried about one of my nurses.'

Denise frowned. 'In what way?'

'Since she started it's been a total shitstorm. Unexpected deaths were eighteen in the last quarter – I think that's around double the usual. She's always around when things go wrong. She was looking after a patient last week who arrested from nowhere and luckily lived to tell the tale, but, I don't know, Denise, I've a very bad feeling.' Aoife shifted on her plastic chair. Of course, patients often arrested from nowhere, but she knew Denise would listen.

'Have you spoken to her?'

'No. I haven't spoken to anyone.'

'Have you witnessed anything specific?'

Aoife shook her head. For a split second she thought about lying. She could easily tell Denise that she *had* witnessed Sophie doing something; giving the wrong medication, for example, or speeding up a potassium infusion. That would surely get Sophie transferred, and things could go back to how they'd been. The status quo would be resumed, and she and Michael could love each other as they always had, without Sam ever knowing or getting hurt. She kept thinking of Sophie and Michael together, images flashing in her head like an alarm. She wanted her gone. Sophie was dangerous, in every sense of the word.

'Tell me about the nurse you're concerned about.'

Aoife sat upright. 'I mean, in terms of performance management, it's not her competence exactly, more a hunch at the moment. It felt like there was a shift in safety outcomes the moment Sophie arrived in ED.'

Denise paused. She pushed her glasses to the top of her forehead. 'Hmm. Well, you guys see – what? – 110,000 patients a year? There's bound to be fluctuations. What's her background?'

'Senior staff nurse. She worked in ED for around eighteen months in a level two, but never on a major trauma or Hyperacute Stroke Unit. I have no idea what she was like there, but on paper she looks safe. I'm really worried, though, Denise.' Aoife let the words breathe. 'I'm not saying she's deliberately hurting patients, but, oh, I don't know. I don't trust her.'

It was true that the death rate had gone up since Sophie had arrived. That alone was concerning enough. 'I wonder if Sophie might be moved sideways.'

'You mean transferred to another unit? HR would have a fit. The red tape involved would stretch around the planet, Aoife.'

'I know, but ED isn't a good fit for her. It's such a high-risk area,' said Aoife. *And she's a total fucking bitch*, she thought.

'OK. Well, at this stage, I'm assuming this is an off-the-record chat between two old colleagues, and you haven't raised concerns with anyone else? My advice to you would be to keep an eye on things.'

Aoife smiled. She'd known Denise would react with this advice, but at least she'd planted the seed. 'I'll watch Sophie like a hawk,' she said. 'I don't think this is paranoia.'

'There's a huge cohort of new starters so it could be any of them making mistakes. It's most likely Sophie needs a bit more experience. The last CQC inspection was pretty clear that it saw evidence in ED about learning from unexpected deaths. I think that's the key thing to focus on, but shout if you need me to see her.'

Aoife didn't answer, but it felt good to have told Denise her concerns. The death rate *was* spiking, after all. People had begun talking about how bad things were getting, huddled together after night shifts, wondering whether it was down to the system or who'd been on duty that day. All Aoife had to do was gently whisper Sophie's name. Gossip spread faster than MRSA.

TWELVE
Sophie

'Ten ambulances backed up outside, and there're no beds anywhere. Entire hospital is full, apparently, so no wiggle room yet to ship anyone out.' Aoife spoke in a quiet, calm voice that didn't match her words. 'Brace yourselves for today, I'd say. Sophie, you're in charge.' She looked at Sophie over the top of her glasses, sizing up her reaction.

Poker-faced, Sophie glanced around the handover room, avoiding Aoife's telepathy: *Are you up to this?* In any case, there was only one answer: *Is anyone?* An article about death rates in ED had been printed off and left on the coffee table. Somebody had highlighted a section titled 'Emergency Medicine' that said 15 per cent of in-department deaths are described as unexpected and a measure of the quality of care. There was a handwritten note in the margin: 'Hahahahahaha.'

Sophie scanned the nurses in front of her. Mary was the safest pair of hands during a cardiac arrest. She was the mathematician, able to manage equipment gone wrong, machine errors, and to calculate oxygen requirements for flight transfers. One glance at an ECG recording and she could tell you if a patient was in sinus rhythm or any number of obscure anomalies. She suffered with type 1 diabetes and had a tendency to skip meals, so could be prone to hypos herself. Aoife always kept a packet of sweets in her bag. Rhian was next to her, kind and capable in her own way, though made frequent drug errors, a by-product of her dyscalculia. Despite that, she could set up a ventilator or haemofiltration circuit with her eyes closed. Obi was self-obsessed but he was also kind and charming. The families loved him, and he could defuse conflict and calm down an angry relative within minutes of entering a room.

Eden had the most red flags. The Emergency Department was an excellent place to work for anyone who got off on trauma. Although she was obsessed with being a good nurse and sometimes appeared capable and caring, her nervousness led to frequent mistakes.

'We've three outliers, and a multiple stab wounds en route from Sussex. We've not much room. There's a gynae patient, Nora, in Majors and stable so the first out, as soon as gynae has a bed. She was booked in for a hysterectomy, but it was cancelled for the second time – strikes and all that – and she came in bleeding; haemoglobin was in her boots but she's now on nasal-cannula oxygen and finishing a third blood transfusion, so basically ready to go. All good?' Aoife smiled. She somehow never looked tired, even after night shifts. Sophie suspected she got Botox. She looked after herself; she'd told Sophie she did reformer Pilates to correct her nurse's back. Most nurses did not look so good as they aged; the job showed on their faces and bodies.

Aoife handed Sophie the keys and the large diary. 'I hope it's a manageable day. I've asked Denise to be around on bleep if the big guns are needed, given how short we are of senior staff. I'll see you tonight.'

She touched Sophie's arm and looked at her so intensely it felt almost intimate. Sophie felt like reminding her that she *was* senior staff, but something about Aoife's expression stopped her. 'Er, are you OK?'

'Could I request Resus today?' Eden interrupted them. 'I've a few final, final competencies left to get signed off.'

Sophie turned to Eden as Aoife headed out. 'There're not enough bodies around for much learning,' she said. 'Doubt we'll be out of here on time. This job is taking over my life.' They all groaned in agreement. 'OK, habibis. Mary, can you cover Resus?'

She nodded. 'Grand.'

'Great. OK, so, Fran: Majors A. Obi to AMU, but can you cover Urgent Care for breaks? Anyone "fit to sit" gets moved off trolleys and let's try to clear the corridor. Non-respiratory patients only in the ambulance assessment area, and mask up – we've got Covid, flu, and now bird flu's doing the rounds.' She smiled at Eden. 'You can transfer the stable patient in Majors to gynae, please, then the equipment cupboard.'

'Equipment cupboard?' Eden flicked her head to Sophie.

'It's a clinical area now. They're calling it a temporary escalation space.'

'Jesus fucking wept,' said Mary. 'First corridor care, then cupboard care? What next? We'll be putting patients in the staff room soon, and then where will we moan about them all?'

'Are you the nurse in charge today?' Ben poked his head around the sluice door.

'Sure am. That's why I'm hiding in here.' Sophie was leaning against the sluice, eating a Peperami.

Ben made a retching sound. 'How the fuck you can eat in here is beyond me. Stinks.' He walked in and stood opposite her. 'I need you to help me craft a Datix. I've fucked up.'

Sophie bit off another chunk. 'What have you done?'

'Put an i-gel breathing tube in a patient's airway with the plastic shell still attached.' Ben grinned, but his eyes didn't.

Sophie pressed her lips closed to avoid letting a laugh slip out. 'That wasn't very clever, was it? Some might say it was moronic, in fact. How's the patient?'

'Multiple lacerations and a bit of soft-tissue damage, but apparently not too terrible. At least I'm stealing some of Eden's thunder. You know people have started calling her the Grim Reaper?'

Sophie laughed at that and chucked her Peperami wrapper into the sluice, then lightly reached over to pat Ben's shoulder. 'It'll be OK,' she said. 'Worse things have happened, and you're right, makes a change from Eden fucking up.' She tried not to imagine Michael's face when he heard about yet another clinical error.

After helping Ben fill out the Datix with careful language that minimised the event and the outcome, Sophie had a typical in-charge day. She had to get involved with a complaint from a relative, staff sickness for the forthcoming night shift, a drug error and a supply issue. There had been no fewer than five Code 10s, where a mental health patient had kicked off sufficiently to put out the security call. They had to store a dead person in the relatives' room, as the porters were so busy and needed an hour to collect the body for the mortuary. Somehow it had got left unlocked and a small child had run out screaming. She hadn't seen Michael all day bar a quick ward round, and that suited her fine. She had no interest in starting a relationship with him and had been crystal clear about that. He was purely a distraction.

When she'd suggested the sex party idea, Michael had laughed and vigorously shaken his head. 'No chance, kiddo. I'd like to keep my job, thanks. Can you imagine the headlines?'

'Consultant who believes in liberation and sexual freedom has a fun night with his lover. Sounds like health promotion to me.' His reticence surprised her.

At work, they kept it professional. They never flirted publicly. Instead, they snatched the odd liaison at his flat. She enjoyed that he went down on her even on her period. He said he liked the taste.

Sophie took a quick break at 5 p.m., bumping into Ethan, an ICU nurse who she often collided with on late breaks in the canteen, and chatted with him for a few minutes as she shoved a chicken sandwich down, and then walked back onto ED.

'Can I have a hand?'

Sophie was at the other end of the corridor but noticed Eden come out of the coffee room and run towards the cubicles, calling out. She followed quickly. 'Eden, everything OK?' Sophie threw open the cubicle doors.

Eden was standing frozen to the spot with her hand covering her chest. Nora, the gynae patient who'd been stable and heading to the ward, was waxy and unmoving. Her alarms were going crazy.

Sophie pulled the red alarm on the wall at the back of the bed. 'Get the crash trolley!' she shouted to Eden. But Eden was still rooted to the spot. She had a strange expression on her face – not terror, but something else. Sophie shouted again as she pulled the head of Nora's bed flat, 'Help! Now!' then performed a head-tilt chin lift, looking down at Nora's chest for any movement. Nora's silk headscarf fell into Sophie's hands, and she flicked it off. It floated down to the puddle of blood on the floor.

'You OK to do this?' Eden still hadn't said a word. They had performed twenty minutes solid of good CPR and Nora had remained in asystole throughout. There was little more they could do. Sophie told Eden to take a break. 'There's enough of us here,' she said. 'Take five minutes, then talk to Jess, her wife.'

After the medical registrar finally pronounced Nora dead, and she and the team had left, Eden sloped back in, her face red and blotchy from crying. 'She's making phone calls, then coming in. She didn't even cry, just went totally pale, then had to sit down in case she fainted. I think she's in shock. I can't believe it.' Eden glanced at Nora, who looked peaceful, as though she were simply sleeping. 'She wasn't supposed to die. This wasn't meant to happen.'

Sophie checked Nora's name tag, then turned around. 'Well, clearly not. Fuck's sake, Eden. "Never events" like this shouldn't happen; they're totally unacceptable in all circumstances. If they find any mistakes here, it'll trigger a Fatal Accident Inquiry and we're under enough probing as it is.'

'I can't believe it.' Eden looked at Nora's face and touched her cheek. 'She was meant to be ward ready.'

Sophie grimaced, then looked around Nora's room, taking in the large yellow clinical waste bag full of gauze and empty cannula packets and defib pads, dirty rolled-up plastic aprons, used latex gloves, empty saline pouches and giving sets. The neon-yellow sharps bin was on the small patient table, overflowing with needles, next to a half-eaten sandwich and a plastic jug of water with a cornflower-blue lid.

The door burst open and Aoife walked in, breathing deeply. She stopped suddenly when she saw Sophie and Eden. 'They rang me at home. What happened?' She turned to Sophie and narrowed her eyes. Eden was crying and putting dirty wipes into the yellow waste bag. 'Stop. Don't touch or remove anything,' she said. 'Eden, you go and get some air.'

'That's OK, I can handle it. You should be asleep and resting, Aoife.' Sophie put an apron on. 'No need for you to come in.'

Aoife looked around the room. 'Every need. Tell me what happened.'

Eden sobbed. 'I don't know. She was sitting up and talking.' Eden stared at the large pool of blood on the floor and picked up the green patterned scarf. She held it in front of her, then placed the scarf on Nora's unmoving chest.

Aoife glanced around. 'Leave all the IVs and i-gel in situ,' she said. 'This could be a crime scene.'

The buck stopped with Aoife. Sophie watched the weight of it land on her, the confusion and pain of a patient's potentially avoidable death. 'It was on my watch, not yours,' she said. 'And crime scene is a bit excessive – it's hardly a suspicious death. Unexpected, yes, but not suspicious. She deteriorated suddenly, that's all.'

Aoife pulled the small slit window open a fraction and then looked straight at Sophie. 'It's *always* my watch.'

Eden was shaking. 'Crime scene? It was me looking after her. Oh my God. How? She was stable. She was. But crime scene?'

'Come on,' said Sophie. 'You're really going to call the police and get a forensic coroner involved? Look at the obs; she was scoring eight when she arrested. I didn't have time to do anything other than put out a crash call.'

Aoife stood frowning a moment or two, and then her face relaxed. 'Well, she still needs investigating. She was ward bound, so something's happened.' She touched Eden's shoulder on the way back out of the cubicle and glanced at Sophie again on the way out. She gave a tiny nod, a morsel of encouragement. 'She scored eight on NEWS?'

Sophie nodded. 'Yup. Gynae, so anything could have happened. She presented as stable, but she clearly wasn't.'

Aoife looked a bit relieved, then left them to it.

Sophie picked up Nora's arm, turning it and examining the line the blood had gone into. 'Let's hope Aoife doesn't escalate, but for now, don't throw out anything at all, not the packets or vials, nothing.'

Eden stopped crying. She stared at Nora's body.

Sophie passed her a paper towel and exhaled. 'I'm not sure how you missed her crashing out, Edes?' Her voice dropped to a whisper. She felt the sweat trickle down the centre of her back – CPR was akin to a dozen spin classes. 'Did you check her BP?'

'I don't know. She was fine.' Eden looked up, finally.

Sophie frowned and thought, *No wonder people are calling you the Grim Reaper.*

But as Eden's face scrunched up, she realised she'd spoken out loud.

THIRTEEN
Eden

There was no train station in Keston, so her dad picked her up from Hayes. Eden watched him pull up carefully, looking left and right and indicating, despite the road being entirely empty. This was the deepest, darkest suburbs. She had a few school friends in the area, all still living at home with their parents, and with no plans to move out. Eden felt like she'd outgrown them, but even so, it was nice to be home.

'Hello, Dad.' She climbed into the passenger seat and kissed him. He smelt strongly of aftershave. 'Phew, is that new?'

He laughed. 'Sauvage. Mum got it at duty-free after her last girly weekend. I think it's a bit flash, but she seems to like it.' He pulled away and drove towards home, making chit-chat and describing his new office, the astronomical cost of rent in London, the dahlias in the back garden that had come out really well this year. 'Anyway,' he said. 'How's the dream job?' He didn't notice Eden's tears until they pulled into the drive, a shingle gravel path with two stone lions on pillars either side that Eden found embarrassing.

Her dad stopped the car and walked over to her door, opening it. As soon as Eden stood up, he bear-hugged her. 'What's going on, sweetheart?'

Eden sobbed into his shirt for so long that when she came up for air, her whole face smelt of Sauvage.

'Come on. Let's go in.' He linked his arm with hers and they walked through the house to the large kitchen where Eden's mum was drinking a large glass of red wine and reading a cookbook.

'Hi, Mum.'

'Oh, Eden! We've missed you. So near, yet so far . . . Are you crying? Darling, what is it? What's happened?' Her mum put down the glass and held Eden's arms, kissing her hard on the cheek. 'Come here, let me get you some wine. I told Dad something must have happened for you to visit on a random Tuesday. I've made chicken orzo, it's a Nigella recipe. Come, sit. Tell me everything.'

Her dad walked to the other side of the large kitchen island and sat on a stool opposite, pouring two more glasses of red wine. He passed one across to Eden.

She sniffed. 'Ah, I'm sorry. My nervous system is a bit dysregulated, that's all. I've had a rough few weeks.' She looked at them both, her dad in his red trousers, her mum wearing a pair of glasses on a sparkly chain around her neck. She was always in the kitchen poring over cookbooks. She watched all the cookery shows, too, on a small TV her dad had installed on the wall, sometimes texting Eden about the dishes she'd seen: *Next time you come I'm making Lasagne of Love. I've seen a pistachio ice-cream recipe that does NOT require an ice-cream maker. Will try: tarragon chicken with crème fraîche, YUM.*

Eden breathed in her mum's cooking, her happy place. 'That smells amazing. I have work tomorrow but I can stay until the last train, if you don't mind dropping me back to the station, Dad?'

He put his wine glass down. 'I'd better have a Coke instead. Right. Tell us what's happening. You sure you can't stay? We've made your room up. Fresh towels and everything. Mum even cleaned the windows in there – you know what she's like.'

Eden laughed. 'I'm hardly a guest.'

'I told you we need new windows, and the Juliet balcony needs replacing. There's a serious condensation issue. Anyway, it's good to be houseproud. How is the new place, darling? Is it the flatmates? Are they nice people?'

Eden let her mum's questions tail off, then she told them about ED. She didn't talk about specific cases, of course – that would be in breach of the confidentiality clause in the Code of Professional Conduct – but she told them enough about the environment that both of them kept shaking their heads. She didn't want to worry them, but it was good to offload. Some things at least.

Eden didn't mention Nora once. And she didn't tell her parents what Sophie had called her.

'God, I knew it was bad, but that really is shocking,' her mum said. 'People waiting eighty hours for a bed? In corridors? The elderly? Sickening, isn't it? Those are the people who fought wars for us.'

Eden's dad shook his head. 'It's not right. You girls out there, angels in my view. They're lucky to have you, but are you sure about this? It's never too late to change your mind. There's a bloke at the golf club who's a foot surgeon. What's it called, love?'

'Orthopaedic.'

'That's it. Orthopaedic. He has a private clinic on Harley Street. Could put a word in, if you like? I'm sure he could find you something there. Weekends off, too. You could come home.'

Eden chugged her wine and looked around the kitchen. A million Sunday roasts. Dozens of parties when she was little, when she'd get to stay up late and watch all the adults get drunk and silly. The time she fell off her bike and her mum had to put her leg in the butler's sink to dig out all the gravel and clean it. The week her parents went to France when she was sixteen and she'd lied about staying at her friend's house and instead had a party that got shut down by the police as someone had posted it on Facebook and literally hundreds of random teens had turned up. The door frame where every year her dad had measured her and marked the date with a line and punched the air as if growing was a huge achievement in itself.

'I don't want to come home. I'm living independently now. It's just been a bad week, but I'm sure I'll get used to it. It's what I always wanted, and I know I'll do the most good at City.' Eden paused. 'I've saved lives already.'

Her mum began to well up and put her hands over her cheeks. 'We're so proud of you, Eden.'

But her dad shook his head again. 'Sounds like Gomorrah. Just come home if things stay that bad. Thank God we've got private insurance. What a shitshow the NHS has become. Nye Bevan will be turning in his grave.'

Fuck Sophie. She should report her. It was beyond offensive. Inappropriate, politically incorrect, unprofessional and cruel. Even to insinuate that Eden had somehow been capable of foul play was beyond belief. This was ED. People died! They died unexpectedly too. More and more people arrived in the Emergency Department when they should have been in a hospice, due to a missed or late diagnosis of something devastating. The palliative care team were increasingly coming to Resus, or Majors – or even the corridor – to have terrible conversations that should never have to happen in ED but often did, forcing the team to give tragic news to the soundtrack of screaming, swearing, alarming. Asking a family's wishes about organ donation. Telling a person on a trolley in a draughty corridor that they had weeks, or even hours, to live. Death shouldn't happen in ED, but it did, increasingly, all over the world. That is what they were there for: people who were imminently at risk of dying. Of course the death rate was high. It wasn't *her* fault.

Nobody cared more than she did about the patients. When Nora had died unexpectedly it felt as if the world had stopped spinning. Eden had acted as quickly as she could and had done everything to the best of her ability. Her chest compressions had been perfect. When the doctor who was leading the arrest had gone round the team suggesting they stop, Eden had insisted they carry on. *Just one more round.*

She'd pressed so hard on Nora's chest that she'd heard snapping. She'd wanted to *save* her. Eden was good at saving lives. There was a reason she attended so many cardiac arrests: Eden could bring people back from the dead better than anyone. She'd done her absolute best to save Nora, but sometimes, despite best efforts, patients died. Sophie was the dangerous one, not her. Sophie was likely a psychopath. She had zero empathy for the patients. Eden *loved* them.

Beryl was shivering in the corridor on a trolley when Eden met her at the start of her shift the next day. She reminded Eden of her great-grandmother, who she had stayed with when she was little and who had been kind, always offering her Garibaldi biscuits and Ovaltine. It was heartbreaking even looking at her. Beryl's eyes were wide open in fear, and her skin icy to Eden's touch. Yet another elderly female patient like Ivy, alone with no family and suffering terribly. 'My name is Eden. I'm your nurse today. Oh dear, you've been in the wars.'

Her arms were splattered with bruises and cuts. Beryl tried to smile, but her eyes were wet with tears. She couldn't speak for a few moments.

Eden gently took her wrist. 'I'm going to check you over and do some obs.' Beryl's pulse was thready and irregular. Atrial fibrillation, like a lot of old people. Eden lifted her hand and assessed her capillary refill time to see if she was dehydrated, though her sunken eyes and cracked lips gave that away. 'When did you last eat or drink, Beryl? Shall I make you a cup of tea? Rustle you up a sandwich?'

'Yes, please.' Her voice was so quiet.

Eden didn't have time to disappear off to the kitchen. But *this* was nursing. That poor woman was somebody's gran. She brought back a cup of sweet tea and the last remaining sandwich in the ED: egg. Always egg. Then she perched on the edge of Beryl's trolley and opened it for her.

Beryl wolfed down the sandwich like she'd not eaten in months, then slurped the tea. Eden sat quietly, waiting, so she could do an ECG, then take her blood pressure. It was so undignified, doing this in a corridor. There was no curtain for privacy, so instead of removing Beryl's blouse completely, she could only unbutton it and stick the ECG dots on blind. Beryl had come in after a fall, so head injury and concussion needed ruling out, but there were no signs of that. Beryl seemed frightened, but not confused.

'Any dizziness? Headache? Double vision?'

Beryl shook her head. 'I'm so clumsy.'

'Me too. I'm always tripping up and falling over. Right, Beryl, I need to take some blood from you, I'm afraid.'

Beryl smiled properly then. Her face was a thousand wrinkles, most of which were around her eyes, Eden noticed. Laughter lines. Her colour had changed to pink, and she was sitting more upright. 'That's all right, love.'

Eden couldn't find a vein. She jabbed her thin skin so many times, but Beryl didn't complain once. 'I'm sorry. There. Got it.'

Eventually she got enough blood for a troponin level and kidney and liver function and white cell count, and a CRP to see if there were any signs of infection anywhere. She smiled at Beryl, slid the blood bottles in to her scrub pocket, then went to get them sent off straight away.

A man on another trolley was at the other end of the corridor, and his wife was shouting as Eden walked past. 'We've been waiting here for seven hours! Seven hours! Nobody has even checked him. Please help us.'

She grabbed Eden's arm and pointed at the patient. He was a man in his sixties with a tracheostomy attached to a portable oxygen cylinder at the foot of his trolley, and his leg had been amputated. Eden recognised him immediately as the man smoking through his trachey, who'd coughed phlegm onto her face and had looked so embarrassed her heart had ached for him.

'He's got throat cancer, and we need to be on the head and neck cancer ward. Can you get somebody, please, nurse? Please.'

Eden could see the desperation in the wife's eyes.

'He's due to have radiotherapy next week.'

'I'll be back in a minute,' Eden said. She touched the blood samples in her pocket. 'Promise.' She glanced at the line of trolleys, the patients on them, and the angry relatives pacing up and down next to them. She needed to get to everyone else, and Beryl seemed medically fine. She'd have been dizzy, that was all – atrial fibrillation was common in the elderly and could have that effect, and luckily it seemed as if she'd avoided a head injury. She was most likely a bit dehydrated, that was all. This man needed urgent care. 'OK, let me check him over and I'll ask the docs to review.'

His wife's face flushed with relief, but as Eden stepped away to get the blood-pressure machine, he started coughing, choking almost.

'Keith, what is it? Keith?'

And just like that, his tracheostomy flew out.

Keith was immediately blue around his lips and mouth. He was making noises that Eden had never heard before: a rasping that sounded somewhere between a woman giving birth and a rattlesnake. He was trying to suck in air, while the hole in his neck got smaller and smaller. Eden grabbed the tracheostomy tube – there was no time for gloves. She leant forwards to try to put it back in, but he seemed to simply burst open, and turn red. 'A hand here!' Eden shouted.

Keith's wife screamed and then fainted, nearly knocking Eden over.

Blood was pouring from Keith's neck with such pressure it hit the ceiling. Eden pressed it as hard as she could with her hand and shouted again, 'Help!'

Sophie appeared in seconds. 'Having fun?'

Eden was covered in bright-red arterial blood, and Keith was grey, struggling to get any air at all. His wife was lying passed out, twisted around the trolley.

Sophie kicked Keith's wife out of the way and pushed Eden onto the trolley. 'Sit on him and press as hard as you can on his neck.' Then she started pushing the trolley with Eden on top of Keith. 'Carotid blow-out to Resus. Make room at the inn: we've got a bleeder.'

Occupational Health was a strange place, a bit like HR: essential, behind the scenes and manned almost entirely by competent, proficient people who for some reason did not find mundane work boring. Eden had the average amount of contact that most nurses did, almost always about immunisations and hepatitis B booster injections. She had never suffered a needle-stick injury or had a colossal mental health breakdown or addiction issues, all of which they also dealt with. There was a sign on the door on the way in: 'Sharps Splashes, Bites, Needlestick Injuries, Take a Ticket from the Machine'.

Eden sat on a plastic chair next to a few other people, all clutching their tickets as though they were at the supermarket deli counter. A screen in front of them flashed up with numbers and the room they needed to go to. Eden had washed the blood from her face and hair, but she could still smell it and wondered if the person sitting next to her would too. Eventually her number was called. She went into room five and described what had happened.

'Right then,' said the nurse, Avril, who was tapping away at her computer. 'You had an eye wash-out in ED? We'll follow up with the patient to see if there's any obvious risk of blood-borne diseases, and whether you might need prophylactic treatment to prevent any.' Avril was smiling. 'You seem OK in yourself, especially after eye irrigation. However, this is the kind of thing that stays with you, so let us know if you start having flashbacks.'

'I'm actually OK,' she said. 'I called theatres and checked, and the patient survived, which apparently is nearly unheard of with a carotid blow-out. He's on ICU now, so I might pop by and see him tomorrow.'

'That's amazing,' said Avril. 'Above and beyond. Still, your job is not easy.'

A look of total understanding passed between them. Eden liked being seen like that. It felt like a club she belonged to.

'You're not a proper ED nurse until you've had an eye wash-out,' said Aoife. 'Honestly, don't worry, these things happen. You'll be fine now, though I'm sure it wasn't very nice.' They were in the relatives' room, which was the only empty place to talk. It was functional, a small cheap table with a single box of NHS tissues in the centre. The rectangular sofa upon which they sat was facing the window, which had bars on it, and a poster on the wall about talking therapy.

'It's a calling,' Aoife said. 'No matter what anybody tells you.'

There was a knock on the door and Michael opened it, Rohan standing beside him. 'Ah, sorry,' he said.

'It's OK, need us to vacate?' Aoife looked straight at him, but he glanced away and simply shut the door.

'I need to get back and clean up,' said Eden. She reached across and hugged Aoife, but pulled back, remembering that Aoife had told her not to.

Aoife stared at the closed door for a few moments, then shook her head and focused. 'You're so conscientious, Eden. Listen, I need to tell you something. In all the drama of Keith, the patient who bled into your eyes,' Aoife pretended to retch, 'there was a death in the corridors. I know it's been a busy day, but it looks like Beryl, the elderly lady who came in, must have been septic after all. Haematology is denying that the admission bloods ever arrived, but Sophie has sworn blind she saw you take them. Anyway, nothing to worry about, I'm sure they'll turn up. You did the obs on her? I found an ECG floating around.'

Eden clenched her jaw. Beryl. The sweet old lady, the nicest patient she'd had in forever. 'I did bloods. Is anyone with her? I mean, has she gone to the mortuary yet?'

'She needs laying out. But I can do that as soon as I've finished drug round in Majors.'

Eden shook her head. 'I'll do it. Where is she?'

*

Beryl looked even smaller in death than she had in life; her face had sunken down. There was no window to open in cubicle one. Eden checked Beryl's name band was correct and attached to her and put another on her ankle. She softly wiped her face with a paper towel. There was a wedding ring around her neck on a thin gold chain. Her collarbone jutted out. 'How long have you been like this?' Eden whispered. 'How many women your age are alone in this world?'

She leant over Beryl's chest and rested her head on it for a moment. Then she closed her eyes and imagined this poor woman's life. There had been no family members with her. Nobody. She clearly hadn't eaten or drunk or had any kind of warmth for some time. Sepsis may be the cause of death on her certificate, but Eden knew she'd died of loneliness. She knew it. She lifted her head and kissed Beryl's lifeless cheek, then took her phone out of her pocket and glanced around before taking a quick photo of Beryl's peaceful face. Then she covered her with a sheet.

For a few moments she stood above the body, head bowed. Then Eden walked out of the cubicle to get a porter, touching her scrub pocket, which still contained Beryl's blood bottles.

FOURTEEN

Aoife

Aoife had been attending local weekly M&M meetings for years, but she'd never been summoned to a hospital-wide one. The Trust Mortality Monitoring Committee meeting was a far more formal affair, held in the hospital boardroom, a grand table in the centre, the walls lined with oil paintings of stern-looking women and men who'd run the hospital over the years.

'Death rate in 2025 ED, same period.' Her colleague, Bill Curtis, a dour-faced haematologist, stood in front of the screen and pointed at the large wave, like a Covid spike. 'And now.'

A few people tutted and two of the managers put their heads in their hands. Denise's face was puce. '*Health Service Journal* last year reported 30,000 excess deaths due to A&E waiting times. So let's revisit that?'

Aoife hadn't expected the slide show. There was muttering around the room. Nobody wanted to see the wait-times slide; they were in constant breach of their four-hour targets and everyone knew it, with staff leaving by the day and an ever-increasing demand for services. The sick were getting sicker, and that included the nurses.

'We are not at the level where external reporting is critical,' Bill continued, 'but there was a coroner's case last week, so let's wait for the outcome of that before we involve the police.'

'Police involvement?' Denise's head jerked up and she glanced at Aoife. 'Suggests intentional wrongdoing, and surely that's not what we are saying here?' Aoife had wanted to plant the seed of Sophie's incompetence and get well rid of her, but it hadn't crossed her mind that any of her nurses might be deliberately hurting patients.

'Let's go through the recent cases of concern.' Bill looked at Aoife too.

'Fine.' Denise tapped on her laptop. 'Beryl Cartwright. Ninety-one. She came in via ambulance, was nursed in the corridor and subsequently died of sepsis. One set of observations recorded in a twelve-hour window, and her BP was 85/40, temperature 34.6. There were no bloods sent for a CRP, and she was not reviewed by the doctors or given antibiotics.' Denise had her game face on. Aoife was sitting next to her at the large boardroom table and looked around at her colleagues. They were professionals at the top of their career, yet Aoife had worked with a few of them long enough to know their secrets.

Bill Curtis had once been arrested for stalking his ex-wife. Fabio Notts was the lead pathologist, a friendly man with a booming voice, who everyone knew had a foot fetish. Mabel Cunningham, the chief nurse, was a gambler. Then there was Denise. Aoife could recall more than the odd night out with Denise that had resulted in liver pain. Denise didn't drink every day, but once she had even one white wine, an entire bottle of gin would surely follow. Aoife had stopped answering late-night calls from Denise, which were inevitably nonsensical.

Everyone had their demons, but NHS staff surely had more than most. The higher up the food chain, in Aoife's view, the more extreme the coping mechanisms.

'I can certainly tell you about staffing that day in ED. We were way off safe staffing levels, which was raised at the time with the lead consultant, and site nurse practitioners. We had to open a cupboard space and literally put patients in the equipment cupboard that week, such was demand. A Datix was recorded, and I've emailed you all copies that you should be able to access. I think this was more systemic than individual failure.' Aoife paused. She had to work hard to keep her voice level.

'For context, we had a patient with head and neck cancer who had a carotid blow-out in the same clinical area and he survived. And while we're on the subject, I'd like to see all my staff involved offered ongoing counselling, or a debrief at least.'

Denise smiled; she, too, was a nurse's nurse. But then a flicker of doubt crossed her face. 'Can I ask the name of the nurse who was allocated the patient in question? Was it Sophie Ibrahim?'

Aoife hesitated. She could throw Sophie under the bus in that single moment. Her colleagues trusted her and took whatever she said at face value. But it might come back to haunt her. After all, it would be easy to access the off duty, and Bill was pedantic. 'Actually, it was Eden Walsh, who's one of my newly qualifieds; she was acting as corridor nurse.'

'Do we know why bloods weren't sent? Would you say there was adequate support for Eden? Did you speak to her after the event?' Bill leant back in his chair and looked at the lawyers. 'Perhaps more importantly, is there likely to be any complaint from a family member?'

Aoife thought back to the day that Beryl had died, and another man had survived. She remembered Eden in the office after an eye wash-out, her clutching Aoife close after they'd chatted, despite Aoife having told her not to. She remembered feeling the shape of the blood bottles still in Eden's scrub pocket, their slight rattle. 'The bloods were sent so I would suggest a problem in the labs.' She paused. 'I don't believe there was any family, so I doubt anyone will complain.'

Aoife watched the lawyers' faces relax a fraction. That was all they really cared about.

It was lunchtime when Aoife knocked on Michael's office door. She'd not spoken to him properly in days. Since he'd told her he was seeing Sophie, it was all Aoife could do to function. She couldn't stop thinking about Michael, their shared history, their mutual desire. Everything had been perfect until Sophie had arrived on the scene, but now the future of their relationship was uncertain. Aoife was not used to feeling out of control.

She still had no idea what she wanted to say to him, but she banged on Michael's office door again anyway. He opened it and shushed her, beckoned her in, locking it behind them. 'I'm presenting Grand Round. Want to listen in?'

'Online? Great.' She nodded a bit too enthusiastically. Pre-pandemic, this bombastic showing-off event for senior clinicians had happened in the large lecture theatre above the post room, the sound of Kiss FM occasionally wafting through the floorboards while the doctor or surgeon presented what they considered to be a fascinating topic. Of course, all senior medics thought their own speciality was endlessly interesting, and there was serious competition between department heads. The nephrologists were the worst, and the weirdest. Aoife knew of one consultant nephrologist who apparently ate steak and kidney pie every single evening, a fact she found more than disturbing.

Michael's eyes momentarily slid over her body. He pulled her over to his desk.

She squeezed his hand. Since that night in the pub she'd been watching his interactions with Sophie but couldn't see any love between them. They looked like any other colleagues, friendly but professional. Still, Aoife had spent several sleepless nights worrying. She'd woken, heart pounding, at 3 a.m., at first hearing Bill Curtis's voice in her dream, but then her mind flipped to Michael telling her about Sophie, and saying they'd never been monogamous in the first place. *I get to be with who I want. Like you do.* Still, she had a plan.

Aoife pulled a plastic chair close to Michael but out of sight, as he turned on his camera and microphone and began. 'My name is Michael Connors. I'm the clinical lead at ED and sit on the ethics committee and governance board. Welcome to the Wednesday Grand Round – it's lovely to see so many faces. The title of this presentation is "Anti-microbial Resistant Gonorrhoea – a Rising Threat", which is far sexier than it sounds, I can assure you. Well, until it isn't . . .'

Aoife smiled. Michael was a good speaker. She heard muffled laughter from people who'd forgotten to turn off their microphones and peeked at Michael's screen. Eighty participants. A good turnout, and no surprise; everyone loved listening to Michael. He had that rare quality of being able to deliver a fun and lively talk while imparting difficult data, meaning people learnt by osmosis, almost without realising they were absorbing the latest research.

She looked around his small office, once a broom cupboard. There were piles of papers and books everywhere, a pair of running trainers covered in mud on a piece of newspaper, a few drawings his nieces and nephews had done sellotaped to the wall. There was a small shelf filled with coffee cups, and a desk upon which were his computer, a photograph of a Greek island, a packet of cigarettes and a well-thumbed copy of *Crime and Punishment*. There was a drawer underneath the desk, no doubt containing a bottle of Grey Goose vodka.

'In 2023, there were over 85,000 new diagnoses of gonorrhoea in England alone, a figure which is the highest since records began in 1918. And while the number of antibiotic-resistant cases are tiny, for now, they should be of significant concern to all of us, for many reasons that I'll outline here.' Michael tapped on the keys, getting various slides up on the screen.

It felt good to be in a room alone with him at last, with him seemingly at ease with her, his usual smiley self. Perhaps he and Sophie had fizzled out already? It would no doubt be a flash in the pan and then, surely, they could slot back into how they'd always been? Aoife moved closer and put her hand on his knee. He let her, or at least he didn't shake her off. Aoife felt her skin prickle with relief.

'Ceftriaxone is the first line used to treat gonorrhoea, and resistance to this makes it extremely difficult to treat, especially gonorrhoea infections in the throat.'

His words bounced around the small room. Michael's voice could make anything sound soft and pure.

She had an idea. At first, she dismissed it, but with each second alone in the office, the *locked office*, it became more plausible. Excitement was the glue that had always held Michael and Aoife together; that's why they loved the job and why they loved each other. They'd had more danger and excitement than Sophie could ever imagine. Aoife had to mark her territory and remind Michael of what they had.

She checked the blinds to make sure they were fully closed, then dropped to her knees and crawled underneath the desk. She'd do *anything* for him, and he had to know that.

Michael froze. She wondered, as she undid his belt, then his fly, and took out his penis, whether he would push her away. He started to, his hands firm against her shoulders, but then he gently loosened his grip. He was hard the instant she put him in her mouth, sucking, licking, steadily, silently.

He stopped speaking a moment and moved his hands. For a few seconds he held her face, his hands covering her ears, and looked down at her. She paused, wondering if that was a signal to stop, but he moved her head up and down, up and down, faster and faster. Somehow, he managed to focus on the screen and talk at the same time, though his voice was a little high.

'Case one, a twenty-year-old woman presented at ED with pelvic pain . . . Oof. Sorry, is anyone else having technical issues?'

FIFTEEN
Sophie

Sophie woke late. A rare and much-needed day off. She planned to take herself to a gallery and a restaurant and listen to podcasts and classical music. She didn't want to talk to a single soul. The flatmates were all at work, and she drank her coffee in total peace, before showering and dressing, despite the hot day, in her cosiest tracksuit and warm socks that Gee had bought her one Christmas. She knocked on Eden's door to double-check she was long gone before sneaking into her bedroom.

Something made Sophie want to know more about Eden. A gut feeling that had escalated not only after Nora had died, but after Eden had reacted so violently to Sophie calling her names. Her room was as orderly as Sophie had imagined, down to tiny printed labels on the drawers, as if she had dementia: socks, gloves, T-shirts, gym kit. The bed had hospital corners. There were a number of stuffed animals and cheap scented candles, no less than three different editions of *A Little Life* on the bedside table. 'Sick puppy,' whispered Sophie.

She rummaged around in the drawers, not sure what she was looking for. A diary, perhaps? There was nothing on her desk except a 'To Do' list with boring odd jobs – 'buy nail varnish remover, portable iPhone charger, Mum b'day' – and a small handmade wooden pot full of pens in various colours. It deeply annoyed Sophie that Eden wrote everything in gold pen. She was about to leave and put Eden's oddness down to a personality clash and Eden's obvious deviancy, but impulsively she crouched down to check under the bed. Pushed into the middle was a shoebox with stickers on the cover. A childhood memory box?

Sophie sat on the bed and opened it. The box was full of nonsensical things, mostly sentimental stuff. A hospital bracelet, a photograph of a premature baby, a pressed flower, a journal, a small bottle of perfume, nearly empty. But then, there were blood bottles, still half full, and underneath them was a scarf, an expensive kind, green silk with a distinctive pattern of bluebirds all over it. There was something else on the scarf too. A splodge of rusty blood.

'Fuck,' she said, out loud.

She opened the journal, which was sure enough covered in gold pen, and flicked through it. Most of it was nonsense – shopping lists, affirmations and shit poetry – but there was the occasional page of writing. Sophie's eyes lingered on the latest entry.

Our patients deserve the best care in the world and my heart breaks for them. Will I ever be a nurse as good as Aoife? I try my best and keep making mistakes, but when I got John back from a cardiac arrest, I knew. There's no greater feeling in the world than bringing someone back TO LIFE! I need to practise and practise and help people in ALL the ways they need it. What greater privilege than holding a hand of a patient at the end of their life. TO BE A NURSE!

She rolled her eyes. Even in text, Eden was annoying, but then she flicked the page:

I wish Sophie Ibrahim would fucking die. I wouldn't do chest compressions on her, not a SINGLE ONE.

Sophie couldn't help but smile.

The next day, at work, Sophie pushed Eden out of her mind. She leant over the patient, pulled the rebreather oxygen mask down from her face and sniffed. She moved the oxygen further away and sniffed again as the girl, Andrea, who was only seventeen and in Sophie's view better off in Paeds, exhaled. 'Pear drops,' she said. 'I can smell pears.' She replaced the oxygen mask and spun around to face the girl's parents, who were hovering next to the bed. 'I think this is diabetes, something called diabetic ketoacidosis. I'll fast-bleep the A&E consultant to come and see Andrea, but while we're waiting, she needs some fluid, and after that she'll need insulin. Everything needs to be corrected slowly so that we don't cause any complications.' Sophie didn't describe the complications she'd seen many times: overzealous colleagues giving fluid and insulin too quickly, causing a child presenting for the first time with type 1 diabetes to have permanent and catastrophic brain damage. Communication in ED was on a need-to-know basis.

Her parents – mum wearing pearls, dad wearing a cravat – looked shell-shocked. 'She's not diabetic,' her mum said. 'What do you mean about pears?'

'Ah, it's a classic giveaway. Pear-drop breath and the way that Andrea is presenting points to diabetes . . .'

'Is it genetic?' Her dad walked closer to Andrea's bed and grabbed her hand. 'We're here for you, darling. Mummy and Daddy are here. The doctors will be here soon and they'll get you fixed up.'

Sophie walked out of the cubicle and grabbed Eden by the arm. 'Can you fast-bleep Michael? She's DKA. I'll get some saline drawn up and given pronto.'

'I didn't know you'd done your nurse prescribing training already.' Eden glanced past Sophie at the patient. 'How old is she?'

'Seventeen and I haven't, but it's fine, I'll get it prescribed later.'

Eden's eyes flashed back at Sophie. 'You can't prescribe fluid or drugs unless you're a trained nurse prescriber. It's part eighteen of the Code of Professional Conduct.'

Sophie laughed out loud. 'I haven't got time for this.' She walked quickly off to the nurses'-station phones, where Rhian was writing something on the board. 'Hey, can you fast-bleep Michael? We've a DKA – Andrea, cubicle two.'

'Sure thing. Need anything else?'

Sophie smiled. 'Arterial blood gas, blood sugar, potassium; another line would be great and start some saline. No insulin yet until we know what's what – slow and steady, etcetera.'

'Gotcha. We've had loads of diabetic nasties recently. Ton of kids taking weight-loss jabs and actively avoiding their insulin to get ketotic intentionally.'

'Depressing.' Sophie flicked her head back towards Eden. 'It's a risky business and I don't want this kid to end up with cerebral oedema, so keep the Grimster away from this patient?'

Rhian followed her eyes, then laughed. 'Ah, she's not that bad, but all right. I'll send her on a transfer.'

Michael was nowhere to be found, but Andrea had stabilised and was now receiving an insulin infusion, yet to be prescribed but saving her life, nonetheless. Sophie whizzed around the unit, eyeballing everyone and everything. A rare good day at the office. Thanks to Rhian, Eden was out of the way on a transfer of a patient with serious burns to King Charles Burn Unit, a good hour away, and the ED was manageable.

'Hi, hi, hello . . .' A man Sophie recognised was standing at the entrance to the coffee room holding a large bunch of yellow roses.

She walked over, squinted, then realised where she recognised him from: the photo on Aoife's desk. 'You're Aoife's husband. Sam, is it?'

He nodded. He was tall, handsome, clean cut. 'Wanted to surprise her, and she texted earlier that she might actually get out on time for once.'

Sophie laughed. 'Don't you dare say the Q word and tempt fate.'

'Ah, don't worry, I've been married to a nurse long enough to know the rules, even though Aoife calls me a Muggle.' He held up the flowers. 'Her favourite.'

A patient hovered nearby, holding a letter and wheeling an oxygen cylinder. 'I need to go,' Sophie said, 'but you can wait in the coffee room no problem.'

It was at least an hour later when Sophie walked off shift, taking the shortcut out of the hospital in the basement, and almost bumping directly into Aoife, who was running in her direction. 'Crash call?' she asked.

Aoife was red-faced and out of breath. She ignored the question. 'Everything OK? Sorry, I got held up in Michael's office and lost track of time – hadn't realised shift was over already.'

Sophie shrugged. 'It's fine, all under control. Sam's waiting for you in the coffee room, though; he's been there a while. Think he's planning to whisk you off somewhere.'

Aoife stopped and seemed to be holding her breath. Her usually neat hair bun was coming loose. She exhaled in a burst of air. 'Right, that's nice, I'll get back to him then. Thanks, Sophie.'

She walked quickly away, her clogs thumping on the shiny floor.

SIXTEEN
Eden

It had been a long day. One of the patients had performed a dirty protest, smearing faeces all over the wall. They'd used industrial bleach to clean it, but it was all Eden could smell, even after showering and scrubbing herself with shower gel and sticking some Vicks under her nostrils, before putting on her dressing gown and flopping onto her bed. She needed to forget. On days like this, Eden used to like watching sad films until she sobbed, until her body was empty of tears and she felt lighter. But now she had something better.

She pulled out the shoebox from where it was hidden underneath her bed and opened it on top of her duvet.

Eden took out the objects she'd collected, one by one. A green scarf. A discharge planning letter, a photograph of baby Jocelyn. A printout of arterial blood results. She touched each item softly, remembering the person it had once belonged to. Her heartbeat quickened and she blinked, wiping her wet eyes before licking her fingertips, tasting salt. She picked up the scarf and let it float down in front of her, before pressing it to her chest. 'Nora,' she whispered. 'I'm sorry I couldn't save you. Rest in peace.'

Three blood bottles marked 'Beryl' were at the bottom of the box, labelled in gold pen. The blood was congealed to jelly, the colour of Ribena. Eden opened one of the tubes and breathed it in, this life-after-death smell.

After placing the items back in the box and then pushing it underneath her bed, Eden scrolled through her phone until she found the photograph of Beryl. *I'll do better. I promise you. I'll be a better nurse.*

They all sat around the living room drinking from the bottle of absinthe that Ben's parents had brought home from Paris. 'Is this actually legal?'

Ben laughed. 'Come on, Eden, they drink it like water in Europe.'

The absinthe was warming, burned a little; still, they drank it neat with no ice. There was a giant packet of Popchips on the table, but nobody ate them. Instead, they snorted lines of cocaine off a book. At first Eden didn't recognise it, but when Ben gestured to the book and nodded at Eden, she looked down and saw immediately what it was.

Florence Nightingale: *Notes on Nursing: What It Is, and What It Is Not.*

'I borrowed it the other day,' said Sophie. 'From your room.'

Eden's face flushed. 'That's not funny,' she said, but she looked around at all her flatmates and closed her mouth before any other words came out. As far as she knew, Sophie had never mentioned what she'd seen a few weeks before when she'd burst into Eden's room unannounced.

Sophie's eyes glowed. 'Useful book.'

Eden scowled at her.

'Do you think this is wise?' Rhian had white powder puffing out of her nostril. She'd told them she could not snort effectively since having her adenoids out when she was twelve. Nobody commented; a bit like Sophie, Rhian did not tend to discuss her adolescence, but in her case, it was teenagers she most loved caring for.

'We have the new doctors starting tomorrow, which means – no shade to doctors or anything' – she glanced at Ben – 'but Everyone Will Die!' She jumped up onto the couch and started bouncing. 'Everyone's going to die, everyone's going to die.' The others all copied her, except for Eden, who poured herself another drink. She downed it. Already, her chest felt warm.

Sophie stared at Eden as she snorted a line, winked at her, smacked her hard on the back. 'Come on, old fella, we're here for a good time, not a long time.' She was clearly enjoying this. She passed the drugs and the book to Eden.

Eden stared at Sophie. There was a new energy between them. She was clearly relishing teasing her about the book, and having seen Eden in an embarrassing situation, but she had no idea that Eden kept a secret too. Many secrets. Eden's mind whooshed with the absinthe. She never took drugs, but then, she never drank absinthe either. She half smiled at Sophie, then bent her head as if praying, and snorted.

They silly-danced around the living room, each kicking their legs from side to side, and Eden felt suddenly part of it. Eventually, when they flopped on the sofa, they all lay half on top of each other.

'Let's have an orgy.' Ben sat up, suddenly serious.

'Fuck off, Ben,' said Obi. 'I know, let's play Truth or Dare?'

Sophie and Eden exchanged another look. 'How about Eden goes first?' said Sophie.

The room was blurred. Eden's face was numb. 'I can't feel my face,' she whispered. 'It's like my heart is busting out of my chest.'

Sophie stroked her cheek gently. 'Sweet Eden. Right, you choose.'

There was a sudden intimacy between them. It felt like they'd stepped into a film, or each other's skin. Eden didn't care about what Sophie had called her, or when she'd laughed at her with Michael or mocked her privately. Something shifted. 'Dare.' Eden didn't care what she was dared to do. She looked around at her flatmates. Maybe they were whispering about her bad luck at work, but they seemed, in that moment, to accept her completely, even Sophie. She was one of them.

'I dare you to let Ben draw on you with a Sharpie, and you cannot under any circumstances wash it off until morning.'

Ben laughed. 'Excellent plan.'

Eden nodded. 'Sure.'

'Really?' said Rhian, giggling. 'Not anywhere visible. Edes, it won't wash off if it's a Sharpie.'

Eden laughed too. Her laugh sounded far away, and it echoed. She was spreading happiness around the room.

'She loves it,' said Obi. 'Our Eden is hardcore. It's not a real tattoo. Look at this.' Obi stood up and flashed a tattoo on his left butt cheek of an arrow pointing to the crack. 'Magaluf, aged eighteen.'

Eden laughed harder. 'I literally cannot imagine you in Magaluf.'

Obi grimaced. 'It was another time.'

Ben disappeared and returned with a black marker. 'Rule is, whatever I want, wherever I want.'

Eden looked around the shiny faces of her flatmates. Her *friends*. 'I'm not taking my underwear off,' she said. The room was spinning a bit, the colour fading. There was loud EDM music playing but Eden couldn't tell if it was inside or outside her own body.

'Ew. Not necessary. Right, lie flat.'

Eden lay down on the couch, all of them crowding around her. Ben climbed on top of her, legs either side, and moved closer to her face. He uncapped the pen and began to write on her forehead. Eden closed her eyes. The couch was comfortable and even the feeling of the pen on her head was soothing. 'This won't hurt a bit,' he said.

The alarm went off in each room simultaneously, loud enough that Eden woke even though she was still on the couch in the living room. It was dark outside; they somehow hadn't closed the curtains. Rhian was first in, switching the main light on, followed by Sophie. Both were bleary-eyed. Eden put a pillow over her head. 'I'm dying,' she said. 'How, how do you guys party like that all the time?' She took a deep breath and began to cough; the air was thick with sweat and smoke and stale beer and there was a faint smell of vomit. Had someone been sick in the night? Had she? Her head pounded. 'Water. I need water.' She slowly removed the pillow and sat up inch by inch. 'Oh my God. I took cocaine? How? I never, ever take drugs. And this is why. How?' Eden stopped talking as she noticed Rhian staring at her face. She pressed her hands to her cheeks; her fingertips were ice cold.

Rhian finally shrieked. 'Fucking hell!'

'Here.' Sophie sat on the chair next to the sofa. 'Paracetamol, water and my phone to check yourself. You should probably take the paracetamol first.'

Eden frowned. Even frowning hurt. But then a fragment of memory. Ben, on top of her with a pen. She took the tablets and water from Sophie and then picked up the phone.

'Oh, mate.' Obi was there in his pants. 'Ben!'

Eden checked her reflection. The word 'CUNT' was written on her forehead.

Sophie pursed her lips but then shrugged. 'If we can't scrub it off, we can always cut you a fringe.'

Eden glared at Sophie, her feelings of anger rushing back. 'I'm going to report you.'

Sophie laughed. 'Hey, I didn't do it! Let me know if you want a fringe. I have a pair of scissors in a *shoebox* in my room.'

Eden lunged at Sophie. It took Ben, Rhian and Obi to hold her down and pull her back onto the couch. Sophie just stood and stared. Eden wanted to rip her head off. Obi had his hands locked around her arms and Ben and Rhian were gently pressing her shoulders so she couldn't move an inch, but they couldn't stop her screaming. 'You're the cunt, Sophie Ibrahim. You are the fucking cunt.' Then Eden took a deep, guttural breath and screamed. It was the biggest sound she'd ever made.

SEVENTEEN

Sophie

It should have been funny, but after listening to Eden for almost twenty minutes, as she scoured the skin of her forehead with a wire brush used for cleaning pans, the joke lost its shine. They had all followed her into the bathroom and stood in the mildewy smell. It was full of condensation, and underwear. Rhian always pegged her tights to the top of the shower curtain, and Ben dropped his pants wherever. There was a wet towel on the floor next to the toilet that nobody had ever claimed, so it was left on principle, making the room smell even more like wet dog. Eventually Sophie and Ben left for work. 'Maybe that was a slight overcook,' said Ben, as they walked away from Rose Cottage.

Eden was off the next day, and didn't answer when Sophie texted her from work: *You OK?* But by the time Sophie got home a little after 9 p.m., Eden was calm and wearing pyjamas, drinking hot chocolate. 'Is it safe to approach?'

'Sophie, I'm sorry. I have never in my life lost my temper like that.'

Sophie dumped her bag on the floor, clicked the kettle on, then walked over to sit next to Eden.

'It looks fine now,' Sophie said. The word was now gone and in its place was an angry graze, with tiny baubles of blood budding out from the now-exposed and shiny upper dermal layer. 'You'll need to put a plaster over that, assuming you're coming in tomorrow?'

'What was I thinking? This is why I don't do shots. This is why I never touch drugs.'

'You're OK. It was pretty brave of you to let Ben write on your head with a Sharpie, to be fair. But you became a bit fierce, literally shaking with rage. Like *Cocaine Bear*.'

Eden laughed, then put her hand to the side of her head. 'Don't make me laugh. Thank God it's gone. It's Ben I should have lost it with.' She stared at Sophie and her mouth twitched as if to say something, but no more words came out.

They left early the following morning. They both grabbed their rucksacks, put on their shoes and walked together to the hospital. Eden was hungover. 'Two days and I still feel terrible.' She groaned. 'I honestly don't know how you all went to work yesterday.'

It was hot already, and only 7.30 a.m.; 7 August, which meant the new doctors' first week. Everyone was moaning about it, especially the doctors, and it kept Michael busier than ever. She'd been enjoying their inventive lovemaking, and he seemed to accept their situation. He clearly had no time for a relationship, even if she'd agreed to one. 'Wonder what they'll be like, the new lot.'

'Hopefully not as bad as Ben.'

'Well, now that's impossible.'

'I feel really sick. Do you have any mints?'

Sophie took some chewing gum from her rucksack pocket and handed the pack to Eden, who took two. 'Do you want to talk about it? The rage?'

'Honestly, I can't remember much about it. My last memory was agreeing to Ben tattooing me, then blackout central. I've killed off more than a few brain cells, for sure. Then yesterday morning screaming at you like a banshee. Sorry again.'

They walked down the long street, and through 'Rape Alley', where there was a large pile of human shit next to a broken bottle. They side-stepped all the London rubbish, tiptoeing down the shortcut alley until they reached the wider road and the traffic lights across to City.

Sophie listened as Eden rambled on. She was more animated than Sophie had ever seen her. It had been the first big night where she'd joined in their antics, and until she realised Ben had written 'CUNT' on her forehead, Eden had clearly felt part of the group. She seemed happier. Sophie had started wondering if she'd underestimated Eden. Still waters ran deep, and maybe Eden was more interesting than she'd perceived. 'Do you want to talk about that shoebox?'

Eden stopped walking. 'What shoebox?'

'Oh, come on. The blood bottles, the scarf. I mean, are you actually OK? Because serial-killer nurse is a little cliché.'

Eden looked ahead and began chewing gum aggressively. 'That's not funny. Look, I'm sorry I lashed out and, trust me, I won't be touching drugs ever again. As for the box, why were you in my room in the first place?'

'I was snooping.'

Eden paused, then glared. 'Well, you should keep out of my business.' She folded her arms in front of her. 'Anyway, it's nothing. You know how things end up in your pocket at the end of a shift. You come home with all manner of crap. I've seen plenty of confidential results and pieces of paper with patient details chucked in the kitchen bin. That day, with the carotid blow-out, everything was out of control. You know I've been having nightmares – or flashbacks, I don't know, but that man's blood was all over the walls, the ceiling. And then the poor woman, Beryl, who died. I'd checked her and I even sat with her a while, held her hand. She was like my granny! I got her an egg sandwich and, honestly, she wolfed it down. I'd completely forgotten about her blood bottles – I was literally on my way to send them off, but Keith needed help. That's all.'

Eden side-eyed Sophie, clearly checking her reaction.

They crossed the road in silence and turned right to the hospital, in between Lime bikes and ambulances, past a bus that had broken down with angry passengers climbing off. Eden stopped walking. 'You won't tell anyone, will you? I'm just in my weird girl era, that's all.'

Sophie belly-laughed. 'You don't strike me as dangerous. But keeping souvenirs from work in a box is a little fucking creepy, babes, no?'

Eden stopped chewing. She resumed her less friendly, more Head Girl know-it-all face. 'Don't forget that I have eyes and ears too. Are you still sleeping with *Michael*?'

Sophie snorted loudly. 'What of it?'

Eden was quiet a few moments as they snaked their way into the hospital through the ambulance entrance. '*That's* creepy, in my book.'

Sophie shrugged. 'It's not serious. He's weirdly kinky. I pissed on him last week, in the bath, and he came spontaneously.'

Eden winced. 'Not our bath at Rose Cottage?'

'Look, we're all a bit fucked up. It's this place. All that darkness, it needs to go somewhere.' She opened the changing-room door, where she and Eden had first met months earlier. It felt like a lifetime. They walked in and stood in front of the sinks and the cracked mirror, the noticeboard next to it.

They both looked into the mirror. 'You need to find an outlet, that's all. Take up ketamine or something – cocaine clearly isn't your drug. That box of treasures is not a healthy hobby, Eden, and I'd hate to have to report you.'

Eden stared at Sophie's foggy, distorted reflection. They both looked far away. 'Are you going to tell Aoife? Because I don't think it's appropriate that you're sleeping with Michael, or doing whatever it is you're doing with him, which is seriously gross by the way. I could literally report you too.' She was breathing quickly.

Sophie turned to face Eden and leant in close, smelling the gum. She touched Eden's forehead gently. 'Don't be a cunt, Edes.' Then she smiled.

Michael reminded Sophie of the drill sergeant in *An Officer and a Gentleman*. He stood in front of the new Foundation Year doctors, who had formed a semi-circle around him, and hollered as though they were in another room entirely. He was showing off, which made Sophie smile – as much as he moaned about FY1 and FY2 doctors, he was a good mentor to them. 'Right, you lot. Listen up.'

The new starters huddled closer. They were dressed smartly, yet to change into scrubs, and Sophie could tell from their clothes which side of the tracks they were from; there was a clear divide between head-to-toe Reiss and head-to-toe Next. One of the blonde, freshly blow-dried women was wearing Louboutins, Sophie noticed, and staring at Michael as if he was the second coming of Christ. Within a week they'd be as scruffy as the rest of them. Sophie hovered by the nurses' station and listened. It turned her on a bit, hearing Michael barking orders.

'Key things you need to know. The hours are longer than your contract tells you. You'll be here weekends and nights and Christmas and New Year. Do not ask for annual leave for a funeral or a wedding – you'll not get it. This place owns you for the next six months. I own you. The coffee is disgusting. The patients are difficult. But there is no finer training camp anywhere in medicine than City ED. You'll learn things here that you'll take throughout your entire career, and the staff are the best people you will ever work with.

'Some of you will not make it. ED is not for everyone. But those who get through this placement without asking for a transfer to Neurology Outpatients or somewhere else you can slowly die of boredom, you'll be rewarded with knowledge, wisdom and the psychological strength of the Dalai Lama. Tips: carry gloves in your pocket, always. Have eyes in the back of your head. Do not use the patient toilets, unless you are actively trying to contract pubic lice. Oh, and be nice to the nurses. Your life will depend on that.'

Sophie smiled. She had no idea how Michael got away with being so un-PC, but it excited her, his personal breed of anarchy. She watched them all disperse, except the blonde in heels, who giggled at something Michael said and then clicked off to the changing room. Sophie leant across to Ben, who was looking at an X-ray. 'I call bingo on her.' She nodded over.

Ben smiled. 'Tenner says it's a man who fucks up first. Have you met them yet?'

'Nope. But she's wearing Louboutins. I'll see your tenner and raise you. Twenty quid she accidentally kills someone first week. And I'll do your washing-up for a month.'

Ben clicked the computer screen closed and shook Sophie's hand. 'Done.'

Jasmine, the girl who'd carved 'HELP' on her chest, had clearly not been granted her wish. She was rushed into Resus after throwing herself into the road in front of a car. Sophie recognised her immediately, but it was still horrifying to cut her T-shirt open with large hospital scissors and see the giant word forming a scar.

Jasmine meant business. Her body was all odd angles. Sophie felt her vision blur slightly. She was not a crier, but this girl somehow reached inside Sophie's chest and touched her in a deep, dark place.

'We need flying-squad blood. All the goodies, massive haemorrhage protocol!' Sophie shouted to Eden, who ran to the phones. It was only her and Eden in Resus today, and two new doctors. 'A very bad day to throw yourself in front of a truck,' said Sophie, as she assessed Jasmine head to toe. 'Somebody call her mother.'

She was bleeding, that was clear, but from where? One of the new doctors, the blonde woman, Amy, who had now changed from Louboutins to clogs, and from head-to-toe Reiss to scrubs, was trying to get a miniscule pink cannula in the back of Jasmine's hand. She looked at Sophie. 'Can you squeeze her arm for me? I can't find a vein.'

'What's with you all trying to get peripheral access? She's shut down — there's no chance you'll be able to get a line in, not unless you do a venous cut-down and there's really no time. Use the IO.'

Amy carried on as if she hadn't heard Sophie, but her face reddened. She was way out of her depth. Sophie tried to remember how stressful that first day had been on ED, especially for the new doctors. It was a million miles from the simulation suite where they practised real-life scenarios on mannequins.

Sophie reached to the trolley for the EZ-IO and stood next to Amy, moving the bloody sheet out of the way of Jasmine's hip bone. She found the landmarks and began to drill through bone until she heard the crunch of the needle going into the right space, and aspirated a few millilitres of bone marrow, before flushing some saline with a giant syringe.

Amy's mouth dropped open.

Sophie began drawing up the saline from the bag into a syringe, then pushing it into Jasmine and repeating. 'Can you do this? She needs fluid resuscitating; she's no blood pressure and will arrest any minute unless we fill her up.'

Amy nodded and stood up, copying what Sophie showed her, the rhythm of it a strange dance. She looked relieved to have something to do, but Sophie noticed she couldn't look at Jasmine.

It was hard to look. Her body was twisted and broken, and she wore knickers that had pandas all over them, which made Sophie's heart ache even more. But she couldn't fall apart. She had to find the bleed, and quicky. Pelvis? Abdomen? Head? Chest? Most people who bled to death did so internally. Our bodies have spaces that can silently be filled with blood until nothing works. Human bodies and minds rely on the gaps inside them. We are made of shadows.

Michael strolled past and nodded. 'Looks like you've got it all under control.' Despite his words his voice wobbled and he looked stunned, like he didn't know what to do. His niece must be close to Jasmine's age.

An animal cry like a fighting fox pierced the alarms sounding. Sophie turned to see the anxious woman she'd met in triage some weeks before. Jasmine's mum. Plenty of nurses asked relatives to wait outside while resus was in progress. Doctors and nurses worried about family members' distress, or them somehow hindering the management of the patient, getting in the way. But really Sophie understood that all that was a defence mechanism. Caring for bloody, broken bodies was easy. The person on the trolley was a slab of meat for a while, and it made things psychologically easier to dehumanise them. But once a family member was there witnessing their loved one at the edge of life, the patient was no longer anonymous. They were someone's mother, father, son, daughter. It was no longer them and us. It was just us.

Sophie grabbed her arm anyway. 'Come. Sit next to her and hold her hand. We're doing all we can to save Jasmine's life.'

Jasmine's mum's face held all the pain in the world. 'Please,' she said. 'Please, nurse, help her.'

EIGHTEEN
Aoife

Aoife woke, as usual since things had gone wrong with Michael, in the dead of night, heart rushing, drenched in sweat. She remained half in the nightmare for a few moments after consciousness; could still hear the alarms and see the blood and Sam standing in ED holding a bunch of yellow roses, moments after she'd left Michael's office. She felt haunted by work in a way that was new, having nightmares and flashbacks with increasing frequency. Aoife would walk around a park and see ghostly figures, only to get closer and understand they were simply trees.

Michael was on her mind constantly. She kept reliving the shock of seeing Sam at work on that day – she'd always kept her marriage separate but now the boundaries were blurring. She could still taste Michael in her mouth. It had been a risk, going down on him while he'd done the Grand Round, but it had felt worth it when he'd held her face with such tenderness like the very first time he'd kissed her. Now, lying next to Sam, she was disgusted with herself. What kind of depraved person performs lewd sex acts at work? In a hospital? Her head pounded, jaw ached, heart crashed. She was coming apart at the seams.

Sam half opened one eye and leant across to her, kissing her on the mouth. Aoife pulled away, hating herself.

'What's wrong?' He propped himself up on his elbow. Even in the near darkness, she could see the concern on his face.

'Ah, I've got toxic breath,' she said. 'Wouldn't want you dropping dead after kissing me.'

He stretched his arm out and rested the palm of his hand on her cheek. 'I'm worried about you, love. You're talking in your sleep.'

There was silence for a few moments, then she pushed his hand away. 'What? No I'm not. What do you mean?'

Sam lay perfectly still, not responding.

Aoife sat up, a stabbing pain in her stomach. 'What did I say?' She flicked on the bedside light, so she could see Sam's expression properly. Had she said anything about Michael? She'd never sleep-talked before, as far as she was aware. 'Are you sure?'

Sam nodded, eyes narrowing. 'Are you OK?' he said. 'You've not been yourself, and I'm getting worried about you.'

'Of course I'm OK.' She hadn't meant it to, but her voice sounded clipped. 'I've been having a busy time, that's all, and a bit of stress with the state of ED. I'm honestly fine.' She fake-smiled, hoping Sam wouldn't see through it. He knew the bones of her; they'd been married forever. 'What did I say?'

Sam turned his head away slightly. 'You weren't making sense, but you were talking and thrashing around a bit.'

'That's all?' Aoife kept her voice steady, her face neutral, but she felt relief fill her up. 'It's just been super-stressful with the new starters – bunch of new nurses, and one in particular who's dangerous, frankly. It'll pass, you know how it gets. Patients dying who shouldn't be, left, right and centre.' She reached for his hand, squeezed it.

But Sam didn't squeeze her hand back, like usual. 'I need to go back to sleep,' he said. 'Can you turn the light off?'

*

Aoife chained her bike in the bike store and made her way to ED, stopping at the small café for more coffee before her first night shift of six, before calling in to the site nurse practitioners' office to collect the bleep.

'Any fun in the sun?' Aoife stood on the patterned carpet in the SNP office, which, for some reason, always smelt like spaghetti carbonara. There was a line of desks, and two fridges, one for staff food, the other for drugs. 'Good day?'

'Nothing major. Well, we had to cardiovert a trauma surgeon in the corridor. She had a bit of VT. But all is now calm on the Western Front.' Beatrice, like all SNPs, was a hospital miracle maker who conjured beds from thin air and managed all manner of crises with unflappable ease. She had an elaborate silver nurse's belt and a fob watch, and looked starched from head to toe. Old school. She yawned. 'Nursing is ageing me rapidly.'

'Indeed. They don't advertise the bad backs, varicose veins and early-onset menopause during nurse recruitment drives.'

'Don't forget the PTSD,' said Beatrice.

Aoife sighed. 'No doubt.' She thought of her nightmares and flashbacks. Perhaps it wasn't Michael and Sophie that was causing her state of mind. Maybe the job was finally catching up with her. 'Feel like I should retire,' she said, out loud.

But Beatrice just laughed. 'We've got a family coming into the bereavement office tomorrow and meeting with the family liaisons. Nora, patient of yours, unexpected death.'

Aoife's vision blurred slightly. 'I remember her. Young woman. Gynae.' She thought of Eden and Sophie performing futile chest compressions on Nora. She hadn't insisted that the police be called and the room sealed off as a crime scene. That had been her call to make, but although it would have no doubt shone a light on Sophie's incompetence, her own judgement might have come into question; after all, Nora *had* been showing signs of clinical deterioration. In any case, since the Grand Round, Michael would surely come back to Aoife and forget about Sophie in no time.

'Apparently the post-mortem showed up a whack of morphine, but there were some metabolic issues and a bleed, too – DIC – her clotting was totally deranged, so the cause of death was inconclusive and recorded as natural, a clotting disorder. In any case, the family have already asked to speak to the doctors looking after her – they seem determined to get answers, quite rightly. Any chance you can stay a bit late tomorrow morning?'

Aoife thought about Nora's wife. Staying after a night shift, although common, was never a good idea; she'd be exhausted and unable to focus properly. But she wanted to make it clear to Nora's family who'd been in charge the day she'd died so suddenly, and that it hadn't been Aoife caring for her. 'I'll ask Sophie to attend,' said Aoife. 'She was looking after her, and the nurse in charge that day.'

She walked the basement way through the hospital to avoid the crowds hanging around and the day shift leaving slowly. The basement was always empty. It was an eerie other world, only one level below the SNP office. The atmosphere changed as she walked down the stairs. The ground floor and upwards were well maintained and refreshed yearly, but the paint below deck was peeling off, the floors dirty and damp. Aoife had walked this route a million times, past the chlorine smell of the hydrotherapy pool, where there was a small fishing net hanging on the wall for scooping shit from the water; past the neuropsychiatry office where the longest-standing professor in the hospital hid away with her Petri dishes full of live viruses. Aoife side-stepped the rat traps, which someone had kicked into the middle of the walkway, and the used needle, dropped and left. She'd once found a human leg down there. It was in a yellow clinical waste bag, and she'd got roped into a discussion with the porters and the mortuary about whose responsibility it was to find out who it had belonged to and why it had been dumped. Everyone had argued it was not their job to dispose of it, as if the leg was a fox lying on a pavement and the mortuary staff an overstretched council waste department.

Michael was rolling a cigarette on the stairs.

'Hey, you.' Aoife smiled and sat next to him. 'I didn't expect to see you here waiting for me. Want to carry my school bag?' Seeing him made the bones in her back feel more aligned. She sat up straighter.

Michael didn't react. He licked the paper, then put the newly made cigarette into the pouch of tobacco and turned to Aoife. 'What you did last week was fucked up,' he said.

She tried to kiss him, but he moved backwards, then stood up. His face was red. 'What? You don't mean—'

'You gave me a blow job while I was fucking presenting.' His voice cracked.

Aoife stood and leant on the stair rail. She looked behind him and glanced up the stairs. They were alone. 'Are you serious? You're kidding me, right? You loved it. You literally loved it.' Surely, he was winding her up? But she felt the ground move beneath her.

Michael put the tobacco pouch back into his scrub pocket. His eyes were red-rimmed. Had he been drinking?

'My body may have responded but it doesn't mean I wanted it. We're at work, Aoife. This is my career. My life. You put everything in jeopardy for, what, some silly fun?'

The words hung in the air and echoed. Aoife opened her mouth to laugh, but nothing came out.

'You literally sucked my dick in a locked room, when I was on live show to a hundred fucking colleagues.' His voice shook. Was he crying?

Aoife took a giant breath. 'It was sexy. You know it was.' A layer of sweat patterned his top lip. She shook her head and stood even taller. She turned to look at Michael. 'You came in my mouth. You *wanted* it. You always do.'

'Aoife, this needs to stop. Us. It's over. We're over.'

She took a step towards him and gently brushed his arm with her hand. 'Darling, Michael, we belong to each other. This is the only way we get through it, this job, together . . .'

He whipped his head back and sneered. She'd never seen that expression on his face. 'I'm not keeping this secret anymore. Us. I won't do it. I'm telling Sophie about us. About this. And that's an end to it. I don't want to keep a dirty little secret anymore. We are *over*.'

Aoife's head began to rush and she stumbled. Pain in waves. Everything was falling apart, all of it. Her entire, steady life was made of sand. Sam flashed in front of her. James. Michael. Her job. 'You wouldn't fucking *dare* share our secret with Sophie. She doesn't give a shit about you, can't you see that?'

Michael put his head in his hands then. When he lifted his head back up, he stared at Aoife. 'There's CCTV in that office,' he said. 'Surely you know there is CCTV in there. You put my entire career in danger. And I am through with this.'

'No,' said Aoife. 'No way. None of the CCTV has worked for decades.'

Michael hung his head low. 'I'd completely forgotten it was in there. Fuck. It's fucked up, Aoife – you, me, us. And I'm done. Finished. I don't belong to you, Aoife. I never did.' He walked away.

Aoife sat on the floor and pulled her knees to her chest and closed her eyes. Then she wept.

NINETEEN
Sophie

Finally, a day off. Sophie had worked six shifts in a row, her long days as rostered and two extra twelve-and-a-half bank shifts on her 'days off'. She used to visit restaurants and spend time wandering around antiques fairs and flea markets, but those things were a distant memory. City ED was short-staffed, but it was money, not altruism, that led her to working extra shifts; London living was not cheap, and she wanted to travel, as well as save for a flat of her own. Both prospects felt impossible on a nurse's salary, but Sophie was clocking up the savings week by week. She had toyed with the idea of getting money from Michael; after all, it was transactional enough, for her at least. Rhian was a sugar baby online to a number of men Michael's age and was building a significant portfolio of stocks and shares, but Sophie wasn't into it. Best to keep it as what it was. They were colleagues with benefits, she'd insisted on that from the start.

With the hours she was working she hadn't seen Michael outside work or been to his flat in weeks, but he'd texted her that morning: *Fancy meeting up today before your night shift? Really could use a chat.* He'd added an aubergine emoji. She ignored him. She needed to get away from work with the Walking Dead and away from men who sent emojis.

'Hurry up, Soph.' Obi was animated. He'd borrowed his mum's giant cool box and filled it with packets of cooked chicken he'd found on the sale shelf in M&S and Ben had contributed an eight-pack of non-alcoholic beers. After the Eden incident, he'd announced he was sober curious. Eden was on day shift – they'd invited her and she'd tried desperately to swap her long day, but with no luck. Sophie suspected they were all a little relieved.

'I'm here, ready for wholesome fun.' Sophie rolled her eyes, 'But can we please stop at the lido on the way back?' Sophie craved the sea. The best thing about living with Gee had been the sea. She liked to swim in all weathers, even in the dead of winter, when there was a layer of ice to break through before getting in. It cleared her head of so much, the shock of the cold.

'Absolutely not for me,' said Obi, 'but you guys knock yourself out.'

'I've already got my cossie on.' Rhian pulled her T-shirt up, revealing a bright-blue swimsuit patterned with sea creatures. 'Narwhals,' she said.

They walked in pairs to Brockwell Park, Ben and Obi carrying the box, Rhian and Sophie behind them. It was a gorgeous day, and they all wore dark sunglasses; an occupational hazard from not seeing daylight often enough. It burned their eyes.

When they arrived at Rhian's favourite tree, she spread a large blanket out for them to sit on. 'I'm so happy we could do this,' she said. 'I made a banana cake and popped that in there too.'

'It's weird without Eden, even if she is a cunt.' Ben laughed but it sounded hollow. He felt bad, clearly. At first, he had complained that Eden was overreacting, but as her forehead skin had healed and left a tiny red raised bump that would no doubt turn into a silver scar, like a fucked-up Harry Potter, he'd softened.

Sophie dumped her rucksack on the ground. The park was humming with activity. Families and crowds of friends were dotted around; one couple had an illegal BBQ on the go. She sat down and flicked off her flip-flops, stretched out her legs.

'Frisbee, anyone?' Obi created a large shadow in front of them, and Rhian began to laugh.

Sophie opened her eyes wide. Obi had stripped down to a pair of gold hotpants and was holding a Frisbee, looking around at everyone staring at him.

'Jesus. You are such a poser,' said Ben, but he stood up and they began to play. Ben, despite the heat, wore a jumper with a shirt underneath.

Rhian lay down next to Sophie and rolled onto her side. 'It's nice, isn't it?' She moved onto her back and closed her eyes. 'This. Friends. Sun. Youth. Salad days.'

Sophie listened to the sounds of the screeching South London parakeets, the park activity and her friends. She'd always been a loner until Rose Cottage. Always. But Rhian was right, it was nice. Sophie hardly recognised herself.

'Right,' said Ben, collapsing next to them. 'Who's skinning up?'

Michael had somehow engineered it so they were both on the crash team the next day, despite it not being the job of ED staff. He was filling in for the medical registrar, who was out on the picket lines supporting the junior doctor strikes, the sound of beeping car horns reaching all the way to the ninth floor. 'Bit thin on the ground today,' he said, as they ran to the first call: *Adult crash call. Public toilets. Pan Wing.* 'We've Gavin from Resus department, and a junior doctor from God knows where. I think that's it.'

Sophie slowed her pace so he could keep up. 'Fine,' she said. 'I'll be your sous chef today.'

Michael laughed. He stopped to catch his breath, waving her on. 'This is a young man's game.'

The crash call came blurting out of the bleep again: *Adult crash call. Public toilets. Pan Wing.* Sophie responded, then slipped the bleep back in her pocket and grabbed Michael's arm. 'I know a shortcut.'

She ran down the steps, pulling Michael behind her, to the basement where there would be fewer people milling around. They flew down the twisting corridor, into the bowels of the hospital, where the place became a labyrinth.

Michael stopped outside Academic Psychiatry and peered in.

'Come on, there's no time for a tour of your own hospital.' They walked quickly up the stairs to level one and past the Cancer Centre, the smell of which was all too familiar. 'Ah, the smell of home,' Sophie said.

Michael looked at her and frowned.

'Leukaemia,' she said. 'Ages eleven to thirteen. Completely cured thanks to our NHS.'

For a second, Michael looked as if he might cry. 'I didn't know that,' he said. Men of a certain age always looked as if they might burst into tears at any given moment. All that repressed sadness. There was a vulnerability to ageing men that Sophie found interesting.

They edged past the Cancer Centre; the Palliative Radiotherapy Suite corridor lined with patients sitting on rickety chairs, too weak to stand. Bald, gaunt, yellow and devoid of all hope, yet still, here they were. *Humans are remarkable*, thought Sophie. She had always thought that.

Eventually they came to the public toilets, Pan Wing, a place where they might find anything. This time it was a stroke. The man was in his mid-sixties, possibly younger, and had fallen and banged his head on the sink, causing a bleeding forehead and the tell-tale racoon bruises over his eyes of a broken nose, but it was his movements that revealed his condition: cycling on an invisible bike, breathing deeply, and he was only moving the left-hand side of his body. Sophie already knew as she knelt next to him that his face would have drooped down too, and he'd be confused and likely unable to verbalise his thoughts.

She looked up at Michael. The porter had arrived moments after them with the trolley, and all their kit. Michael leant across to the man's legs and met Sophie's gaze. 'Let's not dick around,' he said. 'Lift him onto the trolley and get him straight to CT.'

Sophie reached her arms around the man's waist. 'Agree.' They lifted him up in one, and Sophie saw Michael wince. She had back pain already, but he had years on her. There were all sorts of rules about not lifting patients, and using hoists instead, but of course, the emergency teams ignored them. That's why they were the emergency teams.

'Hello, sir, my name is Michael, I'm one of the doctors.' He shouted as if the man was deaf, as they pushed him out of the toilets and into the corridor.

Sophie attached the defib pads and wafted a bit of oxygen near his face. The rest of the crash team arrived one by one, and seeing that they were already on the move, left to go back to their jobs. She squeezed the man's hand. 'The staff in scan and ED will look after you,' she said. 'You'll be fine. Most likely.'

He most likely wouldn't be fine, she knew, but lying was often a kindness.

The porter wheeled him away, and Gavin, the resus officer who arrived as part of the crash team, pushed the trolley from the bottom. 'We've got this.' He was former ED matron and mindful of the fact that aside from the hospital resuscitation nurses, everyone else had theatre lists, clinics and anaesthetic lists to deal with as normal.

'Before we go back,' said Michael, 'let's please grab a coffee.'

Sophie didn't like how beggy Michael was being. She was beginning to regret this situationship. She thought about brushing him off, but there was something extra-desperate about him. 'Sure.'

They wound their way back to the coffee shop, and ordered double-shot lattes, before sitting in the corner, huddled together so that they wouldn't be approached. 'What's up?'

The coffee-shop area was bustling with staff and patients alike. Michael looked around and smiled awkwardly. 'I wanted to tell you something.'

Sophie put her coffee down; the steam was fogging up her glasses. She pushed them on top of her head and leant towards Michael. 'Yup.'

'God, it's so hard to say.' He slurped his coffee and scanned the area, before leaning forwards. 'It's just that I've been seeing someone else. For a long time. I want you to know.'

Sophie shrugged. 'None of my business.'

Michael shook his head, put his coffee down and took off his glasses. 'It is your business. We all work together, and it's complicated.'

'Go on.'

He took a breath. 'I've been in a relationship . . .' He paused, closed his eyes, then snapped them open. 'With Aoife.'

Michael spoke quickly as he told Sophie about the decades-long affair. 'I've never told anyone about this. We've never. Christ, it's been going on so long.'

Sophie leant back and whistled. 'I mean, frankly, it's nothing to do with me, though it's more than a little surprising. Aoife's a dark fucking horse.' She found it hard to imagine Aoife and Michael as lovers, but then she thought back to first seeing them, in that Japanese restaurant, and how the possibility had crossed her mind. It made sense. They were together more than any married couple, and ED was a hotbed of shagging. It was as incestuous a place as they come.

'She doesn't seem the sort. Aoife. She was literally raw-dogging cottage cheese for lunch yesterday; she doesn't strike me as a pleasure seeker . . .'

'You don't know her at all.' Michael's voice had an edge.

'Maybe not, but clearly you're wanting me to give my approval or something?' The words were not meant to be as sarcastic as they sounded. Sophie closed her eyes and tried to imagine Michael and Aoife shagging, then shrugged. It didn't bother her.

Michael stared at her for a few moments. 'Not approval exactly, but I just wanted you to know. In any case, it's over now. With me and Aoife, I mean. We had a big falling-out. Worrying behaviour she's got sometimes. Recently, I've almost felt afraid of her.'

Sophie held up her palms. 'Aoife? Afraid how?' Aoife was hardly the bunny-boiler type. She was married, for a start. Happily, too, as far as Sophie could tell.

'She's a bit unhinged, been coming on way too strong. I don't know. We're very old friends and I don't want to involve you, but when I told her I was seeing you, she went ballistic.'

'Why tell anyone? Why tell me?'

Michael shook his head. 'I didn't want secrets. Felt wrong.'

Sophie pulled a face. 'Everyone has secrets.'

'Well, I do want you to know I won't be sleeping with her, or with anyone else, from now on. I'm only interested in you.'

Sophie rolled her eyes. 'You can do whatever you want. This isn't a relationship. I still worry you're expecting more than I want to give . . . I don't know how to be clearer with you.'

'I know. Oh, it's wishful thinking maybe. I don't understand why we can't see each other. Outside sex, I mean.' Michael's voice was loud enough that a nurse walking past raised her eyebrows. 'But I hear you. I promise.'

Sophie leant in. 'It's not going to happen, with you or anyone else. I'm seeing other people. I fuck whoever I want. I hope you do too. Simple.'

'I don't understand your generation,' said Michael, smiling now, a bit flustered. 'But OK. I'm all in. If this is the only way I get to be with you, let's experiment with polyamory. Or whatever.'

Sophie laughed. 'If you have to label it, we're friends with benefits. As for you and Aoife, I really don't care what goes on, but I'd rather not know any details. But Aoife. Wow. Just wow.'

The ED was buzzing. It felt on the edge of something, like civil war was about to break out at any moment. Sophie found Aoife in the Minors area, stapling a man's arm wound closed. She poked her head around the curtain. 'I'm back. Sorry. Stroke in the loos and took an age to get him to the unit.'

'No stress. Can you take cubicle three round to CT?'

'Sure thing.' She stopped talking but found her legs rooted to the spot, unable to take her eyes from Aoife. She looked at her closely, her face, her body, and tried to imagine her with Michael, naked, but it was impossible to think of Aoife in anything other than her nurse's dress.

Eventually Aoife noticed her still standing there. She stopped stapling. The patient winced. 'Is that it?'

Aoife ignored him. Instead, she stared at Sophie, and for a moment something passed across her face. She had an expression that Sophie hadn't seen before; her eyes changed colour.

Sophie hadn't been planning to say anything. After all, Aoife was her boss. But she couldn't help herself. 'You're a dark horse, Aoife. A dark horse.' She didn't elaborate. She simply left the room.

It was late, and the hospital was quiet by the time Sophie made her way to ICU. Day and night on Intensive Care were pretty much the same. Strip lighting, loud noises, bustling activity. Keith's bed was by the nurses' station. Sophie recognised his nurse, Ethan, immediately from the staff canteen, where they sometimes sat together chatting as they ate a dry sandwich.

She glanced at the numbers on the monitor – all pretty crap. 'Hi-hi, Ethan.' She lifted her hand and smiled. 'Popping in as this was our patient in ED, quite a while ago now.' She nodded at Keith. 'Wanted to see him with my own eyes. My flatmate, Eden, said he was still here, and finally stable after the carotid blow-out on ED. Feels like a small miracle.'

'Sophie! I haven't seen you downstairs in forever.'

'It's been so busy they've literally banned lunch now.'

'That's crazy. Come work here, we've Band 6 vacancies year-round.' He laughed. Ethan was a typical ICU nurse: quietly controlling and always measured. ED nurses were headcases in comparison. Nursing was a language with many different accents, and there was no place Sophie would work except ED. She'd decided that on day one.

'What's his prognosis like?' She nodded at Keith, unconscious on all manner of life support, bloated, shiny and very dead-looking.

He screwed up his face. 'Nasty. You OK to stay here a second while I nip to the loo, Sophie? Thanks, angel.'

He skipped off, relieved to be able to pee. *This job*, thought Sophie, *when a toilet break is a rare treat.*

She walked over to Keith's face. His eyes were stuck closed with Vaseline. There was a thick endotracheal tube attached to the ventilator and all manner of other tubes coming from his neck.

He was barely alive, and this was no life he'd want. Sophie felt no relief or comfort knowing they'd saved Keith for this fate. Head and neck cancer is surely the most grotesque way to die.

The morphine pump began to alarm; Sophie glanced around but the other nurses were busy, so she washed her hands, put on an apron and checked the machine, which was the same make as they had in ED. She took the large syringe out of the driver to make sure it wasn't empty and turned the pump off and on, which usually seemed to do the trick, inspecting the plugs at the back and all the obvious things. The alarms stopped sounding; it was working again.

Before securing the infusion back into the syringe driver, she paused and stared at Keith a moment. He had pain etched on his face. Sophie glanced around again. What if she were to press down on the morphine syringe as she put it back into the machine and allow more of the drug to travel into Keith's veins? Any good nurse would surely want to make a loud, bombastic death a quieter, softer, kinder one.

TWENTY
Eden

It was the morning after a night shift, and Eden walked across the concourse towards the chapel, and to sanctuary. All her colleagues were heading home, climbing onto bikes, rucksacks hanging off their hunched shoulders. A few waved at Eden as she walked past, but even then, she felt alone. While her flatmates had all been having fun together the previous week, she'd had a string of day shifts, then nights, and had to write statements for an internal review into the care of a patient she'd looked after. The hospital management had told staff, after an inconclusive coroner's report, that there would be no police involvement or external review, but that all aspects of a patient's care should be thoroughly examined to see where and how the team could do better. Eden desperately wanted to be a good nurse, yet after each shift her head throbbed with anxiety; bad things always happened when she was around. Even when seemingly good things happened, like the day she and Sophie had saved the life of the patient, Keith, suffering a huge haemorrhage, the ending was the same. He'd survived, against all odds, and after weeks on ICU she'd hoped he might turn a corner, but she'd found out last night that he'd died after all.

The chapel was always candle-lit no matter the time of day or night. It was tiny, and dark, and smelt of washing that hadn't quite dried before being put away. There were rows of pews and giant flower arrangements at each end, maintained by the chaplain, a thick-necked, deep-voiced Welsh man named Stephen, who popped over to ED whenever somebody requested prayer. At the front near the altar was a table of small candles and a large lectern, upon which was the leather-bound book of messages and prayer requests, the saddest book you'll ever read. Eden walked over and stood in front of it. She imagined the many relatives of the dying, all scribbling down their outpourings, as they cried and grieved and hoped. She touched the paper and ran her fingertips gently over the words.

> *Paul, RIP. You were my angel gone to heaven too soon.*
> *Please pray for Damien Buller Ward, 7, having his surgery today.*
> *My rainbow baby. Star. You were perfect in every way, and we will always love you. You are with Uncle Bryan and Grandad in heaven now watching over us. We love you. Mum and Dad.*
> *Edith Swartz. Gone too soon. Our hearts are broken.*
> *Please can you pray for my mum, Martha? She has pancreatic cancer, and they have given her just weeks to live. We need a miracle. She is in so much pain. We are all praying for her recovery and peace.*

Eden held her breath as she read the next page. The handwriting was the same as before, but messier, and there were ink blots on some words. Eden ran her fingers over the marks, over a stranger's tears, and let the words settle in front of her, the weight of them.

> *RIP Martha, Mum, sister, friend. The funeral will be Thursday 6 p.m. at Christchurch, Welling. All welcome.*

All welcome.

Of course, everyone was welcome at funerals. A place to pay last respects, and for those who loved the person to say goodbye, even the strangers who had loved them.

'Who's there? Is that you, Eden? Oh, hello.' She'd met Stephen a few times, but Eden was surprised he remembered her name. 'How are you? I often see you around the place. Settling into nursing life?' He walked towards her, carrying a tray of weak tea in polystyrene cups, and a pile of Bourbon biscuits. He nodded to the tray. 'Want one?'

Eden shook her head. 'No, thank you. I came in to get some peace. I'm finishing night shifts today, last one of five.'

'You all work so hard. Well, stay here as long as you like. That's what the chapel is for. A sanctuary from the outside world.' He looked down at the book on the altar. 'It's tough reading, that one. Always humbling.'

They both stared at the writing a few moments. 'Do you think prayer saves lives?' she mumbled, but then shook her head. 'I'm sorry, of course you do, that's your job! My goodness. It's been a rough week, and I can't seem to help people how I want to. Not even colleagues.'

Stephen smiled. He set down the tray on a pew at the front, then stood next to Eden. 'We mere humans cannot always save people, but healing comes in all forms. I'll bet you're a really great nurse. Do you want any prayer?'

Eden looked up and shook her head. She was moved by his tenderness, but there was a bubbling anger in her stomach too. The Rose Cottage gang were busy having fun without her, most likely laughing at her too, while she was seeking friendship from anyone who'd have her, even the hospital chaplain, who had no choice but to be nice to everyone. 'Oh, no, I'm fine, thank you. Really, I'm OK.' She closed the book with a thump.

The day of Keith's funeral, Eden woke early and lay in the dark, whispering. *I'm good enough. I help strangers. I have much to learn but I will be a perfect nurse. I'll forgive myself. I will do the right thing by my patients, whatever the cost.* She tapped her collarbone in time with her words, a Morse code of anxiety. She knew this would be a good thing for the family, another way she could help; after all, nursing did not stop at the end of a shift. It never stopped.

Eden couldn't contact Keith's family on Facebook; the Code was clear about social media use: *Nurses should not use social networks to build or pursue relationships with patients and service users as this can blur important professional boundaries.* But it didn't say anything about looking patients up and checking how their families were doing, so Eden instead simply watched their pages. Sure enough, all the details of Keith's funeral were posted publicly.

'Where are you going dressed like that, traffic court? Wait, are you wearing those shoes? It's giving Next catalogue, workwear section.' Sophie was lying on the sofa wearing dark sunglasses, knickers and a T-shirt that said 'DADDY ISSUES'.

'I'm going to a funeral, if you must know.'

'Oh. Whose?' Sophie pushed the sunglasses onto her forehead. She had a black eye.

'Oh my God, what happened? Oh, God, it looks so painful.'

'Sexual misadventure. I'll take the rough with the smooth.'

The kitchen door opened as if on cue and in walked a young woman Eden recognised. She also had a black eye. They looked like they'd been in a boxing ring together, the pair of them. She sat next to Sophie and put her legs across her as if they were a married couple.

Eden stood open-mouthed as she realised where she knew her from. Claire, a paramedic from work. 'I had no idea you two . . .'

Claire laughed. 'Us two what?' She looked at Sophie.

Eden felt her face redden. She stood in her suit, shifting her weight from foot to foot, and felt more awkward than she ever had in her life. What on earth had they done? Punched each other in the eye? She had no idea that Sophie even knew

Claire, let alone was sleeping with her, or being violent with her or whatever they were doing.

Sophie stared at Eden without explaining anything or asking any more about the funeral. 'Have fun,' she said, and Eden stood there for a few moments before walking away quickly, her block heels padding heavily on the carpet.

The 68 bus went all the way to the church. Eden sat on the top deck, trying not to think about Sophie at all, as confusing as she was, and instead watching London spilling out on either side of the road: rubbish bins everywhere, people wandering in front of the bus, then staggering back to the pavement, shops selling Congolese groceries and cacti and Korean noodles and healing crystals and fish and multiple law offices advertising immigration services. It was a far cry from quiet Keston, where the only things you could see on either side of the road were perfectly curated topiary and electric gates to huge, ugly cookie-cutter properties with fancy cars and people carriers out front. Eden felt more at home here, with the sounds of shouting and sirens, police cars and ambulances whizzing by seemingly every few minutes. Like Florence Nightingale, she ran towards danger and wanted to be where the action was.

The bus stopped down the road from the church, but she could already see the family in the distance. They were wearing bright colours, as specified on the funeral details posted on Facebook. Eden felt momentarily self-conscious dressed in black, but then Keith's wife noticed her and briefly waved. Walking towards them, Eden could see that Keith's wife was grateful that a nurse had turned up to pay her respects. She waved back and walked towards the mourners.

TWENTY-ONE
Aoife

Aoife tried to catch Michael at work by hanging around outside his office, or in the car park area where she knew he smoked a cigarette before work. She went over to his flat twice, banging on the door and peering into the dark room through his front-door spyhole. When there was no answer she WhatsApped Michael dozens of times:

I love you, darling, and I'm so sorry.
Please don't ignore me.
I LOVE you. SHE doesn't.
I can't do this without you – it's killing me.

He didn't even open the messages. Whenever she checked her phone she could see them sitting there, unread.

At work, Michael couldn't ignore her, but he was cold.

'There's no weaning this patient off the ventilator if they go down that route and admit her to ICU. She's eighty. No chance. Let's stick to BiPAP. Let's get a DNACPR too.'

'Her family want full resuscitation. She does.' Aoife's voice shook. 'Age has nothing to do with it.'

'What planet are you living on? If we tube her, she'll never get off the ventilator,' Michael hissed.

'The family want it.'

They were doing a ward round outside the Resus area, the

new doctors surrounding them both. They looked awkwardly from Aoife to Michael and back again as their voices got louder.

'It's the family who judge quality of life. The patient and the family. Not us.' Aoife was almost shouting. She never raised her voice during ward rounds, not least when discussing confidential information.

'I'm the clinical lead,' Michael insisted. 'It's not a decision for a nurse.'

A few of the junior doctors slunk away at that point, clearly embarrassed. Or afraid.

Everything had changed. He'd clearly told Sophie about them, and she was lording it up, smiling in a sickly way, raising her eyebrows just enough to let Aoife know she'd heard all her secrets. She kept calling Aoife a *dark horse*. Aoife felt constantly sick. That her entire life, her marriage, even her career, rested on Sophie's discretion was unbearable. And how long could Sophie's silence last?

Aoife was no stranger to St Barnaby's Church. It was a rainy day; the grey sky fitting, at least. She'd worked a stint in children's Intensive Care, early in her career, and been to too many funerals where the sun was shining through the stained glass as an impossibly small coffin was carried on the shoulders of a father and uncle or brothers.

Keith Reynolds was a big family man, and it didn't surprise Aoife to see dozens of people lining the pews. His wife, Mabel, was wearing a yellow dress and sitting in the front row. Keith would have loved it; he had been cheerful, even in the face of the worst kind of prognosis. Aoife had looked after him a number of times, blue-lighted in with respiratory infections, or coming back with post-operative bleeding. She'd visited him in the Cancer Centre, too. Mabel had held Aoife's hands in hers and thanked her for saving his life. 'But also,' she'd said, her eyes glistening with tears, 'for recognising that his life is worth saving. We went to A&E on holiday in the Lake District,' she told Aoife, 'and they suggested we go straight to the hospice.'

Aoife looked around St Barnaby's and tried to shake her head clear. She pressed her feet to the floor. As the vicar mumbled some words, Aoife tried to catch the eye of Mabel at the front, to nod before disappearing. This was the role of a nurse at a funeral, to simply let the family know they were there in the background. Mabel would hopefully find comfort in that fact. Aoife certainly did. It reminded her who she was, during all this.

But something grabbed Aoife's attention. A young woman sitting right next to Mabel, head to toe in black, a small veil covering the top part of her eyes. Aoife blinked.

It was Eden.

Front and centre, right next to the spouse of a patient she hardly knew. What the hell was Eden doing here? Aoife glared at her across the church, willing Eden to turn and catch her eye, but Eden was too busy cosying up to Keith's widow, leaning against Mabel's arm.

'We've got a severely psychotic patient in cubicles, and no mental health room, no mental health nurse. We need a bed urgently.' Aoife listened to the sigh at the other end. They both knew that the chance of a Psychiatric Intensive Care bed, even though the patient was now sectioned and identified as critically ill, was zero.

'Eden, wait, I wanted to catch you.' Aoife held the phone away from her. She was reluctant to hang up, having been on hold for so many precious minutes. 'Can we fix a time for your preceptorship appraisal later? And have a general chat, please?'

Eden hovered, put one thumb up. 'Sure.'

'Hello, hello.' Aoife pressed the earpiece close, but there was a dead signal at the other end. 'Fuck's sake.' She felt her face get hot. 'Sorry – right, let's have a quick chat now.'

Eden followed Aoife to the clean utility room, which was the only space empty of people or alarms. 'I went to Keith's funeral,' Aoife said, 'and was quite surprised to see you there, front and centre.'

Eden stared for a moment, then gave that Lady Di smile she seemed to pull out now and then, coy and innocent. 'I didn't see you there. You should have said hello.'

Aoife studied Eden's face – her skin was clear and fresh, and her eyes bright. Eden was impossibly young. Naive. That's all this was, surely. 'It is inappropriate', she said, 'to attend a patient's funeral with his widow. You were right there at the front! In any case, I didn't know you knew Keith or his family that well?'

Eden scratched the side of her cheek. 'Oh, I did. His wife, Mabel, she insisted I sit with her.' She looked suddenly tearful and a bit overwhelmed. 'It's so powerful, isn't it? That we can even provide comfort after death. As nurses, I mean.'

Aoife frowned. 'Eden, you really shouldn't go to patient funerals. It's not appropriate. Of course, if you'd known the patient for months on end, and stood at the back to pay your respects. But at the front? No.' She shook her head. The crash alarm rang out.

Eden's face flashed red from the light above their heads. 'I'm sorry,' she said. 'I really thought it would be OK. It's not specified in the Code of Professional Conduct.'

Aoife smiled curtly. 'Just check if you want to attend any funeral. It's really against the rules – unwritten rules, but still.' She looked at Eden. 'There are hospital-wide investigations going on and I'm up to my ears in PFDs – preventing future death reports – and staff are being dragged to the coroner's court left right and centre. Everyone is looking at morbidity and mortality rates, clinical errors and unexpected deaths, so we're all under extreme scrutiny and this kind of behaviour isn't a good look, Eden. Let's all follow the rules religiously?'

Eden hesitated, opened her mouth, then closed it again. She pursed her lips as if trying to stop words escaping, then dropped her arms to her sides.

TWENTY-TWO

Sophie

Sophie had not fucked Michael since the great confession about him and Aoife. It wasn't that she felt any sense of guilt, or obligation to Aoife; it was simply that Michael had seemed a bit less fuckable after that. Slightly pathetic. He constantly blurred the lines, and, like way too many men of his generation, sometimes had poor personal boundaries.

Sophie didn't care who he fucked, but she was relishing the knowledge about Aoife. Aoife! Who knew that Aoife, queen bee, head honcho, woman in charge of the galaxy, would be having an illicit affair? She was so starched, so buttoned up. Sophie had not been able to resist taunting her. It was a dance between them now.

'Come to the theatre with me. Thursday. I've got tickets to an Ibsen play. Do you like that kind of shite?' Michael walked alongside her outside the hospital. They were on the way into a long day; it was still pitch dark and, aside from the hospital lights, the sky was black. Michael was smoking, Sophie vaping. They stopped at the corner under a streetlight to finish up.

'You'll get popcorn lung,' he said.

Sophie nodded at his cigarette. 'Cancer.'

Michael grinned. 'I reckon I have ten good years left before I start coughing blood.'

'And with that limited time on earth you want to take me to see an Ibsen play?'

'Something different then. I know you don't like restaurants, and I'm willing to watch a boring play just to sit next to you.'

'I do like restaurants,' Sophie said. 'But I like to eat alone. I've told you this.'

'What about Ceroc?'

Sophie smiled. She didn't want to encourage him but she couldn't help it. 'Ceroc? What the fuck is that?'

'It's dance. A mixture of salsa and swing. There's a club in Leicester Square, if it's still there.'

Sophie laughed. It sounded loud and surprising, like a birthday card that blared out music when you opened it.

Michael beamed and frowned at the same time; the top half of his face didn't match the bottom half. He clearly had no idea why he'd made her laugh, or what was funny, but still loved that it had happened.

'I'll give theatre a miss.' She puffed on her vape. 'But fine, we can go out sometime. Ceroc is a no. Tragic.' She smiled, leant towards his face close enough to kiss him. 'This isn't a thing.'

Michael's eyes lit up. 'Whatever you say.'

'Has it ever crossed your mind,' she said, 'that I'm just not that into you?'

Michael laughed. 'Nah.'

Aoife was off sick. According to Mary, that had never happened, ever. 'Sounds like norovirus. She's been projectile vomiting all night.'

They stood in the Rapid Assessment Treatment Room – which had been closed for a deep clean – hiding from the chaos outside. Security guards were rushing around, and the unit was chock full of police, Code 10 after Code 10. 'Today of all days,' Sophie said. 'What are the numbers like?'

'We've poached a few ward nurses but they've no ED experience so might need hand-holding.' Mary nodded towards the door. 'Man with a machete around somewhere and there's about six people on stretchers after a pub fight got a bit feisty. Mostly bottling injuries, one with a definite orbital fracture and a worrying C spine, but they're causing a headache. Nasty facial injury on one guy, scalp lacerations all need gluing, but he'll need a CT, I think. He's complaining of tasting salt so pretty sure it's a basal skull fracture. I'm sure it'll kick off, and the other bad news is that management want to see all the people in charge of any shifts when clinical incidents have occurred, which is basically every shift. They've emailed you a time slot to climb up to the ivory tower and see the head of nursing.' Mary put her hand on Sophie's shoulder. 'Now, I know you're brilliant and all, but it's a lot. Want me to stick around a bit?'

Mary was kind and never patronising – an unusual combination. 'I'm good. We'll be OK, and you need a proper sleep before more fun and games tonight.'

They left the room to face the alarming, strip-lit scene outside. It was like stepping into a nightclub in the morning when the lights had been turned on abruptly to get everyone out. Stark and brutal. Sophie walked to the coffee room and hovered by the door. 'Let's get out there and relieve all the night staff. Rhian, Majors; Fran, can you do AMU? Obi's en route. Eden, just you in Minors until the ward staff rock up. Can you glue that man's head in cubicle one? He was bottled but he can leave straight after gluing. Leave the curtain open – he's a known pervert. Rosy, corridors need clearing. There's a collapsed lung needs moving soonest. I'll be by the nurses' station begging for beds.'

She turned and walked quickly out and across to the area in the centre of Majors where the X-ray screens and phones were positioned, along with the large computer screen of comings and goings that was always slightly out of date. Pamela was there, already pissed off and making it clear to whoever she was speaking to on the phone. Sophie picked up another handset and put the noise around her into soft focus. 'Hi, this is Sophie Ibrahim, senior nurse in ED today, and we need beds like we've never needed beds before. Give me some good news.'

'Sophie! Can you come?' Eden's voice screeched out.

Sophie ran, but when she arrived at the end of the corridor, in cubicle two of Minors, the curtain was wide open, and Eden and her patient looked totally fine. Sophie exhaled.

Eden was setting up the aseptic tray in front of her on top of a trolley, with glue, saline, stitches, wipes and sterile gloves all laid out. She had her hand on the patient's forehead. 'You should put gloves on before going near a wound,' Sophie said. 'What is it? Need stitching after all?' The patient, a curly-haired man with scars all over him and a port-wine birthmark on his neck, was well known to ED. 'Hiya, Gary. You look well.'

'Very funny,' he said. 'Are you having a fucking laugh with me? I know my rights.' His voice was thick with anger. He'd once grabbed Phoebe's bottom, and Sophie had had him thrown out of ED with an untreated broken collarbone.

'That's the problem,' said Eden. Her face was flushed. 'My eczema has flared up so I can't put the gloves on. Stupidly thought I'd just be careful.'

Sophie rolled her eyes and pulled an apron off the wall holder. She put gloves on and moved to Gary's bloody forehead. 'Right, move out of the way and scrub your hands. You'll need Occy Health again and another Datix incident form. Do you have any open cuts?'

Eden shook her head.

'This here is why our fucking country is fucked.' Gary moved his head and Eden held it tightly.

'Let go so I can see.' Sophie reached over and touched Eden's hand.

It didn't move. Eden didn't move. Her hand was stuck.

'I glued it. I mean, I thought I'd be really careful, and I tried warm water and sponging it, but it's stuck. I feel like such an idiot.'

Sophie looked at Eden's face welling up with tears, her hand glued firmly to Gary's head. 'Oh, for fuck's sake,' she said.

'Exactly,' said Gary. 'Now get me a matron who knows what they're fucking doing.'

'I really need the loo,' Eden whispered.

TWENTY-THREE
Aoife

Fear whirred inside Aoife's head, heart, belly. Sophie knew about her and Michael. She'd lose her family and her career. *Loose lips sink ships*, that's what her mother always used to say. It was almost impossible to act normal, but she tried to carry on carrying on, one foot in front of the other. She'd been uncharacteristically off sick the week before, and had dreaded coming back to work, but as soon as she'd arrived on the department, her breathing had slowed down. ED somehow, weirdly, calmed her spirits, as ever. It was impossible to be anything at work except in the moment.

Fatima arrived in agony. Her husband, Mo, was standing beside her when Aoife arrived in Majors to assess her. He was a tall, thin man, with the greenest eyes Aoife had ever seen, even though they were full of tears. Fatima writhed around, unable to get comfortable and crying out in pain. 'She's got colon cancer,' he said, 'but she's in remission. That's what they said. Her oncologist, Mr Bride, he said she was cancer-free at the last scan. That was about ten months ago.'

Fatima's limbs were emaciated but her abdomen was swollen and shiny. 'Fatima, I'm going to give you this pain medication and get the doctors to come and see you, then we'll get you to a ward.' Aoife checked her name band, then studied Fatima's face, creased and pinched. 'How long has she been like this?'

Mo picked up Fatima's hand. 'The pain came on so suddenly. We had a scan booked next week, because the last blood tests were not so good. But she's been fit and well. Working.'

Aoife nodded. 'I've fast-bleeped the oncologist, but we'll get your pain under control, and get you sorted.' Aoife put her hand gently on Fatima's swollen abdomen. 'It might be some sort of blockage to cause this amount of pain, but we'll see . . .'

She stopped talking as her hand jolted. Aoife looked down and felt it again: a definite flutter. Her first mentor had always told her: *If it looks like a sparrow and chirps like a sparrow and flies like a sparrow, it is most likely a sparrow.*

'Mo, is there any chance at all that Fatima might be pregnant?' Before Mo could answer, Fatima was bearing down, gritting her teeth and groaning – a noise that Aoife knew in her bones meant only one thing. 'Help in here, please!'

By the time Obi walked in with the crash trolley, Aoife had the baby's head in her hands and Mo had dropped to the floor. And then with a gush the baby was out. Mo stumbled to his feet. Aoife wiped the baby's face and rubbed its back, patting gently. She was not a midwife; she'd just followed her instincts. The baby screamed. Fatima and Mo looked like they might too.

Aoife grinned from ear to ear, placed the baby onto Fatima's chest and took in the wonder of it all for a moment. This place of life and death. The flesh and bones and blood that connected each and every one of us. The absolute horror. The absolute beauty. The tiny miracles that made it all worthwhile.

The baby blinked. Aoife turned to Mo. 'She has your eyes.'

Aoife managed to avoid Sophie for the best part of two weeks, but eventually they were on duty together. She studied Sophie while she held the breathing mask on the patient's face. People must stare at her and Michael when they were out and about.

It must look a bit pathetic. What did she see in him? He was handsome, of course, in a silver-fox, slightly dishevelled way, but he looked his age. *Their* age.

The patient was sedated, and Kemi was pushing in some pain relief. 'Where's the CT1?'

'Taking his time. I'll do it.' Sophie nodded to the patient's shoulder, which was dislocated and hanging at an odd angle.

'You're not serious,' said Aoife. 'It's the doctor's job.'

'It's really not that hard.'

Aoife glanced at Kemi and they shared a slight eye-roll. 'I'll go find Michael. Meanwhile, do a set of obs.'

Sophie shrugged. She could feel the icy temperature between them.

Aoife rushed off in search of Michael, but he was knee-deep in a lumbar puncture, a thin woman curled in front of him like a comma, her spine protruding, a long needle in Michael's fingertips.

'We've a sedated patient in one, ready-to-go shoulder dislocation,' she said.

Michael nodded but didn't look up. 'Be there in a jiffy. Right, now this is going to sting, I'm afraid.'

By the time Aoife returned minutes later, Sophie had popped the man's shoulder back into the socket and was fixing a sling. Kemi had vanished.

'What? Sophie, did you do this?'

'It's hardly rocket science, though I did have to use modified Kocher's method. External rotation didn't work.'

'It's beyond the scope of your professional practice.' Aoife felt the anger fizzing behind her eyes. 'I should honestly report you. We need to chat about this later.'

Sophie stared and blinked slowly. 'Who's reporting who here?' She fastened the patient's sling, then stood at the sink at the end of the bedspace and scrubbed her hands, wiping them dry with a paper towel. 'I know you had a big meeting with Denise – you both and the Fellowship of the Ring or executive committee or whatevs – about this hospital-wide audit of deaths and adverse incidents. She's scheduled a meeting with me to discuss governance, apparently.' Sophie turned to face Aoife. 'Did you know that women of colour are way more likely to face investigations or disciplinary process than Caucasian women in the NHS? I wonder if you mentioned that Eden is incompetent, or maybe worse – or are you keeping your favourites close? Did you know she glued her hand to a patient's head? Took three hours to soak it free, and during that time we had patients dying on trolleys; she had to pee into a bottle while attached to a patient. Put that in your Datix pipe and smoke it. Also,' Sophie lifted her head up, 'I *know* about you and Michael.'

The words floated between them.

'I know that you were together, and for how long, and that you'd like nothing more than to see me out of the picture. I'm on to you, Aoife.'

Aoife's heart pounded against her ribcage.

The patient began to cough and open his eyes. 'Welcome back,' said Sophie, turning to him. 'All fixed up, don't worry.'

Aoife turned away and opened the curtain to find Michael standing there. Had he heard them? 'You're too late,' she said. 'Sophie has taken it upon herself to be a medically trained doctor.'

Sophie didn't challenge her. Instead, she looked directly at Michael, and he held her eye contact as if they were the only two people on the planet.

TWENTY-FOUR

Sophie

The nursing management offices were above the Sexual Health Unit, at the back of G Wing. Sophie walked up to the first floor where the executive leadership team held informal meetings. The stairwell smelt of prawn cocktail crisps.

She banged on the door marked 'Department Head and Director of Nursing: Denise Fawn'. Somebody had pinned a photo of Hattie Jacques from *Carry On Matron* next to Denise's name.

'Come in.' A man's voice.

Sophie had never been to these offices before, but they existed in every hospital, and she'd certainly spent time in similar offices in Blackpool. Sophie knew all about non-statutory public enquiries, investigations into patient safety, process.

By the time the hospital called people into a place like this — a large, square, soulless office, the windowsill lined with half-dead spider plants, a large jar of Nescafé — bad shit had most likely been going on for ages.

The young man who ushered her in was wearing a shirt and tie and speaking on the phone. He pointed at one of the chairs, but Denise immediately poked her head out from the main office door and smiled. 'Come on in.'

Denise was tall, and painfully thin, Sophie noticed, and smelt of cigarettes covered up by a Smint. She had teeth that were too big for her face, and badly applied make-up. It was hardly an advert for executive life, but then, this was the NHS. Her job was likely a living nightmare.

'Thank you for coming along to see me.' Denise put on a pair of glasses, then glanced down at a piece of paper. 'As you know, we're looking at learning opportunities from things that may have gone wrong. We have a no-blame culture here at City and we all appreciate that our nursing team are universally fantastic.' She smiled too widely. 'But ED particularly has had a period of instability; there's likely to be a police enquiry if this current spike continues, and our insurance rating will not withstand that, as I'm sure you can imagine.' She looked off into the distance, then focused, as if remembering where she was and who she was talking to. 'Patient care is at the centre of all we do, of course, and our total priority is the safety of patients *and* the wellbeing of staff. We're here to support, not criticise. We're speaking with all the in-charges. You came to City from Blackpool Royal Infirmary, is that correct?'

Sophie nodded. 'Yes.'

'How was that?'

'Swings and roundabouts.' Sophie slow-blinked but didn't elaborate. She didn't mention the off-the-scale unexpected death rate there also. Or the day when there had been three cardiac arrests in one hour, warranting a full closure of the unit, and the entire team going through every single piece of kit, from saline flushes to giving sets, to check they were kosher. The manager was worried that something had been contaminated, a vial of water mixed with antibiotics that had some rogue potassium in it, or bacteria that had invaded a sterile needle kit. Sophie suspected foul play. That people found it impossible to believe that nurses and doctors could be psychopaths was fascinating to her.

Denise pushed her glasses up on top of her fringe. 'As a trust we take very seriously the safety of both our patients,' she smiled, 'and our staff. The waiting times have never been worse, so we are committed to supporting and helping all frontline staff on the ground however we can. And, of course, we have a duty both legally and morally to make sure that we are not missing anything untoward, and to investigate patient safety concerns.'

'It's been pretty stressful. I mean, incident after incident. That's the nature of it, I guess.'

'Indeed. I worked clinically on ICU a long time ago. It was stressful even then. However,' she tapped the paperwork in front of her, 'we've been looking for any patterns of concern, and we've had a few relatives complain about nursing care. Your nursing care.'

Sophie groaned. 'Who reported? What relatives?'

Denise's smile vanished. 'Anonymous, I'm afraid, via the patient advice office. There's a feedback box for patients and families, and we periodically get complaints via that route. We don't have details but of course we need to follow up, especially in view of the number of cases from ED.' She pushed her glasses back onto her nose and stared at Sophie with an expression that both impressed her and made her skin crawl.

Denise clearly smelt a rat.

'There's a number of cases I'll go through, which all happened when you were leading the shift.'

Sophie stood up. She wasn't going to listen to any more of this bullshit. Could Eden have said anything? Surely it wasn't Aoife?

'I'll be off now back to the badly staffed ED, to try to save as many lives as possible with the total lack of resources. I'd say when having meetings of this nature, best to have a representative from the RCN and legal present. If anyone is responsible for an increasing death rate, I suggest you look further up the food chain, at systemic failure. Your remit, I believe. Yours and *Aoife's*.' She turned and didn't look back. She didn't need to. She could feel Denise's eyes on her as she walked out.

ED was unusually calm. Sophie pushed the DYNAMAP blood-pressure machine around AMU and took her time chatting with patients as Phoebe did her basic observations.

'Fuck me, that hurts!' Sandra was in bed three, shouting.

'You OK to carry on?' Sophie smiled at Phoebe. She was super-keen and totally out of her depth. Sophie would usually avoid working with students at all costs, but after the chat with Denise, she wanted the distraction.

Phoebe nodded. 'Thanks, Sophie.' She was doe-eyed and spoke in a soft, fragile voice.

Sophie followed the sound of Sandra's shouts and perched on the end of her bed. 'I know you've had some morphine but I wanted to check if you feel nauseous at all? I can get you some anti-sickness if so? We're just waiting for a call from theatres, so it won't be much longer.'

Sandra was rolling around in pain. 'Fucking agony, I won't lie. I don't feel sick, just agony.'

Sophie stood. 'I'll get you some more morphine. Phoebe will be in to do your obs in a minute, OK?'

'Thank you, nurse. Worst pain ever and I've given birth three times.'

Sophie looked at Sandra's pale, scrunched-up face. 'I had my appendix out when I was five, but I can still remember it.' She put her hand on Sandra's. 'We'll get you sorted in no time.'

Sophie saw herself, a small girl, curled into a ball crying out for a mum who never came, then darkness.

Sophie walked away from Sandra, and out into the corridor towards the locked cabinet. She pulled out some morphine to double check it with Obi, who was standing by the controlled drugs cupboard drinking from a Stanley cup. 'Appendicitis. Funny how quiet things can sometimes cause us the most pain.'

'Apparently, we have an appendix from the days when we used to eat trees,' Obi said. 'Helps process bark.'

Sophie opened the packet of morphine ampules and showed him the label. 'Is that true?'

'True story. By the way, I'm through to the next round. *Love Island.*' Obi clapped his hands together. 'Personality tests next, I think.'

'Wowza. Good luck with that,' Sophie said. 'I hope you get it, but I don't want you to leave. Rose Cottage would be far less fun without you.'

'Aw, shucks, Soph. You're such a softie at heart.'

Sophie locked the cupboard and popped the morphine vial into her scrub pocket. 'I'm really not.'

'I know,' said Obi. 'I was just practising stretching the truth for my personality tests.'

She grinned and punched him on the arm before heading back to Sandra.

Eden was sitting cross-legged on the living-room carpet when Sophie arrived home, a packet of tarot cards in front of her. She turned each one face up and read out the names. 'Ask a question,' said Eden. 'Ask the cards. I know you think this is witchery, but ask.'

Sophie took a Diet Coke from the fridge and flopped down on the sofa, glaring at Eden. 'You are almost unreal. OK, I have a question.'

Eden held the cards in front of her, fanned them out into a half-moon.

Sophie put her hand on top of the cards but continued looking straight at Eden. 'Did you report me to Denise as incompetent – or worse, dangerous?'

Eden laughed nervously, but then shook her head. 'What?'

'Someone is spreading rumours that I am the ED Antichrist.'

Eden flinched; her pupils constricted a fraction. 'There's no such thing as a bad nurse. Just a busy day. And no, of course I didn't.'

Sophie laughed. 'God, you've got so much to learn. Of course there are bad nurses. Sadistic nurses, even.'

Eden pulled her hand away and turned her head slightly. 'Well, it certainly wasn't me,' she said. 'But bad things are happening, so it's good they're investigating. And it's no secret that you break the rules.' She lowered her voice. 'Michael, for example.'

'Are you having a laugh? Consensually shagging a grown adult is not breaking any rules. As for you and your fucking Code of Professional Conduct, do you want Denise to know about your shoebox of death mementos?'

Eden dropped the cards she was holding.

'Denise – do you know her?' Sophie said. 'Director of nursing. Looks like Cruella de Vil. She is a total cunt. She said relatives have complained about my care, but she couldn't tell me which ones.'

Eden swallowed hard enough that Sophie could see and hear it. 'You know it's nothing sinister. I *told* you.'

'You'd think they'd look at staffing, but no – good old NHS. Blame the nurses. And no, I didn't mention your creepy-as-fuck box, but I most certainly will, if I get a hint of you implying that I'm responsible for offing patients.'

'Of course – I would never. It's the NHS and the state of staffing, surely?' Eden picked up her tarot cards and put them into a small silk cover, carefully wrapping them up.

Sophie rolled her eyes. 'Surprised you're not using Nora's scarf for your cards. Still, I believe you. But if you didn't report me then who did? No way relatives complained; management are just twitchy, so if I were you, given the accusations flying around, I'd stop collecting dead people shit.'

Eden glared at her with a look of pure hatred. 'Be careful,' she said.

Sophie ignored her meaningless threat and stood and walked to her bedroom. Once inside, she closed the door and leant on it, breathing for a few moments. Then she took out her phone and messaged Michael.

It was dawn when they'd finished fucking; Michael was out of Viagra so had turned over to sleep, but Sophie kicked him gently. 'Thought you wanted to leave in the dead of night before everyone wakes up.'

He moaned quietly. He was sex-drunk; drowsy, flushed, swollen and soft. 'OK, OK, but you're like a freshly baked sausage roll. Too warm and lovely to leave.'

Sophie giggled. Michael's knack of making her laugh unnerved her a bit. 'Nobody has ever called me a sausage roll before. Right, out you go.' She pushed him out of bed with her legs, and he stood and dressed in the near darkness. The birdsong outside was getting louder, and a siren had gone past already. The flatmates would be up for their day shifts imminently, and while Sophie didn't give a flying fuck, Michael had been so concerned about coming over that she felt obligated to help him avoid their gossip at work.

'I am in total like with you,' he said, kissing her shoulder, her arm, her mouth.

'Stop dropping the L bomb. It's tragic.'

He let himself out, and Sophie lay there, listening for the front door, but instead she heard voices. She climbed out of bed and opened her bedroom door a fraction. Eden. She had somehow found Michael sneaking out like a teenager and struck up a conversation with him. Sophie listened for a few moments to Eden waffling on, in a too-high cheerful voice, as if it were a perfectly normal occurrence to see the lead consultant sneaking around Rose Cottage at dawn. Michael would be worried, but whatever. Eden already knew about him. Let her judge away.

TWENTY-FIVE
Aoife

Eden was at work early, hovering around the desk. Aoife wondered if it was about the investigation – after all, Denise was now calling all staff individually, and Eden was next in line to be formally interviewed. Eden smiled. 'I've brought you a latte,' she said. 'Soy milk.' She handed Aoife a large cardboard cup with 'BOSS' written on it.

Aoife smiled back. Sweet Eden. She may get a lot wrong, but her heart was in the right place. 'Thank you.'

'I wanted to talk to you.' Eden perched on the edge of Aoife's desk. She glanced at the door, then back to Aoife. 'Really quickly before the others arrive. I came in early. I've been in two minds, but I know it's the right thing to do. If I were you, I'd want to know, for sure.'

Her face was shiny, Aoife noticed, as if she'd been scrubbing it. 'Shoot.'

Eden leant back and exhaled loudly as if she were blowing out a candle. 'Michael stayed at Rose Cottage a few nights ago.' She paused a few moments. 'With Sophie. In her room, I mean.'

Aoife watched the air between them thicken and become wavy, desert hot. 'Michael was at the nurses' accommodation?'

Eden stared at Aoife's face, unblinking. 'I thought you'd want to know. You deserve to know that.' She went to the other side of the desk, where Aoife sat bolt upright, her palms starfished on the desktop, white-knuckled. Eden put her hand on Aoife's shoulder. 'He's a rat and you deserve better.'

Aoife leant forwards until Eden's hand dropped down. She looked up at Eden's shiny face. 'What exactly has Sophie said to you?' But even as she said it, she could tell by Eden's expression that Eden knew about Aoife and Michael.

'He shouldn't be treating you like this,' Eden whispered.

The secret that had been a forever secret, that would never, ever see the light of day, was no longer a secret at all. Of course, Denise had known for years, but she'd never betray Aoife. Not like Sophie, and definitely not like Eden. Sophie must have told Eden. And now *these* were the people in the world who knew the one thing that could destroy Aoife's life, Sam's life, James's life. Eden knew about her and Michael. Sophie knew. Of all the people in the world to have that power, it was a couple of narcissistic, judgy, self-obsessed Gen Z nurses. Fear clawed at her insides again. There was something else, too, almost worse than fear. Every time she blinked, Aoife could see her Michael and Sophie at Rose Cottage, all night, kissing, fucking. She stared straight ahead and steadied her face.

Aoife wanted to scream. Instead, she smiled at Eden. 'Thank you for the latte. Michael's business is Michael's business, but if you think it's affecting work relationships, I'll have a word with him.'

Eden stepped backwards and looked momentarily confused, then smiled. 'OK.'

'That's all.' Aoife sipped her coffee. She smiled again.

'But?' Eden frowned. 'But I thought you and Michael—'

'That's all,' repeated Aoife, waving her hand.

*

Aoife could barely concentrate all morning. Two junior nurses on her unit held all the cards. What if they told others? Sophie didn't strike Aoife as a tell-tale. But Eden? Would Eden fall apart under the stress of the hospital investigation and do something stupid, like tell them – or other colleagues – about her and Michael? Of course they'd want to get into personal relationships and connections as part of their exploration.

Would she tell Sam?

Surely not? In any case it was Sophie who was dangerous, not Eden. The internal review was escalating, yet Denise said there were no clear patterns of concern, despite Aoife pointing out that *everything* had gone wrong the moment Sophie arrived. She was not afraid to report her if it meant getting her out and far away from her, and from Michael. It should have been easy, too, with everything going on, to get her moved somewhere else in the hospital. A few resuscitations that Aoife was reviewing had been not only unexpected but unnatural. Stable patients who should have been recovering were dying, or attempting to die, on her unit, in her care. People with families and lives and futures. For the sake of her patients, she'd told Denise, and the powers that be, Sophie had to go.

How could Michael trust her? How could he be so stupid? Sophie was already using that knowledge, calling Aoife a *dark horse,* and telling Eden, of all people. He was ignoring Aoife's messages and distancing himself. He was staying at Sophie's flat, making love with her all night. She had somehow bewitched him, and he'd lost all sense of himself. She was messing with Aoife's head too.

But Sophie was fucking with the wrong person.

Della had been blue-lit in with a penetrating abdominal wound, after falling through a roof onto thick glass, a piece of which remained lodged in her lower abdomen, sticking out like a stalagmite. She'd lost so much blood on the scene externally, and no doubt internally, that a cardiac arrest was inevitable. Aoife knew as the paramedics wheeled her in, and announced that she'd arrested, that it was unlikely they'd get her to theatres, or that she'd survive long enough to attend to the thickened shard of glass.

Resuscitation had its own choreography. The opening was the most important part, the placement of the nurses. Who took charge. Still holding her coffee cup – 'BOSS' – Aoife planted her feet firmly on the floor and shouted. 'I'll lead this. Sophie, you get on the chest. Eden, fetch the crash trolley. Can we get a scan lined up, please?'

Michael was next to her in seconds. She could smell his aftershave, and even in that moment, her heart flipped. 'Want me to lead?' He leant against her arm.

'Nope.' Her voice had hard edges.

'I'll scribe then,' Michael said.

'You do that.' She turned towards the rest of the team. 'Sophie, you continue chest compressions,' Aoife said in a loud, authoritative voice. Even during a cardiac arrest, Aoife wanted to keep him away from Sophie. The nurses looked flustered and flushed. 'Be conscious of hand position – dead centre of the chest – and careful of that glass.' Aoife straightened her back, feeling strangely calm. She was in charge here.

Eden had run back with the crash trolley and pulled out a set of defib pads, which she attached to Della's chest. She hovered uncertainly by the machine, waiting for further instructions.

Aoife noticed the high-flow oxygen set to fifteen litres, at the back of Della's head. She glanced at Michael, somehow looking sweaty and sexy even in this scenario. Sophie was performing chest compressions carefully, dangerously close to the glass sticking out of Della's belly. The air sparked with risk.

Aoife turned to Eden. 'Can you be in charge of the defib?'

Sophie and Michael were absorbed in what they were doing and didn't react, or even seem to hear.

Eden's eyes glinted. She nodded enthusiastically and switched on the machine. She spoke as if she were narrating a primary-school nativity play. 'OK, Sophie, continue chest compressions. Everyone else away from the bed.'

Eden wasn't looking at Della as she should have been but instead over at Aoife. At this point, with anyone else, in any other scenario, Aoife would have physically moved her inexperienced colleague away from the defib and taken over. Sophie was still doing chest compressions with the oxygen mask out near Della's face.

Eden looked so pleased with herself. So confident. So fucking dangerous.

Aoife could see the oxygen blasting out from where she stood, some 10 feet away, the oxygen-filled reservoir bag and the mask attached. Were they stupid? Could they not sense it? She heard the screech of the defib machine indicating that it was fully charged.

Eden had time to sweep her eyes across the whole of Della's bed, check for safety, then shout, 'Oxygen away! Off the chest, Sophie! All clear, shocking.' But she didn't.

Before Eden thought to give any safety instructions to Sophie, Aoife stared at Eden's face, held her eye contact, and quietly and firmly said: 'Shock.'

Eden's finger pressed the red button, a reflex.

A spark, a flash of fire over Della's body, and then the oxygen exploded. Sophie was thrown to the floor by the force.

Nobody moved. 'Start chest compressions,' said Aoife, louder, firmer, but Eden looked from Della to Sophie and back again to Aoife. 'On who?'

Aoife stared down at Sophie and simply stood watching her turn grey and lifeless. Then, she looked at Michael.

TWENTY-SIX
Sophie

'What happened?' Sophie half opened her eyes. Everything hurt. The strip light above was flickering, or perhaps it was her own brain.

Michael was leaning over her. 'Holy fuck,' he said, then he looked up and shouted, 'Get a fucking wheelchair!'

'Wheelchair?' Sophie sat up on her elbows but the blood in her head rushed around, glitchy, somehow. It felt like the time she'd overdone the molly and developed nystagmus, an uncontrollable twitching of her eyes. She lay back down and let her eyes open a fraction more until they settled on one fixed point: Aoife.

Aoife was doing chest compressions on a patient to her right. There was a smell of burning. Eden was crying for help. Alarms, chaos, lights, then screaming. Everything felt soft and dreamy. Sophie tried to focus but her head was cotton wool.

Michael pulled Sophie's arm towards him and pressed his fingertips gently on her wrist. 'Get a monitor, please. Is there a space? Who's getting the chair here, please, people?' He shouted at the air around them, but nobody answered.

Sophie felt a sharp pain in her arms, a thick bone-marrow pain that was too deep and strange. 'What's happening?' But her words were far away, and then it was dark.

*

She woke in a cubicle. The smell of Hibiwash, the sink with plastic aprons rolled up on the wall next to boxes of gloves of different sizes. She was attached to an ECG monitor and a blood-pressure machine, and had a thick cannula in the back of her hand. Someone had cut open her scrub top and it dangled over her chest like a rag.

'Hey. You're back with us, then?' Michael was printing out the ECG and looked at it quickly, before putting the printout down. 'Nothing. All clear. Just a nasty shock, I expect.'

Sophie groaned. The dizziness was gone, and everything was in sharp focus. 'What happened? Did I faint?' But even as the words left her mouth, she remembered. Flashes of memory fired at her. She'd been doing CPR for her patient, Della. Aoife had been in charge of the resuscitation. But Eden had been in charge of the defibrillator.

Eden had shocked Sophie with a defibrillator.

She might have fallen straight onto that shard of glass. She might have gone into cardiac arrest herself. Eden had almost *killed* her. Sweet, sickly Eden, with her shoebox of dead-people memorabilia. The one she was desperate to keep secret.

'How's your head? You fell on the floor with such a crack.' Michael gently touched the back of Sophie's head, then took a pen torch out of his scrub pocket. 'Luckily you weren't impaled by the shard of glass coming out of the patient's stomach. That would have been a very bad day at the office.' He shone a light in each of her eyes. 'Know what date it is?'

Sophie didn't answer for a few moments. She was still processing. Then she shook her head and his hand away. 'Eden tried to kill me.'

Michael laughed but then noticed Sophie's expression. 'Now come on, it was obviously an accident. No harm done as it turns out, and in fact, rarely – if ever – does anyone suffer anything major from a defib shock these days. The pads are too good. In the olden days,' he grinned, 'before you were born, we had all sorts of accidents – doctors mainly, naturally, waving around defib paddles as if they were pom-poms.' He glanced at the monitor. 'BP 125 over 72. You're basically a textbook.'

'That's high for me.'

'Running will fuck your knees.'

Sophie sat up slowly. 'How's the patient?'

'She was still in VF when I left, but I'd say the future doesn't look too bright.'

Sophie's head was suddenly fuzzy again, as if she had spotted an old friend and couldn't remember their name.

Michael frowned. 'I'd better get back. You good to wait here for an hour or so? You can go home with all the usual caveats, and we'll need to do the forms, sadly. Heads will roll.' He paused, and kissed Sophie on the cheek. 'Not just yours.'

She groaned. 'Dad jokes not warranted. I don't need to go home; I'll get changed and go back to work. But Eden needs to check herself. Incompetent and dangerous.' She paused. 'There's a reason they call her the Grim Reaper.'

Michael laughed. 'Go easy on her. We all make mistakes. You'll be fine – a short, sharp shock, that's all. Della has a few burns, though, so that's a headache.'

'What the actual fuck? So a patient in cardiac arrest now with additional burns and a member of staff who received 200 joules of electricity, and you think I should go easy on poor, sweet Eden?' She sat up straighter and swung her legs around the front of the trolley.

Michael reached forwards and put his hand on her chest. It was hot, but she couldn't tell if it was her chest or his hand. He ripped the ECG dots off one by one, quickly and firmly.

'Ouch. Are you enjoying that?'

'Absolutely. I like playing doctors and nurses with you, but doctor and patient is pretty exciting too, don't you think?' Michael let his hand rest on her sternum. He leant closer. 'I can feel your heartbeat.' He looked a bit teary then. 'Thank God you're OK.'

Sophie was sent home by Aoife, who was also shaky and pale following the unsuccessful resuscitation of Della. 'Take tomorrow if you need to. I'm so sorry this happened to you.' She looked detached, dissociated even, and couldn't meet her eyes. When she turned back towards Sophie, her face was wet. 'That poor woman. Three kids.' Aoife reached out and touched Sophie's forearm. 'What a near miss for you.'

Sophie took a slow walk home. She hovered outside the newsagent and contemplated buying cigarettes. Real tobacco. There had been an influx of people in ED with coronary artery disease caused by vaping. But it was as though the electricity had drained her of energy instead of giving it.

The flat was empty. Everyone was on days at the moment except Ben, who had gone to Prague for a stag do, after giving himself a preventative shot of prophylactic antibiotic. 'Nobody more riddled with sexually transmitted diseases than supposedly straight men.'

Sophie picked up her mobile and waited for the call to connect. 'Gee, it's me. Can you chat?'

'Always, love. I'm sorting through some photos. There's one of you here in a mood – you must be fifteen. I can't remember where it was taken but you have that devil look in your eyes. Anyway, how are you? How's work? They really do work you too hard.'

'Ah, it's OK, but I did have a rough day today.' Sophie took a breath and suddenly felt very small. Her body folded over.

'Gee.' She let the tears fall out, just a few, then tried to make her face hard and expressionless once more.

Gee breathed heavily on the other end and Sophie heard the radio click to silent, and the sound of the Isle of Man wind. She listened to Sophie trying not to cry for a few moments, then cleared her throat. Gee was a woman of few words; she always told Sophie that most people spoke absolute horseshit, and she was glad to be partially deaf, but she always put her hearing aids on full when Sophie phoned. The sound system adjusting to the microphone squeaked out now and then. 'I'm here.'

Sophie told her what had happened, all of it.

'Well. I don't believe in accidents, as you know,' Gee said.

It was true that Gee was the most superstitious person in the world, and although she didn't believe in accidents, she believed in many things. Never walk under a ladder; don't put new shoes on the table; never, ever break a mirror; if you hear three thuds in the night, there will be a death in the house, and the thing Gee always reminded Sophie: never trust anyone who tells you they are trustworthy. 'In which case, she literally tried to kill me.'

'Maybe not kill you. Just maim you a bit.' Gee's voice was gentle.

Sophie was silent for a few moments, before they both began to laugh hysterically. Gee always knew what to say. Always.

Eden was home first, rushing in and dropping her rucksack on the sofa, then almost running towards Sophie. Her face was blotchy and red, anxious. 'Sophie, I am so, so, so, so sorry. I can't believe it. How are you? Can you forgive me? My God, I thought I'd killed you. Can I get you anything? How are you feeling?' She reached her arms out towards Sophie.

Sophie shrugged and sat on the sofa. 'Calm down.'

Eden sat next to her. 'It was my first time doing the defib and, honestly, I was surprised I was allowed. Honestly, I don't know what I was thinking. I've done the online training, but that's it. Then Aoife said I could do it and I suppose it gave me some sort of false confidence or something. Sophie, I'm just so sorry.' She stopped talking a moment, took a breath.

Sophie studied her face. Eden wore her heart on her sleeve and was genuinely distraught. 'Why did you agree to do it if you aren't trained?' Sophie asked the question knowing full well she did plenty of things she wasn't officially trained to do. All nurses did.

Eden welled up, chewed the side of her fingernail. 'It was a sort of automatic response. I mean, Aoife said I'd be OK to do it, and you were doing chest compressions. Oh my God, that woman, Della. It's all my fault. She had flash burns over her legs. I'll be struck off and I fucking deserve it.'

Sophie awkwardly patted Eden's knee. 'The patient didn't die because of you. She was already dead, remember?'

Eden sobbed. 'When Aoife said "shock", I didn't look, and I didn't look at you or tell you to get off the chest or do the last safety checks. Oh God, I didn't say oxygen away. I just did it.'

'Wait.' Sophie sat upright. Her head still felt foggy with the memory of before she'd woken on the floor of ED, with Michael above her. She remembered doing chest compressions. She remembered the bead of sweat that was falling down her cheek with the force of it all. She remembered Della's face in cardiac arrest, a cartoon face, two-dimensional, the spear of glass still sticking out of her abdomen, a short distance from Sophie's hands. Everything came flooding back. 'Wait,' Sophie said again. She stared at Eden. 'Did you say that *Aoife* said "shock"? While I was still doing chest compressions? With that oxygen blowing out towards me? Aoife told you to shock?'

'Yes. She must have made a mistake and been distracted or something. She told me to shock, before it was safe. But that was my responsibility as the person in charge of the defib. I don't know why I agreed, I should never have—'

Sophie put her hand on the small of Eden's back to silence her. Then she turned to Eden's face. 'Aoife doesn't make mistakes,' she said.

TWENTY-SEVEN
Eden

They sat up talking until late, piecing together the events.

'She definitely told you to shock?' Sophie asked again. 'While I was on the patient's chest?'

'One hundred per cent. She knew I hadn't really been trained for the defib. I thought it was odd, her allocating that task to me. I mean, Aoife is always so careful about everything. I don't get it.'

They lay on Eden's bed, a tray of snacks between them: hummus and peppers, cheese and celery sticks. Eden had popped out to M&S Food, chucked anything she imagined Sophie liking into a basket. Eden's room was stuffy, even with the window slightly open, but it was always tidier than Sophie's. Her black nurse's shoes were the only things not put away.

Sophie leant up on one elbow. 'Fucking Michael. He's obsessed with me, naturally, so much so he felt compelled to tell Aoife. Honestly, what's up with men? And she's in love with him. Clearly.' She lay back down and slapped her forehead.

Eden sat up cross-legged. 'Oh – my – God.'

'Are my eyes flicking a bit?' Sophie stared at Eden. 'I've a banging headache, too. If I've got nerve damage, I'll sue and get myself a one-way ticket to Mexico City.'

Eden was quiet then. She started scratching her neck.

Sophie lowered her voice. 'They've been shagging for a decade, you know? Michael and Aoife.'

She told Eden everything Michael had revealed about his long-standing affair with Aoife. Eden's heart thumped faster. 'I knew they were together. I mean, I saw them disappear into a cupboard when we first started at City. Maybe I should have told you, but honestly, I had no idea she would try to purposefully hurt you. Or get me to, anyway.'

Aoife was off sick again the next day. 'Clearly having a bad run of things, what with norovirus and now a migraine. Poor Aoife,' Mary said. 'But it's left you girls a bit short again, I'm afraid.' She handed Sophie the large black diary. 'Someone in their wisdom has ripped a few pages out of this, despite it being our holy book, so I've re-written the door codes at the back. Right, girls, I'm over and out.' She nodded and walked off.

Eden watched Sophie's face. A flicker of something shadowed her eyes. Guilt? Tiredness? Anger? She was still so hard to read.

'Can you manage Resus on your own for an hour? I'm sorry about that, Eden, but the agency cover has yet to turn up.'

'It's fine,' said Eden. She stretched her arms up and to each side, as if getting ready for a race. 'It'll be fine.'

It wasn't fine at all. She looked around the Resus area, the chaos, the alarms, the lack of staff and the number of critically ill patients in the bay and cubicles beyond, and thought about the Nurses' Code: *13: Recognise and work within the limits of your competence.* Who'd be competent managing this? Aoife flashed into her mind, but she pushed the image away. Aoife wasn't there. And Aoife wasn't who Eden thought she was.

'Help me, help me, nurse!' Eden spun around, recognising the frail voice. Ivy, a patient she had looked after months before, was lying on a bed in bay three, white as the sheet covering her.

Eden rushed over. 'Ivy! What are you doing back here?'

She opened her eyes and grimaced in pain. 'Hello, love. I don't mean to bother you.'

Eden lifted Ivy's hand. She was even thinner than before, paler and frailer. 'You're freezing.'

'I was outside all night,' she said. 'Stupid woman. I knew not to wear my slippers, Matthew always told me that.'

Obi walked past, pushing a trolley. 'Hi, Ivy.' He stopped at the end of the bed and opened his eyes wide to draw Eden closer.

She placed Ivy's hand down and walked over to him. 'Any chance you can get Ivy's morphine?' Eden said. 'She has a fractured neck of femur after a fall, poor thing.'

Obi didn't answer but smiled at Ivy, who somehow, despite the horrific pain, smiled back. Then he pulled Eden to the nurses' station, where the phone hadn't stopped ringing since they'd arrived. 'I haven't called security,' he said, 'as they're maxed out. But there's a patient in cubicle four awaiting theatre who just called me the N word and said he'd rather die than be treated by me. So that's a nice start to the day.' Obi rolled his eyes.

'Oh my God. I'm so sorry, Obi. Are you OK?'

'I'm fine. Fucking fascist twat – hope he does die. To be fair, it's looking likely; his systolic is ninety despite a second blood transfusion.'

Eden put her hand on Obi's. 'It's not right. We should phone the police.'

Obi laughed. 'Sweet Eden. In any case, I'm not stitching him up. He can fuck right off. He's a suspected abdominal aneurism so he's not long for this earth, I reckon.'

Eden nodded. 'Right, let me know if Majors has any magic extra staff floating around. You're busy enough. I'm going to get Ivy's morphine, and if that guy does leave, call security.'

They both looked over to Ivy, who had her head tipped back a bit and was breathing heavily, clutching her hip. Eden hurried off.

By noon she felt numb. Ivy was crying in pain – Eden still hadn't managed to check out the morphine, and the theatres were dealing with a brain bleed, so had bumped Ivy to the following day. It crushed Eden's heart every time she ran past Ivy to the next emergency, cardiac arrest after cardiac arrest.

'Eden, quickly!'

'Nurse! Who's the nurse in charge here! Help, please!'

Eden's head filled with desperate voices until it felt like it would explode. Ivy's crying throbbed inside her. She walked at speed to the clean utility room, to find Sophie running a saline drip through a three-way tap.

Sophie looked up. 'Oh, hey, how's tricks?'

Eden burst into tears. 'I can't do it,' she said. 'I can't do this job. It's too much, all of it. Who can work like this? Ivy is about a hundred years old and has a broken hip and is crying out there, covered in urine and faeces and sobbing. She's in pain with zero dignity because I haven't had a minute to breathe. And in cubicles, a man – Gary Kennedy, that guy whose head I accidentally stuck my hand to, so he's going to go ballistic when he sees me – is racially abusing staff again, and *he* still gets treatment and this is not why I became a nurse. I can't – I just can't do this . . .'

Sophie put the saline down and turned to face Eden. Eden thought for a moment that Sophie was about to hug her but instead, Sophie slapped her, hard, on the cheek. 'You're hysterical,' she said. 'Stop.'

The shock had Eden bending over the sideboard. 'What? Why did you hit me?' She touched her stinging cheek.

Sophie shrugged. 'Right. Let's get Ivy some morphine, and sort this day out.'

Eden blinked a few moments and then nodded. 'Thank you,' she said. 'I think. That hurt, though.'

'Not as badly as a defib shock,' said Sophie as she reached into her pocket and took out the keys to the controlled drugs cupboard.

They checked out the morphine and walked back over to Ivy, but the emergency alarm from cubicles screeched out. Sophie grabbed Eden's arm and pulled her in.

Gary Kennedy was moribund. Eden stared at him, a large man, instantly recognisable with his port-wine birthmark. His eyes were rolled back but he was breathing and groaning. There was a blood transfusion hooked up to his arm, half full, still going in. 'Think he's taken something?' His monitors were alarming, his blood pressure dangerously low. 'Shall I get the crash trolley? He's got an aortic aneurism, apparently, so probably the highest-risk patient we've got in here at the moment. Crash call? Get the team in here? Or we could wheel him straight to theatres and fast-bleep the surgeons?'

Sophie shook her head. 'Nah, go back to Ivy. She deserves all our care and attention.'

'What if he arrests? That BP?'

Sophie looked at Eden and smiled. 'What if he does?' She reached over and touched Eden's cheek where she'd slapped her. 'You're a good nurse, Eden. Today's a bit shit, that's all. Go give Ivy her pain relief, then come back here. I'll sort this out.'

*

Eden knew exactly what she had to do. She was no longer Team Aoife, and she'd tell her so. She hated confrontation, but her new friendship with Sophie gave her the courage she needed. Aoife needed to explain herself. If Sophie had fallen on Della when she'd shocked her, when *Aoife had made Eden shock her*, she'd be dead. The thought of it chilled Eden to the bone.

She looked up Aoife's address – easy to find in the old-fashioned birthday and address book that Aoife still kept in the office top drawer: *65 Lobrake Road, Catford SE13 4TY*. She made sure to leave on time and got the bus straight there. No way was Aoife sick; she knew exactly what she'd done. Eden would tell Aoife that she had to report herself to the NMC. Time to speak truth to power. If Eden was investigated for accidentally defibrillating a colleague, then what else would they try to blame her for? Murdering patients?

As for hurting Sophie, Eden felt sick about that. Sophie was brittle and could take things too far, but she was also a brilliant nurse. Everything had shifted at once. Sophie was Eden's friend, and Eden would do anything to protect her friends.

The mid-terrace house had a neat front garden and there was an olive tree in a pot so giant it would be difficult to steal. The front door was painted red and had a bird-shaped knocker and one of those video-camera doorbells. Eden ignored it and hammered on the front door with her fist.

The lights flicked on. Aoife's husband, Sam, stood in the doorway. They'd only met once before, when he'd turned up to surprise Aoife at work.

'Oh, hi.' Sam smiled. He clearly recognised Eden but couldn't place her.

'Eden. I work with Aoife. Last time we met I was rushing around ED while you waited for her . . .'

Sam smiled. 'That's it. I'm sorry, but Aoife is still at work. She said she's staying late today; it's all kicked off in Resus.'

Eden stared at Sam's soft face. The face of a man who trusted his wife. 'She's not at work,' Eden said. 'I really need to speak with her. Can I come in and wait?'

Sam frowned, clearly confused, but he beckoned Eden in and they walked through to the kitchen, then sat at the table. 'Do you want a tea?'

'No, thank you.' Eden's eyes scanned Aoife's kitchen, which was exactly as she'd imagined it would be, right down to the fridge magnets clearly collected from various holidays over the years. A large wall clock, a kitchen-roll dispenser, spotlessly clean surfaces. Eden looked at Sam. He had gone a bit pale.

It made her even more angry with Aoife. He didn't deserve this. None of them did. 'I wanted to talk to Aoife, but perhaps I actually need to talk to you.' This man had every right to know who he was married to. Eden knew the Code of Professional Conduct by heart. Aoife had violated it. *13.3 Ask for help from a suitably qualified and experienced professional to carry out any action or procedure that is beyond the limits of your competence.* 'She's not been at work today. She's lying to you.' *She's lying to all of us.*

Sam sighed. 'I wish I was more surprised. I've been sick with worry lately.'

Eden thought of Sophie thrown to the floor after she'd shocked her and was ready to tell Sam about the defibrillator, and perhaps even about Michael. But he had already disappeared into another room, trying to call Aoife.

He came back holding a crumpled piece of paper.

'It's been like living with a stranger these last weeks. She hasn't slept. She's so anxious and jumpy. Not herself at all. I've been so worried about her mental health. Then I find this.'

He waved the paper in front of Eden. She couldn't properly see what it was, but then she recognised the lined paper from the black diary at work. One of the missing pages. 'What's on it?'

'I hid it in my sock drawer, thinking – oh God, I don't know. I didn't mention it to Aoife or ask her about it, and I'm sure it's nothing, but I can't figure out why she'd write such a thing. I do know she'd *never* hurt anyone, but it's like she's irrational at the moment, you know? Losing her mind a bit. Menopause, maybe. I mean, my sister was the same. But this . . .' He waved the paper around, then slammed it onto the kitchen table. 'Maybe she needs anti-depressants.'

Eden glanced at the paper in front of her. A list.

'You don't know where she is?' he asked. 'I mean, she's depressed, that's for sure, but to lie about going to work? It's totally out of character.' He picked up the phone again and dialled, holding it close to his ear. 'Aoife, love, it's me again. I've got Eden here. Just let me know you're OK. Call me back?'

He carried on speaking as Eden stared at Aoife's handwriting. She read every word. Then she read them again. When Sam walked out, leaving another desperate message for Aoife, Eden took out her own phone and took a photograph of the list:

Ways to Kill a Patient

Drug error: NB nanograms/micrograms look similar
Omit basic patient observations
Do not escalate deterioration
Administer known allergen
Dislodge endotracheal tube
Paralysis before/in absence of sedation
Potassium in infusion
Unplug haemofiltration/ventilator
Air/blood/fluid in arterial line

Lack of oxygen – empty cylinder
Insulin/morphine overdose
Turn off/speed up infusion pump
Give intramuscular drug intravenously
Contaminated blood/drugs
Non-sterile/bad aseptic technique
Equipment failure
Misreported scans
Badly managed resuscitation

Allocate the patient the worst nurse on the unit

TWENTY-EIGHT
Aoife

Aoife spent the entire day crying and eating Maltesers in an almost empty cinema in Leicester Square. It was the kind of overpriced multiplex that only tourists visited, a good hiding place. Nobody noticed her, or spoke to her, not even when she bought a ticket for the third film in a row. She'd chosen action films that she figured would be loud enough to cover her sobs.

She had tried to kill Sophie. Worse, she had got Eden to do it.

Aoife replayed the scene in her head, imagining Sophie shocked, thrown heart-first onto a piece of glass. She'd tried to take them both down in one fell swoop, and in doing so committed the ultimate sin: to hurt another nurse. Two of them. Two birds with one stone.

She had no idea who she was anymore. She was no longer Aoife, senior sister, City ED, lifesaver, trusted colleague, beloved confidante. She was a crazy old woman who belonged in prison.

She drank another large 7UP, then vomited in the toilets and left well after dark. When she arrived home, Sam was still awake, pacing up and down.

He rushed towards her, almost knocking her over. 'Oh my God. Didn't you switch your phone on? I've been out of my mind with worry. Bloody hell, Aoife, I was moments from calling the police.'

She put her bag down, disentangled herself from Sam and undid her coat. 'What's the issue? I told you I was going to be late. My phone's lost charge, that's all.' But her voice shook.

Sam held Aoife's arms by her sides. He looked at her and into her, in the way only he could. 'I know,' he said.

Aoife felt the ground beneath her fall away. 'What are you talking about?'

He took her hand and led her to the kitchen. 'James is staying out tonight, which is lucky because Eden has just left.'

'Eden?' Aoife's head spun. 'Eden was here? Work Eden?'

Sam turned and looked at Aoife. 'Yes.'

They were silent for a few moments. The clock ticked on the kitchen wall. What had Eden been doing here? What had she said?

Sam sat opposite her and held her hands across the table. 'I've been so worried about you.'

'I'm sorry,' whispered Aoife. She looked at Sam. Her husband. She had fucked up her life, and his too. 'I'm sorry.' She waited for him to say the words that Eden must have told him. That Aoife and Michael had been having an affair. That Aoife had intentionally tried to get Eden to defibrillate Sophie. That Aoife was so jealous of Sophie she could barely stand upright and wanted her dead. But Sam didn't say any of that.

'You've been so distant these last weeks and now lying about being at work.' He took something from his pocket and unfolded it. 'I found this, Aoife. What is going on? I'm really very worried.'

Aoife held her breath, expecting him to say Michael's name, and hear her whole marriage come crashing down around them.

But he didn't. He just placed the paper on the table between them. Her handwriting. That awful list.

*

'Here's what's going to happen.' Sophie and Aoife sat side by side on a trolley in the back of an empty ambulance. Claire and another paramedic had let them in, giving Sophie a knowing look. 'We'll let you guys chat,' Claire said. 'Probably the most private place you can be at the moment.'

Aoife felt sick. Did everyone know what she'd done?

Sophie swung round to face Aoife. 'You are going to take a sabbatical. A nice long break, because frankly this job is getting to you.'

Aoife almost laughed but stopped herself. Sophie was a powerful young woman, but she was no match for Aoife, even now. 'Who'll run this place if I'm not around? You?'

Sophie didn't even raise a smile; she simply nodded. 'Acting sister. I've spoken to Denise already.'

Aoife should have felt nothing but guilt, but still, there was anger bubbling up inside her. 'Oh, that's rich. Denise is well aware that the death rate is up since *you* arrived on the scene. All eyes are on you, Sophie. You think they'll promote you?' Aoife leant forwards. 'I *know* you told Eden about me and Michael.'

Sophie smirked. 'It's the worst-kept secret on ED. She knew forever ago. And, honestly, I couldn't give a flying fuck who you sleep with. But I do care that you tried to kill me.'

The words floated in the chlorine-scented air.

'I know about your "How to Kill a Patient" list. Given the recent events on ED, I'd say it's pretty damning. Wouldn't you?' She took out her phone and flashed it in front of Aoife. A photograph of Aoife's handwriting on the torn-out page. 'Evidence.' The ambulance was suddenly a cage. Sophie stared, unblinking.

Aoife could barely catch her breath. It wouldn't matter what she said, or if she was believed or not. That the ED had unexplained deaths and she'd written such a list would be the end of her nursing career, her life.

'Like I told Sam, I jotted that list down because of *you*. I wanted to get into your head.' A large tear dropped down her cheek. 'I wanted to know what was happening with my patients. I would never, ever hurt a patient.' She watched Sophie cock her head to one side, as if summing up Aoife's face. Aoife waited for her to smirk, or spit at her, or dial the police and report her then and there.

'I'd never hurt a patient. Ever,' Aoife said again.

'I believe you.' Sophie shrugged. 'But thousands wouldn't. *Juries* wouldn't.'

Aoife's chest felt tight. They had too much on her. Sophie and Eden held her life in their hands.

Sophie looked at the chair next to the trolley they were sitting on. 'I did a transfer once. We had to collect this kid from Leeds, so I slept on the way. Ambulance stopped and collected this old guy in a high-vis jacket, bright orange, pretty nasty cut on his head. We had a little chat, and I must have dozed off again – late night and that. Anyway, when I woke up, he had vanished. I asked the paramedics about him, and they got me to describe him. They went a bit pale and sick-looking. Apparently, the man I'd described had died in the ambulance the day before.' Sophie sighed and then smiled. 'I literally see dead people now.'

Aoife frowned. Why was Sophie telling her this story?

Sophie tipped her head back and exhaled. 'Fuck. This job. Makes you fucking crazy.' She sat up and looked at Aoife, leant in. 'There's no need for the NMC to know about any of this. There's no need for this list to ever see the light of day. Just take a sabbatical.'

*

The last day of any person leaving ED usually meant hurried cake in the staff room and a large card passed around. If they'd been there a long time, there would be a whip-round, and a John Lewis voucher presented to the leaver. Aoife was part of the furniture, so there was no sneaking off quietly, even though she'd only be gone for six months. They'd hired out the boardroom and posted flyers. From 3 p.m. until 4 p.m., when they hoped ED would be quiet enough, she stood greeting colleagues from all areas of the hospital. The long table was filled with snacks, tubs of flapjacks and rocky roads, and small glasses of Shloer. It was like a children's birthday party. Aoife had spent the night awake, heart thumping with anxiety, and was convinced she'd fall apart, but when it came down to it there was relief. She was bone tired and burnt out and crazy; she had tried to harm her colleague. Perhaps it was the decades of deceit. The affair that had lasted too long. She was ready for a new chapter. Her and Sam.

Nursing was like the mafia: nobody ever really left. But the world outside had suddenly become not only possible, but hopeful. There was life on the other side of the fence. A wholesome, less extreme, less fucked-up life.

'No vol-au-vents?' Sophie stood in front of Aoife, holding a paper plate full of cakes. She wore the usual dark-blue scrubs but had a new name badge: 'Acting Sister'.

Aoife nodded at it. 'I've put in a good word to make that permanent. Not that you need it. I'm sorry, Sophie. Hell hath no fury, and all that. I've loved him a long time, you know?'

Sophie popped a square of rocky road in her mouth and chewed. Then she shrugged. 'No hard feelings. I mean, I Jolened the fuck out of you, and you tried to end me.' She put the plate down on the side. 'I respect that.'

Aoife laughed. This was the future of the NHS. Six months ago, that thought had filled her with terror, but perhaps the

Sophies of the world were the saviours of the NHS. It needed a few more badasses like her. 'Michael's a good man. She'd seen him once since all this, just once. He'd hugged her tightly, and she'd whispered *sorry* in his ear, and that was that.

'He's totally fine. Says he's off women for good and he's taken up pickleball, apparently. He'll get over me, and he'll get over you too. I have less than zero interest; it was supposed to be fun, that's all. I'm not sure he'll cope without you being in charge at work, though. He could probably do with early retirement.'

They were both quiet for a moment, imagining Michael without his job. It was impossible.

Sophie looked around the room and Aoife followed her gaze. The room was full; staff had even come in on their days off to wish Aoife well. Quite a few managers had also turned up – Denise, for one – as well as the cleaning staff, the healthcare assistants, the porters. Aoife was loved by many. By most.

'They asked me to consider early retirement.' She nodded at the HR team, and Denise. 'After the defib incident. The patient's family wanted to sue the hospital and were claiming negligence during the arrest, which I guess it was, really.'

'I know,' said Sophie. 'They've had me in for meetings.' She took Aoife's hand and squeezed it. 'I told them that they had it all wrong. It was Eden's responsibility to be in charge of the defib, and if she wasn't trained to do so, that was on them.' Sophie stepped towards her. She lowered her voice, her eyes glistening. 'Someone is killing patients, though.'

Aoife shook her head. 'I don't believe that. I mean, who would do that? I only suspected you because I was mad with jealousy. And with this job. A nurse intentionally killing patients? Not on my watch. Not at City.'

She glanced back at Sophie. She was smiling.

TWENTY-NINE

Eden

Making kites wasn't as easy as you'd imagine. Despite the dust sheets on the floor, Eden had managed to get paint on the carpet. 'END CHILD LABOUR' was painted in red, for added effect, onto the purple paper kite that she planned to fly as soon as the wind picked up. The kite-flying had begun as a local community project, with an anti-war display. A dozen or so young women in the local area gathered in Ruskin Park near the bandstand, carrying pro-Palestinian signs and flags. Someone set up a speaker playing some music that a woman said was Moroccan and had nothing to do with Palestine, and they'd had a small argument among them as to authenticity and appropriation. Eden ignored them and concentrated on the loudspeaker. They wanted the biggest impact and to attract the local press. She had sent emails to all the news channels, and to the hospital media and communications department, but nobody had got back to her. Activism was not easy. If it was, surely everyone would do it? A bit like nursing.

'Hear ye, hear ye,' she said, the loudspeaker squawking into action. Nobody laughed. 'Right, I'm Eden and we all know why we're here.'

People clicked their fingers at her. She looked around at the group. 'We are here to demonstrate peacefully and with power about the disgusting practice of child labour. We must not let this archaic business continue. Let us lift our kites and our hearts to the sky and get the attention of the world.' She paused. A man to her left was picking his nose. Eden ignored him and lifted a finger in the air. 'Wind is coming from the east,' she said. 'Let's go.' She ran towards the middle of the park, throwing her kite out behind her and waiting for the wind to catch it.

It was a good distraction from work, and all that was going on. After they'd flown the kites for an hour or two and sung some protest song that a woman with a ukulele had taught them, they folded their kites away and collected the aluminium water bottles in a pile at the centre.

Eden arrived home to a quiet flat and made a matcha tea. She couldn't get enough of the stuff but monitored her intake carefully. Her kombucha phase had led to severe diarrhoea. The cup was steaming hot, and she stood blowing on it, looking out. The windows of Rose Cottage were filthy. Sophie wandered in and stood behind Eden. 'Hey, you,' she said.

Eden sipped the tea and watched Sophie stretch, like a cat.

'There's a senior staff nurse position coming up. Mine.' Sophie reached out, taking the cup from Eden's hands and setting it down on the rickety coffee table. She stood close to Eden. She wore shorts pyjamas with small stripes on them, and still had yesterday's make-up on; a line of mascara blurred on her eyelids. Eden could smell Sophie's breath – minty, and a bit sour: cup of tea after brushing breath. 'I think you should go for it.'

Eden walked through the ED staring straight ahead, avoiding eye contact. She strode past the frail-looking man trying to reach water from the cooler. She held her large coffee in front of her like a shield and marched on, all the way to Minors. There was nobody else there, bar a student nurse and an HCA, and a room full of angry punters. Eden had developed a way of closing her ears a fraction, only to fully open them, and hear effectively, if there was a serious problem, a kind of internal communication triage. A defence mechanism.

She looked around the waiting area, where all the chairs were full of people clearly in pain, fed up, anxious or all three, and others were lining the wall, leaning their heads back and staring vacantly at the television screen that was bolted to the wall lest anyone try to nick it. There were patients on the floor too, as always, sitting on coats or bags, hunched over, open-mouthed. The air was thick and the room musty; it smelt of BO no matter how often it was cleaned, and it was too hot. Despite that, people kept their coats on, year-round – a comfort of sorts, she suspected. Eden glanced around the room, mentally calculating how busy her day might be, then disappeared to the nurses' station. She opened the computer and scanned the triage admission details.

'Another day, another dollar.' Phoebe was smiling. She had a rainbow lanyard, and a Disney name badge. Her hair was tied up in a glittery scrunchie. 'Shall I do some waiting-room obs?'

Eden could almost smell the eagerness coming from her skin. Her face was clear and her eyes bright. Eden wondered how long it would take for ED to break her spirit into something more real. Not long. 'Sure. And tell anyone who asks that the current wait time is about eighteen hours, in case they want to go home.' She knew she was sending Phoebe to the wolves. Patients were waiting in pain, for too long, despite their best efforts, but there was no sugar-coating the situation. ED was creaking like a boat about to sink, beyond capacity. It wasn't the nurses' fault, and it wasn't the patients' fault.

Michael ran past, dishevelled and late. His skin was waxy and puffy, and he smelt of whisky. He hadn't been the same since Aoife had left. Things on ED had never been this bad, he kept repeating. But on they went.

Eden's bedroom was always organised, unlike the others'. Her bedspread was arranged neatly, with hospital corners, every morning. Her pillows were symmetrical and in order of colour coordination. She had a desk upon which were textbooks: *Advanced Life Support*, *Gray's Anatomy*, the *British National Formulary*, *Immediate Life Support*, *Oxford Handbook of Emergency Nursing*. She had pot after pot of coloured highlighter pens, and a board above the desk with carefully arranged pins, and postcards from various places she'd visited: Canada, Bali, Santorini, Costa Rica. Next to her bed, her copies of *A Little Life*. There was another book under her bed too, now. A large, heavy book, full of prayer requests and funeral details. The saddest book you'll ever read.

Eden liked to read it with Sophie. 'Compassion is overrated,' she'd once told Eden, 'when your head is hanging off your spine.' Eden looked at her postcards and briefly wondered what it would be like to go travelling with Sophie. Or even to become more than friends. She climbed on her chair and reached up to the back of her wardrobe for the now-locked container she kept there. She took the key from her pocket and unlocked it, taking out the items she'd been storing one by one. Nora's headscarf. Jocelyn's photo. A tiny lock of hair. Beryl's blood bottles, now rust-coloured and solid. Eden let her face swell with tears and the pain sink into her chest, right above her ribs. She leafed through the printouts of results, numbers that had been meaningless to her but now she understood. A pH 6.9, incompatible with life. A list of blood tests that she had performed, sometimes, after her patients had died. A final look at what can happen inside a human body when their soul has flown out of the window.

Maybe she was weird, but these small items reminded her of the gravity of their job, the enormity of what nursing meant. It was a strange privilege to nurse, to be there at the most intimate or significant moments of a stranger's life and to sit with another human's pain. She carried the weight of it around with her.

She thought back to the time when she'd cared for a woman with meningococcal disease and had been given rifampicin that had made her cry red tears. Michael rarely spoke to her, but after that he'd explained something about the nature of that illness. 'The antibiotic kills the bacteria,' he'd said, 'in this case the meningococcal bug. But it doesn't simply make the bug evaporate. It breaks it up into tiny, tiny particles, and those particles whizz around the body and get stuck in organs, so you get multi-organ failure. You have to give the antibiotic, or the patient will surely die, but the disease has to go somewhere, so the particles remain – and they do serious damage.'

She could nurse a patient and take some of their suffering away, but she'd have to swallow that suffering, and it would soon clog up her own body. The price of love is grief. The cost of loving strangers is much more complex. All nurses cry red tears.

THIRTY
Sophie

Sophie was still sleeping post night duty when Obi shouted from the kitchen. At first, Sophie half dreamt she was hearing a tropical bird, then he hammered on the bedroom door, almost knocking it open. 'Soph, get up quickly. Like now.'

She sat bolt upright and stood up, stretching. 'What? OK, coming.'

She put on her dressing gown, and walked out to find Rhian, who was also emerging from her bedroom, bleary-eyed and confused. 'What's happening? It's like 3 a.m.'

Sophie shrugged. 'Beats me, but it better be good.' She followed Rhian to the kitchen, where Obi had the television on loud. He shushed them both.

'Breaking news – we can now confirm multiple casualties following a series of large explosions at a factory in South London. We are receiving reports of possible arson, but these are so far unconfirmed, and we will of course bring you more details as they unfold. A spokesperson for Performance Manufacturing – which produces tyres and other materials – has confirmed the presence of multiple acetylene cylinders, a highly flammable gas.'

'Fuckadoodle.' Rhian clapped her hand over her mouth.

Obi switched on the main lights and opened the curtains. It was pitch black outside. Nothing was moving; in the near distance was a warm glow, and smoke rising against the inky dark blue.

'Well,' said Sophie. 'I guess we'd better get dressed.' The others stared at her, but then ran back to their respective bedrooms to chuck clothes on.

They were all out the door in minutes, running towards the danger.

The hospital was a hive of activity. Ambulances lined the entrance, and on the other side of the road, media vans and a cluster of women and men with large spongy microphones and film crews. Sophie swiped her ID and pushed open the doors to ED, where the sound of alarms, sirens and screaming was at fever pitch. Michael was standing in front of a group of police officers, who he waved out of the way, almost running to Sophie. 'Major incident and mass casualties. We're above capacity already; Guy's and Tommies are taking overflow. They're estimating dozens of seriously injured, many more with shrapnel injuries. Four dead on the scene already.' He was in automatic mode, Sophie could tell. He spoke in a clear and calm voice, as if talking about something inconsequential, as a man with serious wounds was pushed past them on a trolley. They breathed in and ignored the smell of burning flesh.

'Right.' Sophie turned to Rhian. 'Get everyone in here. All leave, days off, holidays, sick days cancelled. Let's gown up.'

Rhian ran off towards the phones. They were all still dressed in jeans and hoodies. Sophie grabbed a few plastic aprons, put one on and passed one to Obi. 'Divert anyone and everyone who isn't trying very hard to die. You can act as HALO, please. Liaise with the ambulance teams. Where the fuck is Eden? Michael, see you in Resus. I'll chuck scrubs on.' She paused. 'Get all the FYs in – I don't care if they're drunk or getting married; we need bums on seats. And call Aoife in, please . . .'

Michael glanced at her. He nodded a fraction, then ran towards Resus.

Sophie took a moment in the staff changing room, while getting into scrubs at speed, to close her eyes and breathe. She tried to imagine Gee's voice in her head and arms around her shoulders. *It will all be OK in the end. And if it's not OK, it's not the end.*

Eden poked her head around the door and stared at Sophie, blinking back tears. 'Soph.'

'Let's walk.' She took Eden's arm, and they walked quickly past the cubicles where patients who were already in ED, sick enough, were anxiously peering out. 'Help me,' a man said. They ignored him. What else could they do? 'I know. Can you set up a discharge area in Minors? Get the chaplain or imam in, whoever is around. You'll need to deal with the media too, and the mantra is: we don't have information yet but are working as hard as we can. Give bad news to whoever needs to hear it and ship them out. We don't want relatives of dead people clogging up the hallways.'

Eden made a sobbing noise but didn't comment. It sounded cruel, what Sophie was saying, but it was reality and they both knew it. Major-incident and mass-casualty training was not something anyone took lightly anymore, not after terrorist attacks and nail bombs and chemical warfare and mass stabbings. Like all healthcare workers, they understood that this day was a possibility. This day could be any day.

'Crowd control,' said Eden. 'I'll get right on it.' She pressed her hands on the outsides of Sophie's shoulders. 'You've got this,' she whispered.

*

Sophie ran into Resus to find the bedspaces doubled up with people, doctors and nurses flying around each other, squeezing in blood transfusions, portable X-ray machines, doing cardiac compressions. The patients were all unconscious and some clearly dead: bits of them had been blown off. A few people were unidentifiable, and there was a body on the floor, half covered with a plastic sheet, only a torso, neck and bloody face visible. Someone had pushed the deceased to the edge of the room, leaving a large streak of blood. There was blood everywhere and, worse, pieces of flesh on the floor. Sophie stepped over a pile of what looked like intestines in a large sharps bucket. Everyone was shouting, but there was no closed-loop communication going on. People cried out to the air, as if the help they needed might magically appear:

'We need a pelvic binder!'

'Get neurosurgery down here now!'

'Thoracotomy kit.'

'Massive haemorrhage protocol. Porters need to bring eight units of packed cells.'

'Where's the bear-hugger?'

'Lorazepam. Get the fucking lorazepam.'

All niceties had left the building. Sophie opened the small filing cabinet at the 'Trauma' drawer and took out a patient summary sheet, a tick box of columns, one for each patient, with rows for name, hospital number and then a quick assessment of injuries: abdominal trauma, closed fracture, maxillofacial trauma, spinal-cord injury. She thought back to her major-incident training, and how they'd been told that if they were lucky, they'd never have to use it during their entire career. *Triage: if they're walking, get 'em out; if they're clearly dead or thereabouts, leave them until there is time to declare it; if not breathing, just assume dead – don't hang around to assess; if they have injuries that are compatible with life, and they are breathing, think haemorrhage and high priority for intervention, then run through ABCDE.*

She turned around. The team doing cardiac compressions on the person in bed three had stopped and covered the patient with a sheet. Michael was running out into the corridor as a paramedic pushed in another patient who looked as if they'd been barbecued.

Sophie stood still in the centre of it all. Her heart boomed inside her, skipping beats, and her legs wobbled. She had to swallow hard lest she throw up. She felt human.

Suddenly, a body beside her, a voice, and someone holding her hand. Aoife.

She was wearing a rain jacket over pyjamas. 'Who has time to get dressed these days?' she said.

Somehow, Sophie smiled. Michael walked back in, and Sophie watched his face almost melt in relief, then immediately scrunch up again.

This was too much.

But it was not too much for Aoife. 'Having fun in the sun, I see?' She turned to Sophie. 'Deep breaths. Right, Sophie, I'm going to get changed and you can be the crowd control. See you in a jiffy.'

After Aoife had run towards the changing room, Sophie felt a shift in the impossible air. She scanned the flesh and blood and bones around her and heard death whisper in her ear, but instead of dismissing the sound, or telling herself she was crazy, she faced it front and centre. 'Not on my watch,' she whispered back.

'Right,' she said aloud. 'Michael, you're the boss. Look lively. What's next?'

Aoife was back in moments, wearing a visor and two aprons. They all looked at each other and got to work.

THIRTY-ONE
Eden

Ways to Kill a Patient

Drug error: NB nanograms/micrograms look similar
Omit basic patient observations
Do not escalate deterioration
Administer known allergen
Dislodge endotracheal tube
Paralysis before/in absence of sedation
Potassium in infusion
Unplug haemofiltration/ventilator
Air/blood/fluid in arterial line
Lack of oxygen – empty cylinder
Insulin/morphine overdose
Turn off/speed up infusion pump
Give intramuscular drug intravenously
Contaminated blood/drugs
Non-sterile/bad aseptic technique
Equipment failure
Misreported scans
Badly managed resuscitation

Allocate the patient the worst nurse on the unit

Eden had printed off her photo of the list and kept it folded up in her locked treasure box. Every now and then she'd look at it and imagine Aoife writing it; how crazy she must have felt to imagine Sophie bumping off patients. But something had been keeping her up at night. Now, she took the list and knocked on Sophie's door.

'Yup.' Sophie was reading.

Eden plonked herself on the bed and leant back. 'I wanted to talk to you.'

Sophie looked at Eden and lowered the book. 'Fire away.'

'It's Aoife. I've been thinking about that list. The "How to Kill a Patient" list.' She put the printout down on the bed and Sophie moved over to sit on the end.

'It's not the best list,' Sophie said. 'There are many more ways to kill a patient than those. I mean, if someone dies unexpectedly outside hospital, at home, on the street, well, that's a murder investigation. If someone who is *expected* to die dies a bit earlier than expected in hospital, then there are a million more ways to make that happen. She's missed off about twenty.'

Eden laughed. 'You are a psycho, you know that, right?'

Sophie shrugged. 'Takes one to know one.'

'Anyway,' Eden continued. 'Don't you think it's odd that since Aoife has gone on sabbatical there have been no unexpected deaths? The numbers have gone right down.'

Sophie turned on her side to face Eden. 'That is odd, I agree.' She grinned and pointed. 'I like this last one.'

Allocate the patient the worst nurse on the unit

'Subtle,' said Eden. 'Why would Aoife ever hurt patients, though? She's not that person, even if it was the right thing . . .'

'Hurt or help is a fine line. All nurses bump patients off,' said Sophie. 'Cancel them. All the time. You know that. Nurses get the midazolam and morphine out when *they* judge it's time. Perfectly legal, and all in the name of pain relief, but every nurse in the country knows that giving the drugs will kill a patient who's already dying if they're administered at the right moment.'

Eden nodded. 'Like a form of assisted dying.'

Sophie leant up on her elbow. 'Exactly. Nurses have always finished people off. Killing them softly.'

'God, imagine if the public knew what we know.'

'Come on. People know. They've all seen Grandpa get an injection from a nurse then slip off ten minutes later.'

They were quiet for a moment, but Eden's mind was still whirring. 'Do you think Aoife was killing people on ED? In order to get you sacked. Because of Michael, I mean?'

'Absolutely not.' Sophie shook her head. 'I know that for a fact.'

Eden tilted her head at her.

'Look,' said Sophie. 'When you're in charge of a unit, and there aren't enough nurses, and too many patients, and they're all dying left, right and centre, and the sickest patients of all are a neo-Nazi handcuffed to the trolley, about to die, and a young woman who's been raped and attacked, also about to die, which one do you save?'

Eden frowned. 'All patients are deserving,' she said. And then whispered, 'But some are more deserving than others.'

Sophie smiled. 'You're learning.'

When they arrived at work, the ambulances were stacked up around the corner, and patients were lined up past the entrance. 'I'll triage,' said Sophie. 'Eden, you take charge. The A Team.'

Eden stood a little straighter. Sophie believed in her. She was a good nurse – a great nurse – the thing she'd wanted her whole life. She'd run a tight ship, like Aoife did, and keep the patients and her staff in check, bringing order to the chaos. Help people.

'You've got this,' said Sophie. Her voice sounded a bit like Aoife's, somehow.

Eden waved Sophie off and went into the changing room. She lifted her head high and straightened her back. Instead of affirmations or gratitude, she spoke the truth: *People will die here today because staffing is not safe. Fate plays a big part. Disease does too. But as the nurse in charge, it is also me who gets to decide which people live, and which people die.*

There were not enough nurses. At least one nurse per shift was totally incompetent. Some patients were good people, others were not. It was Eden's job to choose who to allocate and who to prioritise. All patients were deserving of care. But some were more deserving than others.

EPILOGUE
Aoife

It felt strange walking into City after a month away. Aoife hovered at the coffee shop where Denise said she'd meet her, glancing around in case she bumped into Michael, or Sophie. They'd worked together as a cohesive team after the critical incident, but still, she wasn't ready to spend time with either of them. She was quietly healing, focusing on Sam, and trying to ignore the hole in her chest.

'Hello, hello. Sorry I'm late, you know how it is.' Denise side-hugged Aoife. She smelt of stale tobacco.

'Nothing changes, then.' Aoife smiled.

Denise smiled back but it didn't reach her eyes. 'Thanks for coming in. I know I said we'd grab coffee, but we need to pop into the security office, then we'll head to my office upstairs afterwards.'

Denise was quiet as they walked through the main entrance. Aoife had been caught off-guard by her call and had asked what it was about, but Denise had simply told her to pop in as soon as she could. 'Ideally tomorrow,' she'd said. What was so urgent that they couldn't even have a cup of coffee?

The security office hadn't changed much over the years, aside from the topless Page-Three cut-outs no longer sellotaped to the wall, and a bit more tech. 'Feels like a million years ago since we queued up to get in here for our ID photos.' Aoife shook her head. 'I can't believe how much time has passed. How we've changed.'

Denise half smiled. 'Do you remember how nervous we were on our first day as qualified nurses? How keen? We wanted to change the world.' In the windowless room, sitting opposite the CCTV screens, Denise's skin was blue-tinged, her eyes sunken.

'We did change the world,' said Aoife. 'For many, many patients and families.'

They sat with that a moment, and Denise reached across and squeezed Aoife's hand. 'Appreciate you coming in. I honestly didn't know what to do, and the last thing we need is a police investigation. Things are only just getting back on track.'

Aoife squeezed Denise's hand back. Her skin was cold.

'I came across it by chance really, but then I went back over CCTV footage, and oh God, Aoife, I wish I hadn't seen it.'

Aoife's head fizzed, then a sharp pain stabbed the top of her chest. CCTV! Her mind flashed back to the day Michael had done the Grand Round in his locked office, and she had crawled underneath the desk.

Aoife sat back in the security guard's chair and turned to fully face Denise. She closed her fist, pressing her fingernails into the palm of her hand. There was no point denying it. Denise was not stupid, and they went back a long way. None of them were beyond reproach. Denise had known for decades about Aoife and Michael, since she'd walked in on them after an away day and hadn't batted an eyelid. She'd even made Aoife laugh. *What is an ED team-building day for but extra-marital affairs?* After all, it was Denise herself who'd been the reason the policy had been brought in that no alcohol was served at any of City Hospital's social events, including the annual fundraising ball.

'I was a bit surprised you called me in from sabbatical. I really wouldn't even worry about it to be honest; these guys don't check old CCTV.' Aoife nodded around the security office, a windowless square room, the large screens in front of them showing various rooms and areas of City Hospital. 'They're busier than the nurses these days, firefighting one incident after another.' She looked at Denise, who was holding her fingertips to her temples. Aoife's eyelid twitched. Underplaying this was clearly not the answer. 'I'm sorry you saw what you did, Denise. We're old friends and the best of friends, but still, it must have been disturbing to watch.'

'It's serious, Aoife.' Her voice trembled. Denise's voice never trembled.

Aoife's neck felt hot and her skin itchy. 'Oh, come on, you've known about me and Michael a long time. Sure, it was unprofessional, but the door was locked and, believe me, there won't be any more of that kind of behaviour at work again. You've my solemn promise that when I return from sabbatical, there'll be no sneaking off into dark corners with Michael.' Aoife laughed. 'Or noshing him off under the desk.'

Denise didn't even smile. Instead, she tapped on the keypad in front of them and glanced at the closed door. Then she opened a file and pressed play.

Aoife stopped talking. It wasn't Michael's office on the screen. It was Sophie in a cubicle with a patient.

Denise looked up over her glasses. 'Brace yourself.'

Aoife recognised the patient at once. Mary had mentioned him at the M&M meeting, but they'd moved straight on. *Gary Kennedy. Triple A. You'd know him, he has a Gorbachev birthmark on his neck, always a bit handsy with the junior nurses.*

Aoife leant forwards and stared. His monitor was flashing red, and he was lying unconscious, a blood transfusion hooked up to his arm. 'What are we watching here?' Aoife said. Even as the words came out, her bones ached with knowing.

Sophie pottered around for a while, looking busy but doing little. Then she glanced at the entrance and took an opened vial of morphine out of her pocket. She placed it on the small metal equipment trolley next to the patient's bed, flicked open a syringe, and began drawing up the drug.

Aoife stared at the screen without blinking. They kept watching.

Moments later, Eden arrived. They both held eye contact, then Sophie nodded, before pulling more morphine vials from her pocket, lining them up, one after another, drawing medication from each of them into the syringe.

Slowly, carefully, Sophie disconnected the blood transfusion and injected the drug until the syringe was empty. She reconnected the blood, stood up and spoke to Eden before leaving the room.

Eden stood there a few moments after Sophie had left. Then she switched off the monitor and watched the patient change colour from pink to white to blue.

Aoife gasped. She hadn't realised that she'd been holding her breath.

Denise pressed the keypad, and the screen froze on Eden's face, her smile. 'I checked his medical notes. It didn't get referred to the coroner,' she said. 'But his toxicology levels were off, and his potassium levels were also high. She made a mixture, I expect. Leftover morphine and leftover potassium. Because he was so critical it wasn't even considered an unexpected death.'

'Mother of God. Has anyone seen this?'

Denise put her hands over her skull. 'We're fucked. The insurance rating. The press! We're totally fucked. I don't know what to do, Aoife. I don't know, in all my years, in all our fucking years. If this gets out? We'll all lose our jobs.'

Aoife closed her eyes and exhaled. When she opened them, Denise was crying. It felt like the universe was cracking open. 'You're crying. Actual tears.'

Denise touched her wet face, then looked at her fingertips as if checking for proof.

The room was silent for a few minutes, other than the pounding inside Aoife's head.

'That patient,' said Aoife eventually, and slowly, careful with her thoughts, 'Gary Kennedy. He was not a good man. I'm not saying anything here except the truth.'

Denise wiped her face and sniffed. She flicked her head at Aoife's face and stared. Waited.

'The death rate in ED has stabilised. If we lose Sophie and Eden we'll have two fewer staff, and surely the death rate will go up again. More patients will die. Even more.'

'You're not suggesting . . .? I don't know, Aoife . . . If this ever got out—'

'These girls are no doubt dangerous in their own ways. But the NHS is a dangerous place. It's not safe for anyone, not least patients, we all know that.' Aoife stared at Denise. 'We've buried worse.'

Denise sighed and reached for Aoife's hand once more.

They sat holding hands, staring at the screen, two old nurses. 'Sophie is reckless, I've always known that. The thing that niggles me is that that's maybe the only way to survive in this climate. The system is so fucked; it's a literal war zone.'

'We're veterans, that's the truth.' Denise let go of Aoife's hand. 'I don't think this is right, though. My nurse heart won't allow it.'

'It not about what's right or wrong. Not anymore. All that matters in the end is what is the least harmful impact we can have on our patients. For our patients.'

Denise tipped her head back. 'God, who knew it would come to this? I don't know what to do, I really don't. One more thing will have dire consequences for City, no doubt. But we can't let this go. We can't.'

Aoife pressed her hands together in front of her chest. 'I know exactly what to do, and this decision will be on me,' she said. She reached in front of Denise and pressed the button. *Delete*.

Aoife had lain awake all night but did not feel tired at all. She'd never felt more awake. She pushed open the coffee-room door with such force it banged against the wall. Sophie was standing at the sink, eating a piece of toast. Eden had the large black diary on her lap, sitting on the threadbare sofa.

'Aoife, you're in uniform! We're not expecting you back for months!' Eden grinned. She had the drug keys attached to her bumbag, which was on the sofa beside her, and there was a biro pushed into her ponytail.

Sophie nodded and waved her toast in the air. 'Did they call in the cavalry? I think the numbers are actually OK for once – they're naughty getting you in from leave . . .'

Aoife stood in front of Eden. Sophie wandered over to them, and the two of them sat down, Aoife on the chair opposite the sofa.

'I'm back, resuming my role as senior sister, and I'm in charge again from this moment on. Forever.'

Eden side-eyed Sophie. Then she giggled. But when she looked back at Aoife's expression, she stopped. 'What's happening?'

'Sophie Ibrahim, Eden Walsh, it seems that you are short of, and frankly need, mentoring. I put you both under too much pressure, and I'm sorry for that. It won't happen again.'

Eden's face was draining of colour, but Sophie stared at Aoife, cool and calm. 'Go on . . .'

Aoife looked at these idealistic, self-righteous young women. She had been them once, but in a very different ED, in a very different world. 'I know what's been going on,' she said. 'All of it. I have been a nurse longer than you've been alive, and I see everything. I *know*.'

A flicker of panic crossed Eden's face.

Neither of them tried to deny anything, or to ascertain exactly what Aoife knew, or thought she knew.

Aoife leant over, and took the large black diary and bumbag from Eden's lap. She unhooked the drug keys and put them in her dress pocket. 'Here's what's going to happen . . .' she said.

Eden nodded, wide-eyed. Sophie stared at Aoife with an expression in her eyes that Aoife hadn't seen before. Something new and clear. It made her face look softer and younger, more nurse-like, somehow.

It was respect.

Acknowledgements

I'd like to thank a few people for their help and support during the writing of *Killing Me Softly*.

To Sophie Lambert and Alice Hoskyns at C&W for your incredible hard work championing authors like me, and, despite challenging times in book world, your utter conviction that storytelling is more important than ever.

Francesca Main, my extraordinary editor who is whip-smart, sharp, wise and thoughtful, as well as an all-round lovely person. Thank you to all at Phoenix Books, for meticulous, careful thinking, intense creativity and the best editorial notes of all time. Extra special thanks to Sarah Fortune for seamless process, and to Tomás Almeida for the perfect cover.

To Camilla Young at Curtis Brown, for trusting my instincts, and being at once extremely kind and extremely Bad Ass. You'd make an excellent nurse.

Sister Bartimaeus and the nuns at St Mary's Abbey: thank you for the writing space and peaceful sanctuary during a difficult time.

I am indebted to the nurses and doctors who read early drafts of this novel. Jessica Davidson, Simon Newman, Chris Kurt-Gabel, Gareth Grier, thank you for sharing your expertise with my research, while understanding that this novel is a work of fiction and not fact. Any factual errors are mine. And to the writers who offered to read very early (pre) proofs: M. J. Arlidge, Nathan Filer, Bryony Gordon, Anna Mazzola, Holly Seddon, Emma Jane Unsworth.

To my UEA colleagues, for allowing me a sabbatical to write this novel, and huge thanks for particular help to Sarah Barrow and Richard Hand.

My wonderful friends and family: Tom for always making me laugh, Mum for constant support with writing and everything else, Ann and Peter for being the most loving in-laws a person could ask for.

Amanda and Cheryl for DFA. Laurie Fisher for saying you're my number one superfan.

Huge gratitude to my grown-up children, Ethan, Jesse, Rowan, Tay (and Alex!), for understanding and respecting that if I didn't have a (sometimes metaphorical) room of my own, and all that entails, I would lose myself.

Daniel, for not being at all phased that your new wife was writing a novel about potentially murder-y nurses while you lay unconscious in ICU. Thank you for sticking around.

About the author

Christie Watson is Professor of Creative Writing at UEA and a writer of both fiction and non-fiction. She has written eight books, including *Tiny Sunbirds Far Away*, which won the Costa First Novel award, and a nursing memoir, *The Language of Kindness*, which was a number one *Sunday Times* bestseller. Christie is a contributor to *The Times, Sunday Times, Guardian, Telegraph, Observer* and TedX. Her work has been translated into twenty-three languages and adapted for theatre. She lives in London.

Credits

Phoenix would like to thank everyone at Orion who worked on the publication of *Killing Me Softly*.

Agent
Sophie Lambert

Editor
Francesca Main

Copy-editor
Holly Kyte

Proofreader
Amber Burlinson

Editorial Management
Sarah Fortune
Alice Graham
Jane Hughes
Charlie Panayiotou
Lucy Bilton
Patrice Nelson

Audio
Paul Stark
Louise Richardson
Georgina Cutler-Ross

Contracts
Rachel Monte
Ellie Bowker
Phoebe Miller

Design
Steve Marking
Nick Shah
Deborah Francois
Helen Ewing

Photo Shoots & Image Research
Natalie Dawkins

Finance
Nick Gibson
Jasdip Nandra
Sue Baker
Tom Costello

Inventory
Jo Jacobs
Dan Stevens

Production
Hannah Cox
Katie Horrocks

Marketing
Lynsey Sutherland

Publicity
Aoife Datta

Sales
Dave Murphy
Victoria Laws
Sammy Luton
Group Sales teams
  across Digital, Field,
  International and
  Non-Trade

Operations
Group Sales Operations team

Rights
Rebecca Folland
Tara Hiatt
Ben Fowler
Maddie Stephenson
Ruth Blakemore
Marie Matuschka

RAISING READERS
Books Build Bright Futures

Dear Reader,

We'd love your attention for one more page to tell you about the crisis in children's reading, and what we can all do.

Studies have shown that reading for fun is the **single biggest predictor of a child's future life chances** – more than family circumstance, parents' educational background or income. It improves academic results, mental health, wealth, communication skills, ambition and happiness.[1]

The number of children reading for fun is in rapid decline. Young people have a lot of competition for their time. In 2024, 1 in 10 children and young people in the UK aged 5 to 18 did not own a single book at home.[2]

Hachette works extensively with schools, libraries and literacy charities, but here are some ways we can all raise more readers:

- Reading to children for just 10 minutes a day makes a difference
- Don't give up if children aren't regular readers – there will be books for them!
- Visit bookshops and libraries to get recommendations
- Encourage them to listen to audiobooks
- Support school libraries
- Give books as gifts

There's a lot more information about how to encourage children to read on our website: **www.RaisingReaders.co.uk**

Thank you for reading.

---

[1] OECD, '21st-Century Readers: Developing Literacy Skills in a Digital World', 2021, https://www.oecd.org/en/publications/21st-century-readers_a83d84cb-en.html

[2] National Literacy Trust, 'Book Ownership in 2024', November 2024, https://literacytrust.org.uk/research-services/research-reports/book-ownership-in-2024